THE SURVIVOR

DON BOURASSA

ISBN 978-1-957220-60-4 (paperback)
ISBN 978-1-957220-61-1 (hardcover)
ISBN 978-1-957220-62-8 (digital)

Rushmore Press LLC
1 800 460 9188
www.rushmorepress.com

Printed in the United States of America

1

April 16, 1947. Fifteen-year-old Max Douglas was being feted by his family on his birthday. His father, Ian, had just returned from service in World War II. He had fought at the Battle of the bulge against Hitler's last push to drive the allies out of Europe. Ian had lost a foot that had been frozen in the wet fox-hole that he had shivered in for three nights while the battle raged. The V.A. had fitted him with a prosthesis that enabled him to resume his work as a blacksmith in his shop in the old barn. Ian was 5'8", solidly built, with black hair that was starting to turn gray.

His mother, Ilsa, was as tall as her husband but weighed far less. She was a lean, well-proportioned woman that brooked no nonsense from her children or her husband. She was an excellent cook, housekeeper, mender of clothes, fixer of all problems that cropped up in their rural life.

Max's sisters Leah, the elder, Orla, the youngest, were two years either side of their brother. Max thought well of his sisters, treated them with respect. Max had been born over a month early at home. He owed his life to his grandmothers, who sucked the phlegm out of his lungs as he struggled to breathe. The infant struggled to breathe for over two weeks. He was not expected to live, but although he beat the odds, he did not grow properly. He was the smallest member of his family, always seemed a bit behind the other children his age. As he grew, he helped his father in his shop, manning the forge and aiding him in any way he was told. He worked to make his family's lives better; it was a common theme in families spread out in northern New England. French and English were taught both at school and at home. All the children were bilingual. Their French-Canadian heritage was an important aspect of how they viewed themselves in their world.

Max was born of an independent nature. He did not really believe all that he was taught or told. He stood out, apart from his classmates. Although he was the smallest boy in his class, he refused to be bullied. He would fight to defend himself at the drop of a hat, show no quarter to anyone. He used his fists, sticks, stones, anything else that readily came to his hand. He was reprimanded by the nuns and the priest, but he persisted in defending himself in any manner he could. His family paid no mind to his troubles at school. He was rarely punished at home, never felt an angry blow from his parents. An angry word from his mother was enough for him to get back in line. His father often severely instructed him, "Do the right thing."

He started roaming the woods when he was twelve years old. He found himself completely at home in the wilderness of the great north woods. As he roamed, anything that was edible was fair game at all times. When he shot deer with his Winchester single shot, he cut them up into manageable pieces, carried the meat and organs home to his family. Although snowshoe hares were abundant, he never shot them unless requested by his mother. Grouse were always on the menu; they were his favorite game. He hunted them year-round.

Their little farmhouse was situated on 35 acres of sloping hillside on the western side of the Androscoggin River. It was a picturesque, beautiful place to live in the warm months; it was a downright dangerous place to live in the bitter winters. Their water supply would freeze every winter because of the ledge cap between the house and the well. The line could not be buried, only covered with sawdust, branches, tar paper in an effort to stop it from freezing. By mid-December every year, the line froze, would stay frozen until mid-May at best.

Ian first saw the property in 1939. He fell in love with the conifer forest surrounding it. The scenic river across the highway was beautiful to see from the elevated farmhouse. The small attached barn was a perfect place for him to pursue his blacksmith's trade. The realtor failed to point out that the water supply froze solid in the winter months. Ian only saw an ideal property to raise his family. He liked the isolated location, didn't mind that it was thirty-plus miles away from the mill town of Berlin, N.H. The small town of Errol was just seven miles away.

It was Max's job to keep the water barrel, in the kitchen full, at all times. It had been his job since he had been big enough to carry a pail of water. He was 5'4" now, 130 pounds of muscle and bone. He was strong for his size, paid heed to the level in the water barrel at all times. His mother never ran out of water, never had to remind Max to keep the barrel full.

Ian did work for loggers, farmers, some paper mills, horse owners, anyone who wanted metal work done. Ian was famous all over the north country for his ability in making steel springs from iron-loaded with carbon. He would heat them yellow-white in his forge and plunge them into an oil bath precisely at the right time. It was considered art to make springs in this manner. His homemade jump traps were in use from the north country, into Canada, and as far west as Minnesota. Most of his time was spent filling back orders for the traps.

Max had little interest in making them, great interest in using them to trap the much-desired mink that roamed freely through the waterways of his home. Max knew every rivulet, brook, creek, marsh, or culvert the mink would utilize in their travels. He longed to cross the big river, trap on the opposite shore. He had been warned repeatedly by his father, "Never cross the river on the ice."

This cold January morning found him standing on the river, looking across its icy expanse. He had a few traps in a leather pouch across his back, a hatchet to aid him in making sets. He cautiously started across the icy expanse. He was walking alongside a frozen, fallen tree when the ice caved beneath him. The plunging water turned him like a cartwheel under the ice. He didn't know up from down as the icy water pushed him along. He didn't know if it was fate, God, or an unseen hand that forced him up into the branches of a fallen tree. His hands had no feeling as he desperately clawed at the tree limbs that would lead him back to the riverbank. When he finally reached the bank, he was shivering uncontrollably. His pants were frozen so hard; he couldn't bend his legs. He shuffled along like a ninety-year-old man, and with each step he took, he lost more of his resolve.

He doesn't remember passing out at the bottom of his driveway, doesn't remember his mother and sister's pulling him into the house. Doesn't remember being immersed in hot water, had no memory of laying in bed with a sister on each side of him.

He awoke looking at the stern visage of his father. His father puffed on his pipe, said to him, "If you can't obey the things your mother and I tell you, there's no place in this house for you." He watched his father walk away.

Max did not comprehend how close to death he had come. He had surely felt death's icy fingers pressing against his flesh, but the folly of youth stopped him from seeing the true picture. He was standing on the riverbank watching the current fed by the melting snows make its headlong rush to the sea. Orla came to stand by his side. They stood watching the great river passing by them.

"You almost died, Max. I've never seen mom so anxious before. She wanted dad to get the parish priest, but dad wouldn't. He told mama that God doesn't suffer fools."

Max hadn't raised his head at home since the accident. Mother called it an accident; Dad called it arrogance and stupidity.

I van Petrov was a young fourteen years old when the Nazis captured his village in Ukraine in 1941. They assembled everyone, separated the ablest young men. The rest of the inhabitants were shot after digging their own graves. They were herded into the trench, shot to death. Men, women, children made no difference to the Nazi death squads.

Ivan watched in horror as baby's skulls were crushed by the rifle butts of the Nazis. More and more men joined their march to the camp in Lamsdorf. If you fell during the march, you were shot, left laying by the roadside. At the camp, Ivan witnessed the killing of about three hundred more men. What food rations that were passed out were insufficient to sustain life.

After a short stay, Ivan was one of about 1500 men sent to Auschwitz-Birkenau to build barracks and other buildings. The brutal treatment by the Nazis resulted in daily deaths. You could see, smell, the smoke rising from the burning of your comrades pouring out of the chimneys of the ovens. You could never escape the smell that permeated your nostrils. Along with others, Ivan sustained himself by eating the flesh of his dead comrades. His group was kept alive because of their skill in carpentry.

Ivan was one of 92 prisoners alive when the camp was liberated by the Russian army on January 27, 1945. It took Ivan more than a year of care to recover from his wasted condition. Through the hospital, he learned that his uncle in Canada wanted to sponsor him.

He knew nothing of Canada or his distant uncle. After his body was fully healed, he set sail for Quebec, Canada.

He was greeted warmly by his uncle and his family. They provided a small room in their basement, worked with his uncle's construction crew. Although they constantly questioned him, he could not share his anguish with them. He would talk to no one. He could not share with anyone. The sight of a man in uniform would bring back the terror of Auschwitz. The sounds of hammering and sawing would bring back the terror. The sound of cars and trucks on the busy roads would bring back the terror.

He dreamed of his youth with his parents. Tramping through the woods hunting with his father. The smiles and Laughter of his mother and his siblings resonated in his mind. In his dreams, their laughter turned to screams of terror just before they were murdered by the Nazi death squads. He would awake covered in a cold sweat, a clammy feeling all over his body.

His dreams always started out good. Setting traps with his father. Fleshing pelts with his sisters, feeling the warm arms of his mother as she pulled him against her ample bosom, laughter ringing in his ears. When the laughter turned to screams, he awoke.

In his mind, he was still behind the wire fences of Auschwitz. Armed guards walked the perimeter. Their laughter and the smell of their perfumed cigarettes would not leave him. The only difference was the wire fence enclosed the city he lived in.

He fought for his sanity. In his mind, he formulated plans to escape the fences of the city. He started to use the money he earned to buy the things he would need to survive. His first purchase was the finest .22 rimfire rifle he could find, a Winchester Model 52 Sporting rifle. He next bought a Winchester Model 54 rifle in caliber .30-06, a powerful cartridge suitable for the big game. He bought boxes of ammo for them. He bought traps, snare wire, a mummy-style sleeping bag that would keep him warm to 40 degrees below zero. He bought staples he would need, strong nylon string to help construct the shelters he would need to keep him warm and dry.

After a year had passed, all he needed was a place to escape to, a place where his soul could rest, a place where his dreams would leave him, a place where his mind would be clear. He practiced using a fire starter; striking the pieces against one another created red hot sparks that would ignite his dry tinder, giving him life-saving heat. He studied plans for building simple survival shelters in the woods using basic materials. He read all he could find on how to best utilize the animals he would kill to sustain himself. His determination to free himself had become a reality.

After much thought, he chose the Allagash forests of northern Maine. Although it was not a true wilderness, somewhere within its three and a half million acres was a place for Ivan. The continuing logging operations replenished the forest with new growth for wildlife. The many brooks, ponds, and lakes created prime places for wildlife to flourish.

He traveled to the small town of Allagash. The 200 residents paid no attention to the man from Russia unstrapping the canoe from the roof of his old station wagon. He paddled the waterways, searching for that spot that would hide him from society. He pushed up every creek and rill he came to, explored areas on foot. He finally found a spot that would hide him from the eyes of the timbermen who traveled extensively through the forests. No tourist would find this spot. Perhaps a hunter following his dogs or a trapper looking for a game might stumble onto him. He was sure there were other spots where he would find the seclusion his mind hungered for.

He rented an old, abandoned shack on the edge of town. He built two shelters deep into the marshy areas away from the mature timber that would draw the lumbermen. His shelters were far from established trails. He spent months preparing his area for trapping. He walked his trap lines many times to become familiar with their every unique aspect. After six months, he applied for a driver's license and a trapper's license. With the onset of fall, he spent his time preparing for the winter and trapping season. He only had the month of November to trap mink, his most desirable, lucrative prey. He made doubly sure he was ready to make the most of the short season.

He made up humane drowning sets to ensure the mink wouldn't suffer needlessly well before opening day. Opening day, he would start to arm the traps. After three days of setting traps, he started to collect fur. He took eleven prime mink out of his sets the first day he checked them. He had a long night fleshing and taking care not to overstretch the pelts on his homemade drying boards. He was careful to keep his shelter neat and clean. He stored the carcasses out of reach of predators, saving them for bait on future sets. The experience he had learned from his boyhood enabled him to handle the pelts in a professional manner. For the first time in years, he slept a dreamless sleep. The calmness, the serenity of the woods calmed him, helped him heal. He felt no need for the company of people.

On the second week of trapping, he came upon a nice adult doe. He carefully took aim, shot the doe cleanly through both lungs. The animal only went a few yards before staining the pure white snow red with her death. He took every bit of usable fat and meat from the animal. He wasted nothing. That night he ate backstraps in his shelter, the fire throwing flickering shadows on its walls. A feeling of contentment passed over him as he climbed into his sleeping bag. He didn't awaken until the sound of scolding jays reached his ears. He poked his head out of his shelter to see a fat black bear sniffing at the ground where he had processed the deer. He faced the bear, hollering, "Go bear, go bear." The animal seemed to ignore him but slowly moved away out of his sight. He didn't want to shoot it. He had no way to preserve the meat and didn't want the hide. He would not kill an animal only to waste it.

By the close of the mink season, he had 85 mink pelts ready to market. He made up a bundle of pelts wrapped in the pelt of a prime red fox. He paddled, walked, made his way back to the town of Allagash.

The fur buyer was a gray-haired, older man with a weathered face, squinting as he smoked his pipe, graded the pelts in front of him. Ivan took his place in the line of trappers to await his turn. Ivan watched as the buyer flipped through the pelts, grunted, told the trapper, twenty-four dollars per pelt. The trapper angrily took his pelts off the table, walked out.

By the time Ivan reached the table, he had heard quotes from a low of twelve dollars to a high of thirty-one dollars. He held his breath when he placed his pelts on the table. The fur buyer looked his pelts over carefully. He offered thirty-eight dollars per pelt, told Ivan it was the highest offer he had ever given, commended Ivan for his excellent preparation of the pelts. The buyer gave him a card with the dates he would be in the area buying, passed him $3,230.00. The fur buyer's granddaughter watched the tall, well-muscled trapper walk away. His steel-gray eyes had caught her attention when he was patiently awaiting his turn to present his furs. Unlike the other men, he had not glanced at her once as he waited. She could see something in his face she had never seen before. Although it was ice cold in the unheated building, it appeared to her as if he was standing on a beach with warm tropical winds blowing in his face. He didn't fidget, hop from one foot to another as the other men did. He appeared completely detached from the conditions. She glanced at him again as he was leaving. He finally became aware of her interest. He gave her a very small nod to indicate he was aware of her. No one in the small town she talked to knew anything about him. She asked her grandfather about him, he replied, his name is Ivan Petrov.

"What kind of name is that grandfather?"

"I think he's Russian from his name. He is an expert in the handling of pelts; he must have had a very good teacher."

She stood in the doorway, watched the tall Russian go into a shabby building on the edge of town. Her Grandfather exclaimed, "I forgot to pay him three dollars for his well-cared-for fox hide."

Marie offered to bring the money to him.

Ivan had just put the coffee on to heat when he heard the knock on his door. He opened the door to see a lovely dark-haired young woman holding out money to him in her small fist. He hesitated, asked her, "Why?"

She gave out a small laugh, told him, "I'm Marie Carrier, my grandfather, Amos Carrier, forgot to pay you for the fox hide." Ivan reached for the money, but she pulled her hand back.

"Won't you offer me a hot coffee? It's cold out here."

He hesitated but stepped back so she could enter. She had eyes only for his face as she sat at the table. The heat from the small stove was very hot. She leaned forward, removed her short jacket. Ivan poured them a cup. She asked, "Do you have milk?"

He shook his head, "Only sugar."

She studied his face. The strong lines of his Slavic face appealed to her. The old scar across his cheek did not diminish the fact that he was a handsome man. His hands looked strong as they were folded around his coffee mug.

"It's too bad such a fine fur is worth so little. I will trap no more fox this winter."

"What will you trap now that the mink season is over?"

"I thought otter, fisher, maybe a few pine martens I have seen a sign of."

"Try to catch as many fishes as you can; they will bring the best price. try to catch a few lynxes if you can; they always bring good money."

"Thank you for the advice."

"Where are you from, Ivan?"

"My family lived in Ukraine in Russia."

"Did they teach you how to handle pelts?"

"My mother taught me. In Russia. It is a job for women and children."

Marie smiled at him as she sipped her coffee. Ivan seemed a little anxious to her as he waited for her to speak.

"I live in Fort Kent with my parents John and Ethel Carrier. Grandfather is trying to teach me to be a fur buyer."

"Your grandfather knows his business. I hope you learn well."

"Why do you look so sad, Ivan Petrov?"

"I do not talk of such things. I don't know if I will ever be able to talk of such things. You should find yourself a man who is happy, a man who can make you happy."

His comment disturbed her. She guessed something had happened to this young man, but she couldn't even guess at the depth of his sorrow.

"Tell me, Ivan. Share your sorrow with me."

"It is better that you go now. I have to get ready to leave."

Marie reluctantly rose from the table.

"I will talk to you again, Ivan Petrov. I think you may have caught me in your traps."

He watched as Marie walked away from him. She seemed to him to be a determined woman of substance. He tried to put her out of his mind as he gathered his belongings, but her smile, her forthright manner, would not leave him.

The next day, he arranged to buy the old shack and the half-acre of the ground it stood on. He paid the princely sum of $1800.00 to buy it. Before he left town, he asked the fur buyer to put his money in a bank account in Fort Kent, took the hand of Marie, told her he hoped he would see her in the Spring when he sold his pelts. Marie stood on her tiptoes, kissed him on the scar on his cheek.

Ivan welcomed the solitude of the woods. It was so quiet you could hear the falling snow glancing off the bare tree branches as it fell softly to earth. The sound of rushing wings got his attention as a grouse was fleeing from a Goshawk in the snowstorm. We, all have, to eat, he thought as he entered his furthest shelter. He had made eight good sets for Fisher this day. He had used the flesh of mink, along with a bit of the fluid from their glands, to enhance the aroma of the sets. This same set would catch Pine Martin just as well. He reheated the stew he had made the previous day, drank a hot, steaming cup of good coffee flavored with a spoonful of sugar. He stoked the fire in his barrel stove before climbing into his sleeping bag. The quiet of the northern woods was slowly healing him. He didn't think he could ever live amongst a crowd of people, but the few people in Allagash did not disturb him. It had been months since his dreams would awaken him. He went to sleep thinking of the dark-haired woman that had thrust herself into his life.

He stood on the bank, watched the great moose feeding in the alders. He watched as it took great swathes of vegetation into its mouth. He was armed only with his .22 rifle but had no thought of shooting the animal. Spring was not far away, and he had sufficient foodstuff ahead to see him through. He was just about to leave when the pack of eastern coyotes attacked the moose. He shot two of them when they bayed the moose. The moose would not run. She lashed out with her great hooves, determined to fight in place. Ivan helped her out by shooting three more of the animals before the remaining coyotes ran away. The moose looked down its long nose at him, calmly walked away from him through the marsh. He quickly rough-skinned the coyotes, put the pelts over his shoulders. That night he carefully fleshed the pelts, put them on stretchers. He knew these rough-coated furs wouldn't bring much money, but he wouldn't waste them.

The last week of trapping, the skies had stayed dark, the snow falling softly most days. When the morning dawned with a brilliant sun, he packed his canoe with all his furs, reached town just before nightfall. The fur buyer was due on Saturday. He knew his pelts wouldn't bring as much as the mink, but he was hopeful prices had held.

The old man looked the same as he sat next to his granddaughter who was grading pelts, handling the transactions. He puffed his pipe while she examined the pelts presented to her. She was a tough grader. A few trappers left with a look of disgust on their faces. She never looked up at him when she came to his table to inspect his pelts. It took her less than five minutes to sum up his winter's efforts. She looked him in the eye, said, "$2,240.00."

Ivan nodded his okay. The old man paid him his money told him he had received top money for his hides. He handed Ivan a passbook with a smile. Ivan shook his hand, thanked him. He sat at an empty table until Marie finished grading pelts.

Marie sat with him.

"You had a good season, Ivan. You had many fine fisher pelts done up properly. Can you come to Fort Kent with us tonight? I think you need to buy me a good meal in a fine restaurant."

Ivan laughed at her forwardness, took her hand.

"Hold off until tomorrow. I will meet you at the bank when it opens, then buy you the finest meal in town."

Marie kissed him full on the lips.

"I will hold you to that, Ivan Petrov."

He watched her hips sway as she walked away. He got up early the next morning, put the battery in his old station wagon, finally got it to start up. He let it run to warm it up, melt the hard frost on the windshield. He met Marie at the bank. After his business was done, he bought her the best breakfast in town. Ivan had not been this happy since he was a boy in Ukraine.

Marie insisted he come to her home, meet with her parents. They welcomed the couple, made Ivan feel comfortable. They politely listened to Marie tell them of Ivan's furs. Her father was a lawyer; her mother was a, stay at home homemaker. He met her strapping brother, Paul, and his bubbly blonde wife, Florence. It was a good visit; he hated to leave Marie. She told him she would meet him in the morning.

He stopped at a lumber yard, bought cedar shingles for siding, asphalt shingles for his roof. His station wagon's hood was pointing at the sky as he drove to Allagash.

He was working on his roof when Marie drove in with her black Chevy Coupe. Seated at his kitchen table, she asked,

"Tell me what happened to you Ivan, don't leave out a thing."

She was the first person he talked to since he had been liberated from Auschwitz. The tears were flowing down both their cheeks when he finished.

"Oh my God, of course, I had heard of the atrocities committed by the Nazis, but I really had no sense of the reality of what they did."

"The reality of the war is over sixty million dead. I don't know how anyone can conceive of that figure. They say that the bulk of the dead were Russians. The survivors of the camps were only in the thousands, I'm told."

Ivan felt cleansed somehow. The telling of what he had endured, what he had witnessed, seemed to have lifted a dark cloud from his persona. Marie was silent. His hand was clamped between her two hands. She went into his arms, wouldn't stop kissing him. He held her tightly against his chest, his tears dampening her shoulder. They finally broke apart. Marie cooked a meal for them, tried to really comprehend all she had just heard.

Ivan used his construction skills learned at Auschwitz to put an addition onto his home. With the help of Marie, they transformed the shack into a cozy, comfortable cottage. He added a screened porch that overlooked the forests that had brought him back to life.

As the summer waned, he was faced with the reality of Marie. She had broken into his shell, showed him he could love again. She was making him human. They married in the city of Fort Kent with Marie's family all around them. Ivan told his mother-in-law how he wished his family could be here. She embraced him, had no words to comfort him.

Ivan saw them in his thoughts as they were when he was a boy. They were real in his mind; they would always be real in his mind, would always be a part of him. Marie stirred in her sleep. He cradled her in his arms, felt her warm breath against his neck, felt the warmth of her body pressed against him. He fell into a dreamless sleep.

Ivan's skills as a carpenter brought him much-needed work. Marie's grandfather helped him get a job building a greenhouse for one of his neighbors. Ivan did a fine job, received other offers for work.

The trapping season was fast approaching. Marie helped him get ready to face the long winter months. Together they stocked his shelters. Together they roamed the forest, making love under a canopy of stars, forging an unbreakable bond between them that drove the terror from his mind. His nights were dreamless. The memory of what he had endured pushed into the dark recesses of his mind.

It started to snow as Ivan escorted his wife back to town. Through the falling snow, they saw two does and a few yearlings bounding through the hardwood. Ivan took her hand, pointed to where a magnificent buck was scenting the air as he pursued the does. Ivan told her the buck would pursue the does until they would stand for him. The buck paid them no heed as he bounded after the does. Marie was thrilled to have seen this spectacle of the whitetail's life.

Back in the woods on his own, the snowstorm was causing Ivan great anxiety. All his carefully placed sets were buried under two feet of snow. He exhausted himself resetting them. He knew the soft snow would cause many of his traps to remain empty. Mink would be scarcer this year because of the storm. They must have freedom, of travel, in order for Ivan to catch them. He had no choice but to hope the snow would firm up, enable the mink to resume their hunting. He switched to trapping for bobcat, lynx, fisher, martin, even fox, and coyote to make up for the loss of prime mink. He was faced with hard work for less money.

A slight thaw finally firmed up the snow. He started to catch a few mink. The last two days of the mink season, he was grateful for the 18 prime mink he pulled from his traps. He had to break the ice in order to paddle back to town to sell his early pelts. Marie and her grandfather were buying pelts in the town hall. Ivan waited patiently in line as trapper after trapper sold their furs. His furs brought top dollar, but the lack of mink resulted in a paycheck of just over $2,700.

Snug and warm in their cottage, Marie told him she didn't think it was wise to continue trapping. The heavy snowfalls and the bitter cold were taking their toll on those brave enough to try and endure it. She thought he should seek work in Fort Kent for the remainder of the brutal winter. Ivan was, disappointed, but didn't respond to her. It was obvious to Marie that her man had not made up his mind. She could only spend the night with him because she was going on a buying trip with her grandfather.

After a lot of thought, Ivan decided he would return to his trapline, concentrate on fisher and pine martin, try to salvage the season. He drove himself to his physical limits. He doubled the area he trapped spending cold nights fleshing and stretching pelts. The bitter cold made the work that much harder. He was exhausting himself trying to cover all the sets he had made.

Back in his primary shelter, he gorged himself on the meat, drank the broth containing what little fat was in the meat. He cracked bones, sucked the life-giving marrow into his stomach. He rested two days before he pulled all his traps. He made the trek home with a warm breeze signaling the end of winter. It took him a week to recover from the hard winter. He started the old Plymouth, drove to Fort Kent to sell his furs.

The sale of his pelts salvaged the season for him. His payment of $3,700 made his efforts worthwhile. Marie scolded him for the chances he had taken alone deep in the woods.

"You risked your life for these few dollars. It's just not worth it to take the chance of losing your life. Four trappers died this winter, you may well have been one of them. If you care for me, you won't take these chances anymore."

"I'm a trapper, Marie. I was a trapper when you met me; I will continue to be a trapper."

On that sour note, Ivan kissed her goodbye and drove back to Allagash.

Ever since he had fallen through the ice, Max continued to drift farther and farther away from his family. His father was distant, constantly complained about the pain in his missing foot. The doctors couldn't convince him that the pain was in his head, not his missing foot. His pain was alienating the whole family. His sisters had become silent, isolated. His mother had become morose, distant from her family. Max was greatly affected by his father's actions. He felt like he was no longer accepted by his parents. Max's solution was to lose himself in the woods. His schoolwork suffered to the point that he quit school on his sixteenth birthday. He knew very little except for the woods. With the idealism, energy of youth, he decided he would live his life as a free trapper. He would earn his living in the woods that he loved. His thought was, I don't fit in with people anyway.

What Max didn't know, would fill a very large book. The ignorance of youth didn't stop him. He boldly set out with a pack on his back, his only concern, shooting something for his supper.

Animals in the deep woods are scarce, wild, and extremely wary. It is the clearings man makes in his never-ending quest for timber that spurs the growth of new, tender, plants that sustains life in the forest. The deep woods hold little food to sustain a large population of wildlife. Max was well, aware of this. He knew prey was to be found close to those areas that held abundant food. He followed his compass. The needle pointing north was his guide.

It is, a little known, fact that without a compass, or the sun, people will walk in circles. Many a deer hunter has been surprised to cross human tracks in the snow, only to realize that he had crossed his own tracks. Max was aware of this fact. He followed his compass without fail. When he crossed Route 26 in Errol, he entered a vast network of logging roads. He used his compass to keep his line, wound up almost in Maine the first night. He spent an uncomfortable night in the woods. His canteen was almost as empty as his belly when he awoke. Around nine in the morning, he shot a plump grouse that had probably never seen a human before.

It took him three hours to cook the bird. While it was cooking, he followed a small stream, found a rill that flowed into it. He followed it until he could see the ledges it was flowing from. He drank his fill, filled his canteen.

What Max didn't realize was, this is not the 1700s when every rill held potable water. Today's waters hold vastly more bacteria, bacteria that would eventually poison a person to death if untreated. Max continued his trek north crossing road after road in his journey. He ate squirrel, hare, grouse, to try and stop his belly from grumbling, but as he traveled, he lost weight almost daily. He cut new holes in his belt to keep his pants up.

It was an almost famished Max that found himself deep into the forests of the Allagash. He was past reveling in the beauty of his surroundings. His mind had become a little hazy. His rest stops had become longer, more frequent. His thirst was becoming a living beast inside him.

Ivan looked at the boy kneeling over the rushing water. His head was down almost to his chest. His arms were dangling at his side. Ivan had seen this many times before. A memory of the camps flooded into his mind. The boy was on the verge of starvation. He watched the boy closely. He hadn't yet made the decision to intervene. He was frightened by his own memories. He turned away from the boy in front of him, started to walk away, and left the boy to his own fate. Something in him, made him turn back.

"Don't drink that water."

The admonition caused Max to turn his head towards the sound of a human voice. He took the offered canteen, drank his fill. Slowly Ivan led the boy to where he had stowed his canoe. The boy sat quietly in the bow chewing on a piece of pepperoni.

"That's enough, don't eat anymore."

Ivan's advice fell on deaf ears as Max continued to eat the rich sausage. Ivan took the remaining piece away from the boy. Two minutes later, Max was heaving his guts out into the cold black water. They drifted in the canoe as Max drank more water, drained the canteen. Ivan gave him a small piece of ham from his sandwich, drove the canoe towards home.

The doctor had treated Max with antibiotics to cleanse his system of the poison running through him. Marie made the boy nourishing soups and broths to slowly bring him back to the point where he could eat solid food. While Ivan worked, Marie listened to Max's story. She made him write a letter to his parents telling them where he was. Max slowly came back to himself, put weight back on, was able to work, try to pay Ivan and Marie back for their kindness and generosity.

Max was asleep on Ivan's porch when he awoke. A weak sun was showing red all along the horizon. Ivan gave the boy a cup of coffee, sat next to him.

"Have you thought about going home?"

"There's no place for me anymore. I want to be a free trapper."

"You have much to learn my friend before you're able to earn your living from the woods."

"Will you teach me, Ivan, will you help me to learn?"

"It will be a hard lesson for you, and I can't pay very much. There's only so much fur to be caught no matter how hard you try."

"I don't care about the money; I want to learn."

Marie joined the conversation telling Max he needed to be outfitted in order to spend the winter in the woods. She added that he needed a good rifle, warm clothing to see him through the bitter months.

Max listened politely. Marie told him that Ivan had suffered more horribly than he could ever imagine. Never talk self-pity to anyone. She told him he was an ignorant boy, listen to what Ivan tells you.

Max finally learned that he had to learn from others. Life was not so simple that an ignorant boy could leave his mother's breast, make his own way in this world.

Ivan had studied the square jump traps that Max had and was impressed enough to order two dozen from his father.

Ivan and Max spent the month of October in the woods preparing for the trapping season. Ivan expanded their traplines over twice the previous area he had trapped. They made mink sets together until Max could be trusted to make them on his own. Ivan stressed to the boy that over trapping an area was only hurting yourself, you must range out, in order to safeguard the species, you were trapping.

They split up on the first of November to set traps on their drowning sets. It took them two long days to arm all the traps. Ivan taught Max how to properly handle the raw pelts to maximize dollars for their efforts. Max tended to over-stretch them. Ivan corrected him. Overstretched pelts brought little money. Attention to the smallest details was beaten into Max's head.

Ivan had found the track of a moose that had been attacked by a pack of coyotes. These animals were not, coyotes despite the States' insistence that they are. They were, in fact, a hybrid of the gray wolf from Quebec that had mated with, who knows what. Their heavy weight, short, wide snouts, grasping teeth, attested to this fact.

Ivan and Max followed the moose to where it was quietly standing on the edge of a marsh. Ivan could see the moose, was almost gone, the coyotes had torn open its abdomen. He told Max to shoot the animal in the head. Ivan could sense the coyotes padding softly through the surrounding undergrowth. Together they removed the choice cuts, and all the fat they could carry. Ivan knew once they left, the coyotes would claim the carcass. Max soon learned to cherish every bit of fat he could garner from the forest. Always think survival was Ivan's lesson to Max.

When November ended, Ivan sent Max to town to sell their early catch of mink to Marie. Max had the feeling he was returning in triumph to the small town. Marie quickly sorted their catch of 116 mink. At an average price of forty-one dollars, the value amounted to $4.756. She gave Max a hundred-dollar bill, told him his debt was paid.

Max bought a few things at the general store before heading back to Ivan. Ivan had not been idle. He worked with Max showing him how to transition to mainly fisher and Martin sets. Bob cat and lynx were plentiful. Ivan taught Max how to build cubby sets to catch the wary predators. They worked until they could no longer see. After taking care of, the, days pelts, they celebrated by cooking up the bacon Max had bought in town.

They spent long days checking traps, moving sets, rebaiting as necessary. Max shot three coyotes during his travels, Ivan caught three, lynx, a brace of bob cats. At season's end, they had a canoe load of fur to show for all their effort.

After they sold the pelts to Marie, Ivan handed Max $2,500, told him to find work in Fort Kent, come back in October if you want a trapping partner. Max nodded, solemnly shook Ivan's hand, thanked him.

Max bought a used Ford coupe, decided to visit his family. He left Fort Kent late at night, had to lay over in Rangeley until the gas stations opened. He ate a good breakfast before reaching home early morning. His parents were happy to see him. His father had overcome his pain issues, was, a lot, calmer, glad to see his son had started to find his way in the world. Max decided to work with his father for the summer. His dad would pay him with traps, and room and board. Max studied trapping manuals by the light of an oil lamp during the long evenings of summer.

His elder sister had married, was gone from the household. His younger sister, Orla, had a beau that stopped over every evening. He worked at the paper mill in Berlin, rode his Indian motorcycle to see his girl every night. His parents expected to lose another daughter very soon.

The leaves of late September were starting to turn when Max returned to the Allagash. He met with Marie and Ivan, camped out on their porch awaiting the start of the trapping season. Ivan spread out a map to show Max where they would trap them. Ivan told Max they would share equally on the line. That suited Max just fine. They all appreciated that two trappers were better, safer than a lone trapper.

Ivan had studied hard with Marie to become a citizen. He felt that there was no comparing the life he had grown up with to the freedoms he had in America. In America, people were free from the oppression he had grown up with. In America, people were free to say whatever they wanted, free to pursue whatever they wanted to do. He passed the test easily, became a citizen in 1957. In Russia, he had been taught from boyhood never to criticize the Government. To do so was to put your life in jeopardy.

Ivan was rebuilding a porch on a house halfway to Fort Kent. He was expecting Marie to bring him his lunch, share as much time with him as possible before the start of the trapping season. Marie's grandfather, Amos, was in the car with her, Ivan was surprised to see him. Ivan knew that Amos was an influential man. Marie had told him her grandfather had become rich from the fur trade and his wise investments in the stock market. She told him that through marriage, he was related to the current Governor, was said to have his ear.

They laid out the contents of the lunch basket on the tailgate of Ivan's old station wagon. Amos lit up a cigar, tilted his head to blow the smoke away from them.

"How would you like to become a Game Warden for the State? You would be able to work from your home, work in the area that you're most comfortable with."

Ivan was stunned. He hadn't realized how much influence the old man had. Marie was beaming at him, nodding her head yes. Old fears of a uniform flooded into his mind. Bile started to rise in his throat. He choked down the bile, took a long drink from his thermos.

"I don't know how to answer."

Marie angrily shook her head. "For Christ's sake, just say yes."

Ivan turned away from them, looked out over the magnificent forest that had helped to restore him.

"Alright, I'll try it."

Ivan's odyssey started in Augusta, Maine in front of an oral board. He was bombarded with questions about every outdoor activity. General questions about respect for the laws were frequently thrown into the mix of questions. He impressed the board with his knowledge of trapping and hunting, was a little, weak on fishing laws and recreational vehicles. Marie tried to comfort him after the ordeal. He confessed to her that he felt he hadn't done very well. The reality was that the board was really impressed with his knowledge, and especially his honesty and demeanor. Ivan carried himself very well in their eyes.

Ivan faced a long road in front of him. The second step was an 18-week-long training course in Augusta. With Marie's help, he studied hard, passed the course. He complained to Marie that so much information given so fast, wouldn't stick. She helped him out by condensing the information into a handy notebook that he could carry with him while on duty.

Marie couldn't help him during the 12-week special training course, but this involved practical applications that he had no problem with. He was commissioned on the shores of moosehead Lake with a proud Marie and her grandfather in attendance.

He was assigned to Warden Jake Fellows for a sixteen-week on-the-job training before he would be assigned his district.

Marie laid out his uniform on their bed. He looked at the green uniform, couldn't help but bring back memories of the green uniformed soldiers of the Nazi death squads.

"Get that out of your head. This uniform represents only good. Think only of the good, let the Nazis die in your mind."

Jake was a veteran of over thirty years. He was a constant source of valuable information. He treated Ivan like a son, made him feel comfortable. His first big arrest were two family members of a farm shooting deer at night using a spotlight in their fields. They had the attitude that game on their land belonged to them, they found out different. The Wardens were being helped out, by new, stiffer, penalties being handed out by the courts.

A day on the water resulted in more than a dozen citations. Ivan was surprised that so many people were ignorant of the laws or just didn't give a damn about them. Ivan was quickly learning what was required from him. He noted that he met many fine sportsmen and women who obeyed the laws, showed respect for his uniform.

Jake made sure he was introduced to all law enforcement personnel in his area. Jake made sure he was well versed in all areas of his responsibility. They spent the weekend ticketing off-roaders and snowmobilers for non-registration, speeding, and reckless operation. He was again surprised at how many violators there were out there.

Even after his training program was over, Ivan still felt overwhelmed by what he didn't know. His pickup was full of rules, regulations, Marie's notebook. All these items helped him, but they couldn't fill in the areas he was ignorant of. Although he lived, trapped in the Allagash, he was ignorant of how to travel through his huge area, how to navigate its waterways, how to solve the puzzle of the myriad of private timber roads through his area. The first week he was on his own was a nightmare of nervousness for him. He enlisted the aid of Marie's grandfather to learn all the dirt roads that actually, went somewhere. The old man calmed him down with his knowledge, the aroma of his pipe, the quiet companionship that Amos instilled in him. He enlisted the aid of tour guides that bought him through the waters of the Allagash, showed him all the major and minor waterways of both the Allagash and Saint John Rivers. Marie made him a map of all the streams, creeks, rills, that were passable by canoe or kayak. The timber companies supplied him with detailed maps of all the private roads that bisected the properties. His last guided tour was along the border between Quebec and the Saint John River through the Appalachian Mountains. Almost ninety miles of unguarded border with many crossing spots evident to him. After two weeks had passed, he had just begun to understand the enormous area he was responsible for.

Max had taken over Ivan's trap line. He had refreshed the sets he would utilize this season, built another shelter, set up leaning pole sets for fisher and martin, built cubbies for lynx and bobcat, put up firewood to keep him warm during the long season. He was completely at home in the woods except for that time every day between light and dark. A feeling of fear, born of ancient man, always crept into his mind until he reached the safety of his shelter. His fears were brought to the fore when he encountered an aggressive black bear Just at dusk, the animal had surprised him. He didn't know what made him turn around, but when he did, the bear was advancing on him. Armed only with a .22 pistol, he hollered, yelled at the bruin to no avail. He fired two rounds into the ground in front of the bear which only made the animal hesitate. When he was convinced that the animal wanted to eat him, he fired between the animal's eyes, causing the bear to finally turn, slowly walk away, pausing often as he did. When he related the story to Ivan and Marie, Marie said, "For Christ's sake, carry a bigger gun." Ivan just nodded.

Ivan sold him many traps and supplies he would pay for when he sold his furs. He spent the last week in September fishing for lake trout and the plentiful brook trout in the cold deep waters in the Allagash. He was living the life of a free trapper, enjoying every minute of it.

Max had shot a nice Spring bear. He wanted the heavy hide for warmth, the meat he turned over to a Native American woman that made pemmican from the bear meat. He wanted to put up as much protein as he could before winter arrived. The pemmican tasted foreign in his mouth, but the longer he chewed it, the easier it became to eat it. Ivan was busy learning his new job, had little time to spend with Max. Max and Marie went to Fort Kent together to buy winter clothing. It seemed as though people in the area did little else except prepare for winter. He bought a new Marlin lever action .22 to help him supply camp meat, a .44 Magnum pistol to take care of any future bear problems. Max had just about spent all his cash, but he was ready for the bitter winter. When the leaves turned their Autumn colors and the mornings turned frosty, it was time to hit the woods.

Ivan was using the early mornings to gain familiarity with the dirt rods in his area. The rest of the day he spent checking fishermen scattered all over the Allagash region. He issued quite a few citations during this period, received an "atta boy" from his superiors. He was checked on by the district sergeant from time to time, received some good advice from him.

Ivan had been the recipient of violence, not the aggressor of it. He was wholly unprepared when an irate four-wheeler operator punched him while he was writing out a ticket. He caught up with his attacker, beat him to the ground, arrested and handcuffed him. It was his first felony arrest. Marie was aghast when he came home with his nose packed, his eyes the colors of the rainbow, his shirt front drenched with his blood. She ranted and raved at the stupidity of the man who had struck him. Ivan told her the attack had opened his eyes, he would be more careful in the future.

The revolver strapped to his waist was completely foreign to him. He prayed that he would never have to use it. He was fairly accurate with it, but actually resented the fact that it was mandatory that he be armed at all times. He had been outfitted by the State with everything he needed to fulfill his job. His yard was cluttered with a three-wheeler, a snow machine on a trailer, an aluminum boat, motor, trailer, and a green canoe. He had his issued revolver and shotgun, and his own rifle in his state pickup at all times. Through his radio, he was in constant contact with law enforcement, he was well outfitted.

While on a check of a dirt road bordering Quebec, he spotted tracks crossing the border. He could tell little from the tracks but reported the breach to headquarters. He was not surprised the next morning when a stocky, blonde-headed border patrol agent knocked on his door. The agent introduced himself as, Jack Murphy, agent for Ivan's district. They shared coffee before heading out to the site in Ivan's four-wheel-drive pickup. Jack told him it could possibly involve drug smuggling.

Ivan and Jack returned to the area of the breach and noticed two, tow-headed teenage boys racing away from the area on three-wheelers. They followed the tracks that led to an old farmhouse surrounded by open potato fields. Two three-wheelers were parked in the yard. After talking with the boy's parents. Jack warned them it was a crime to illegally cross the border. He wrote out a warning for the parents, decided no further involvement was necessary.

Marie's grandfather reported that a certain trapper always turned in unprime mink pelts every year. Ivan checked the man's area, cited him for unlawful trapping. The man lost his trapping license for the year, besides paying a hefty fine. The irate trapper threatened Ivan who took him into custody. The man wound up in the county lockup and was not a happy trapper.

Ivan quickly learned that his unform could be a target with a bullseye on his back. When he checked on Max's trapline, he was pleased to see the preparations the young man had made. He shared lunch with Max deep in the woods. He cited a few other trappers for early trapping. The word soon went out to all the trappers that Ivan was strictly enforcing the laws.

Ivan was making a difference in his huge area. Increased penalties also helped. In general, a new appreciation for wildlife had started among the population. During deer season, Ivan's phone was ringing off the hook. People reported hunters shooting from Vehicles, even standing in the road shooting. Farmers reported lights in their fields at night, alien tracks going across their green fields. Ivan teamed up with Sergeant Shultz in the placing of a buck decoy on the edge of a farmer's field. Ivan was in the woods holding a rope that made the decoy's head bob up and down. When a vehicle would stop on the road, Ivan would gently pull on the rope. In the event of a shot being fired from inside the vehicle, the Sergeant would pull his cruiser in front of the vehicle with his blue lights flashing while Ivan walked to the driver's door. In two days, they issued nine citations, confiscated seven firearms. Ivan was amazed at how easy it was to catch these men. One old man stopped his truck, got out, and tried to stalk the decoy. He was embarrassed when Ivan told him, "Don't shoot."

"I thought the damn thing was real," Ivan laughed with him, wishing him luck. Two, twelve-year, old boys were caught shooting from the road resulting in some unhappy parents being written up for allowing their minor children to possess firearms and hunt without the presence of an adult. The Sergeant's cruiser was full of impounded weapons when he left Ivan.

Ivan received a tremendous education in his first year as a game warden. He was fully accepted into the ranks of law enforcement. Ivan grew as a person during this time, his horrible memories locked into the recesses of his mind.

Marie's father was closing the sale of a potato farm to a couple from Lodz, Poland. Abraham and Eve Lecenski had met at Auschwitz, were among the few survivors of the camp. The horrors they had survived would never leave them. The isolated potato fields reminded them of their childhood in Lodz. Relatives in Boston had helped them start a new life in America. They were unable to adjust to the busy life in a major city. They had witnessed the deaths of their parents, grandparents, siblings, residents of their home. Their family's homes, lands, had been stolen from them. There was no compensation from Poland, no place for them to live in the place they were born. The fact that they were Jewish, had imposed a death sentence on their families.

Marie's father told them of his son-in-law's experiences in Auschwitz. They actually seemed frightened by the information. They told him that many Russians had persecuted many Jews in Russia.

Marie's father dropped the conversation, wished them well in their new endeavor. He gave them Ivan and Marie's phone numbers. When Marie heard about them, she encouraged Ivan to meet with them. When she questioned Ivan, she was thrilled to find out that Ivan had no bad feelings about Jewish people. He told her he had been raised around many Jewish families, had played with their children. *They are just people, same as us*—this was his attitude.

Marie, phoned them, was invited to come to their farm, meet with them. Ivan was not thrilled with the idea but dutifully drove them to the farm. After the introductions were over, coffee and pastries were shared; they all sat in silence around the table. Eve finally broke the silence.

"Did you see what the Germans did to our family?"

"We all knew what was happening. When the Jews arrived, they were brutally separated. Most went directly to the gas chambers herded like cattle by the Nazi guards. The chimneys would belch smoke for days after their arrival. The Germans considered Russians as animals, undeserving of life. We were separated from the Jews and everyone else.

As Marie watched, tears began falling from her husband's eyes. Abraham and Eve were crying also. Words tumbled from their mouths that she couldn't understand. They were babbling in Russian, Yiddish, German all at once. She tried to understand the depths of their emotions revealed to her. She looked at her strong husband, saw him return to the horrors he had experienced, saw the pain and anguish that was deep in his being. No one that had not experienced it could really understand it.

Their talk gradually turned to childhood memories of their parents, relations, childhood. They became as children as these few good memories passed their lips.

When they parted, they hugged each other, sought solace in each other. Marie could not stop crying as Ivan slowly drove towards home. She had witnessed the breaking of a dam that let out the absolute horror of the German brutality. Ivan was quiet on the ride home, drained of all emotion. She pushed her body against him, wanting to give him comfort. He placed his arm over her shoulder, hugged her to him.

"You saved me, Marie. I'm sorry you have to hear these things, I'm sorry for the millions that died in the camps, were murdered by the Nazis."

"Abraham had to load the bodies of his own family, deliver their bodies to the ovens."

"It kept him alive Marie, it kept him alive."

Ivan was glad to be alone in his pickup. Glad for the heat pouring out of the truck's heater. Glad for the comfort that Marie added to his life. Normal was not a word that would ever describe a survivor of the camps. Normal was for people that had not experienced death and tragedy.

ans Muller was a former prison guard at Auschwitz. He had used his position to steal gold teeth, gold fillings, wedding rings, other jewelry hidden in the seams of prisoner's clothing. Just in time to avoid the on-rushing Russian army, he had been transferred to Berlin to help stem the Russian tide. Hans Muller was a thief, a bully, a murderer, a coward, who fled to West Berlin in civilian clothing, managed to make his way to, Switzerland. Emigrated to America where he used his stolen gold to buy a lumber mill on the banks of the Saint John River. His mill employed mostly French Canadians whom he considered as little more than the Jews he herded into the gas chambers of Auschwitz.

He had built an imposing manse on a hilltop overlooking his mill. He often tracked his workers through the scope of the World War Two German sniper rifle he had bought. He often wished he could pull the trigger on the animals that worked for him. His home was full of Nazi, memorabilia that he had bought from dealers. He had earned none of the medals on display in his glass case, had never worn the SS insignia on his uniform. The SS dagger in its original sheath had never been on his belt. The SS uniform was proudly on display; he had never worn it. His trophy room held the mounted heads of animals he had never hunted. He laughed inwardly when he imagined the mounted heads of the Jews and Russians he had shot, mounted on his wall.

The only people invited into his trophy room were other, former, Nazi soldiers. They had not waned in their adoration for Adolf Hitler and the havoc he had unleashed upon the world. He had created the illusion that he was an SS Obefuner. He was very careful never to invite anyone to his home that could shatter that illusion. He had made himself an SS colonel in his own eyes.

Herr Muller enjoyed fishing in the deep-water lakes. He especially liked catching large lake trout and brook trout that made these cold waters their home. When Ivan moored his boat alongside the fisherman's boat and asked for his license, Herr Muller didn't have a license. Ivan wrote out a citation, confiscated his fishing gear. Herr Muller was incensed at this Slavic-looking Game Warden who dared interrupt him in his pleasure. Ivan warned him, told him to desist in his tirade. Herr Muller got control of himself, lit up a cigarette. Ivan instantly recognized the aroma of the perfumed cigarette smoke.

As Ivan pulled away in his boat, he wondered about the background of this man, Herr Muller. He dismissed the man from his mind as he motored towards another boat he wanted to check. As he was driving towards home, the memory of a prison guard flashed into his mind. The memory of a man watching a group of Jews being unloaded from the train. He was smoking the same perfumed cigarette.

At home, Ivan told Marie about Herr Muller.

"Are you sure he was a guard at Auschwitz?"

"I think he was."

"You can't just think he was. You must know he was."

Ivan shrugged, walked over to the stove to put the coffee on. That night he awoke in a cold sweat. Marie asked him,

"What's wrong?"

"Muller was a guard at the camp, I can see him in my mind."

"Go to sleep Ivan."

Ivan would not let it go. He called Marie's father, asked him for his help in finding out who this man was. Marie's father agreed to do what he could to find out more about, Herr Muller.

Ivan carried out his duties for four more days with no word from Marie's father. If Muller had been a guard at Auschwitz, Ivan wanted him punished to the full extent of the law. He received a call from John that night telling him he had not come up with anything on Herr Muller except for the data on his citizenship papers. He added he had sent a letter to the Israeli embassy asking for their assistance. Ivan thanked him, tried to stop himself from getting worked up by Herr Muller.

Two weeks later, Ivan had just returned home after sealing pelts, to find two young men in business suits sitting in his driveway. They introduced themselves as being from the Israeli embassy. Ivan shook their hands, invited them into his home. The taller man passed him a loose-leaf notebook full of pictures. He asked Ivan to look at the pictures. Ivan took his time looking at the photos. He pointed out five faces he remembered from Auschwitz. Herr Muller was among them. The shorter man told him he had identified known guards from the camp. He confirmed that Muller hadn't even changed his name. He added that other survivors had accused Muller of murder as well as theft, general brutality. Muller had been picked out by over a dozen survivors.

Ivan asked them the obvious question,

"Why hasn't he been arrested?"

The shorter man told him that the West German Government felt that the Nuremberg trials had ended the matter. They would not prosecute for war crimes. Ivan got irate, demanded to know what could be done? Both agents explained they could do nothing unless the United States agreed to deport him to Israel where he would stand trial. They advised they had made authorities aware of Muller. Ivan was not happy, but what could he do? He had no power to act in this situation.

When Marie returned home from her buying trip, Ivan related what happened. Her main concern was to keep Ivan away from Muller.

"You are a Game Warden. A member of the oldest law enforcement agency in the State. You can do nothing to mar the oath you took!"

Ivan angrily shook his head, "Of course I will do nothing, just like the rest of the world is doing nothing to punish these criminals."

Marie stayed, overnight, but had to leave early to hold to her buying schedule. The more furs, she owned, the better deal she would get from the large companies that bought her furs.

Ivan also left early. He would spend an hour or more sealing pelts at various locations to aid the trappers. Trapping was serious business. Almost every farm boy was after every expensive mink he could catch. Ivan's responsibilities did not slow down in the winter. Snow machines, ice fishermen, hunters, trappers, sealing furs, aiding law enforcement kept him busy.

When Spring arrived, the ground was still covered with more than three feet of snow on level ground. Max paid them a visit, settled his debt, reported a decent year on the trapline. Ivan envied the young man, missed the quiet woods that had helped heal him. Marie gave Max hints to improve his fur handling, told Ivan the young man was hard-headed, didn't take advice very well. Ivan grabbed Marie around her waist.

"It takes a strong woman to tame a free trapper."

They laughed, giggled, made love like newlyweds.

Ivan was called out on a search and rescue for a farm boy that had ventured too far into the forest. Ivan headed a search party that found the boy unharmed, but very cold, just before dark. The boy had walked towards the searcher's portable siren. Ivan was thrilled to find the boy unharmed. Ivan had received a tip from a worker at a sawmill on the Saint John River. He turned onto the road leading to meet the man at the mill.

Herr Muller looked down on the unloading area of his sawmill. He saw his foreman, and two others, a short, ugly, Frenchman, and the Slavic-looking animal that wore a game warden's uniform engaged in conversation. He quickly got his sniper's rifle, centered the crosshairs on the Warden's chest. Just a few pounds of pressure, he thought, and the Russian would be no more. But Muller was a coward, not a man of conviction. He would never commit an overt act that would expose him for what he was. His way was the cowards, way. If he ever got a chance to snipe the Russian, he vowed he would.

Herr Muller was enjoying the spring day. The sun was warm, the trails still hardpacked with snow. He had passed many snowmobilers this fine day. Tourism brought many groups riding the well-groomed trails. Slowing down to navigate a sharp bend in the trail, he spotted the Slav Warden checking a group of riders. He huffed and puffed as he manually turned his sled around in the narrow trail, drove to an elevated position above the trail, got his sniper rifle ready, intending to shoot the Russian when he passed below him.

Herr Muller was hidden from the trail below him. It was a long shot, but he felt confident in his 98 Mauser 8mm. Ten good strides would put him back on his sled and then, out of the area in a hurry. He would show this animal, he thought.

Ivan's sled was an older model. Big and clumsy, its saving grace was its reliability. Ivan had ridden it many miles, made sure it was maintained properly. He was riding behind other machines slowly following the trail. He had just passed an old, dead, pine tree when the bullet tore through his bulky clothing, cut a furrow along his neck. He fell off the machine onto the hard-packed trail. In a daze, he realized he had been shot. He heard a snow machine accelerating away from him. By the time the sound abated, the snow under him was stained red with his blood. A couple stopped to help him, put a pressure bandage on his wound to staunch the flow of blood. They drove Ivan back to town, brought him to the home of the local nurse.

Mary Reese had been a nurse for over twenty years. She was highly competent, able to handle most emergencies. She quickly recognized the bullet wound, called for the doctor as she made Ivan as comfortable as possible. Marie beat the doctor to the nurse's home. She was silent as she sat by Ivan. A rage was building inside her as she recognized how close to death her man had come.

Doctor Martin arrived. He quickly sewed the wound, gave Ivan some anti-biotic to fight any possible infection. Ivan refused to take any pain pills, could feel the stitches pulling as he struggled to sit up. Ivan thanked the couple, MR. and Mrs. Larry Murphy for their kindness in coming to his aid. Marie hugged both of them before they left.

Marie drove Ivan home in complete silence. When she approached their home, local law enforcement was there to greet them. A search had been immediately instituted, but little had been found beside the spot the sniper fired from. They all agreed on one thing, a killer was loose in the Allagash.

Sheriff's detective Mark Schaffer had remained at the scene. He was squatting where the sniper had fired from. He lit up a smoke, scanned the snow to his right. He was trying to find an extracted cartridge in the deep snow. He stood up, studied the surface of the snow. He carefully dug through the snow with his fingers. He felt lucky when he pulled an 8mm casing out of the snow. Standing up, he could barely see the blood-stained snow below him. He put the fired casing in a plastic bag, slid it into his jacket pocket. He noted there was a big, dead, pine tree close to the stained snow. Could it be, he thought. He went to the tree, saw a bit of bark laying below the tree. Looking closer, he saw where the bullet may have entered the tree. Using his pocket knife, he carefully dug a slightly deformed bullet out.

Forensics determined it was an 8mm "solid" bullet. It was definitely a military bullet from the Second World war. If they could find the rifle that fired it, they would have their man.

Ivan sat very still as the nurse Reese removed the stitches. His wound had healed well, showed an angry red line across his neck. Mary smiled at him as he left. The bitter cold attacked his wound. He wrapped the wool scarf around his neck, got in his pickup to resume his duties.

7

Deputy Mark Schaffer was determined to check every gun shop from Fort Kent to Augustus to see if anyone had ordered a supply of 8mm military ammo. Not many gun shops carried that caliber in stock. He hoped they would have a record of the people who had ordered it.

After checking, 29, gun shops and other outlets, Deputy Shaffer had a shortlist of people who had ordered that ammo. Each bullet from each rifle is as distinctive as fingerprints. The Deputy simply asked the people he interviewed if he could take their rifle for test firing. Everyone on his list voluntarily handed their rifles over except for Herr Hans Muller.

Deputy Schaffer waited patiently as judge Fairbanks read his application for a search warrant for an 8mm rifle, and ammo that fit it. Schaffer had listed the man's accessibility to the trail that led to the site of the shooting, the fact that he had bought 10 boxes of military ammo, the fact he owned a snowmobile, the fact he had a previous run-in with the Warden. Judge Fairbanks signed the warrant.

Sheriff Tower, Deputy Schaffer, and Ivan knocked on the front door of Muller's house on the hill. The Sheriff handed the warrant to Muller while Ivan and Schaffer conducted the search. They found the rifle and ammunition in Muller's game room. Muller stood amongst the Nazi memorabilia with a sneer on his face as he saw the rifle in the hands of the deputy. When Muller drew a Walther PPK emblazoned with a Swastika on its grips, Ivan tackled him to the floor, cuffed him. Ivan leaned very close to Muller's ear.

"Now you will pay for Auschwitz."

Muller was sentenced to twenty years in prison for attempted murder. After he served his sentence, he would be deported to Israel to face war crimes. Ivan was satisfied justice had been done. It took quite a while for the talk about the Nazi being arrested to die down. Ivan and Marie had invited Detective Schaffer and his pretty, blonde girlfriend for a meal in Fort Kent. Ivan was starting to form a friendship with the tall, lanky Deputy who had caught Muller. Marie and Carol hit it off pretty well. The Deputy didn't bring up the fact that Ivan had identified Muller as a Nazi. Detective Schaffer was not one to spread gossip. He was a young man that had demonstrated outstanding ability to catch criminals. Sheriff Tower gave him full credit for the arrest. Marie was happy to close this unpleasant episode of their life.

They spent a pleasant evening, slept over at Marie's parent's house. Marie's father, John, told them about the increase in drugs in the area. Ivan was, not too concerned, about them, but promised John he would check the border with Quebec as soon as the dirt roads firmed up.

For the first time in his life, Max had money in his pocket. He had paid his debts, filled his belly with the finest foods, had a comfortable apartment that didn't cost him an arm and a leg. He had bought four deer hides from Marie to have the Native American woman who he knew as Agnes, make for him a shirt, and a vest. He planned to hunt for another black bear to make pemmican from, he had gotten fond of the taste in his mouth.

She was a Micmac Native American, spoke English, French, and Algonquian. She was about 55 years old, lived alone on a dirt road just over the border with New Brunswick. It was a pleasant drive. The sun was shining brightly, the air was full of the aroma of spruce, pine, hemlock, and balsam.

The morning sun illuminated the small Air-Stream trailer that she lived in. She was a tall, graceful woman with an unlined face, a serious demeanor. She wasn't one to waste words. Max started to tell her what he wanted when, over her shoulder appeared an oval face, framed by short, straight, black hair. The maidens, eyes were alert, Max thought they were focused only on him. He tried to sidle to his right to better see, the maiden but was unable to see more than her rounded shoulder. Max hesitated, cast his eyes around the neat yard uncluttered by anything. Someone had turned the earth over to either side of the entry. On her picnic table, Max could see two flats of multi-colored flowers.

"Isn't it too cold to plant?"

The maiden answered, "Pansies are very hardy, they will do well."

"Did you come to talk of my flowers trapper Max?"

Max gave a short laugh, stood fidgeting from foot to foot.

"Come in and have a coffee while you tell me why you have come."

As Max sat down at her small table, he was completely taken with the young maiden sitting across from him. He burned his lip on the hot coffee, drew a smile from the maiden.

Max was completely flustered. His face had turned red with embarrassment at his inability to control himself.

Agnes couldn't help but grin at the young trapper.

"Have you never seen a maiden before?"

"Not one as pretty."

Both women laughed. Max finally told her why he had come, asked Agnes the maiden's name.

"She's my granddaughter, Lucille Agnes. She is a member of my tribe, The people of the dawn."

Agnes gave Max a price for making his items. Max insisted on paying for them now. He asked her, "May I come to see your granddaughter again?"

"You must ask her Max. She makes up her own mind."

Max shyly asked, her if he could see her again?

"I teach school in Fort Kent. You can reach me at this number."

Max watched her write out her phone number, was completely taken with her beauty. Max was riding on air as he drove back to Fort Kent. He needed to check on his bear baits, see if any of them had become active. The woods were full of bears, he only needed one to fill his needs.

Lucille thought the young trapper had a sturdy frame. He had a pleasant face with a shock of hair hanging down onto his forehead. He was an inch or so shorter than her, but she thought she might let herself get to know this shy young man. Lucille was wary of men. Men with their lustful eyes and their groping hands. She'd grown up in poverty with her father who got drunk at every opportunity and a mother who was worn out from too many children, too much to bear in her life of poverty and neglect. Lucille had won a scholarship, studied to be an elementary teacher. She hoped she could influence young minds, help youngsters escape the bonds of poverty and despair. She soon found out that the reality of life usually won out over any idealism. Many young women in her district were barefoot and pregnant, carrying on the tradition she had been born into. Grandma Agnes had escaped the culture that dragged her people down. Her grandmother had provided a safe place for her to live and grow. It was a debt she could never repay, but she was devoted to her, would never abandon her.

Max had his first date in a restaurant in Fort Kent. Once he started talking, the words tumbled from his lips non-stop. Lucille listened quietly as Max told her of his early years. Living where she did, she was used to men's dreams of living a free life in the woods. She calmly tried to tell Max the need to prepare for his future by getting an education, finishing high school. Max could only see as far ahead as the next trapping season. There was something in the young man that called to her, brought out the woman in her. She decided that she had to be very careful around him lest he unleashes something in her that she couldn't control.

Max was high in his tree stand. The black flies forming a cloud around his head were only made worse by the biting mosquitos that stung him with a vengeance. He finally lit up a foul cigar to try and hold the horde of flies at bay. Dusk was falling when the small bear came in to, feed. Max was getting tired of feeding this small bear, but this was his most active site, he had little choice other than to wait for a bigger bear to come to his bait. The darkness was complete when Max came down from his stand. At home, he scrubbed his face, hands, and wrists trying to alleviate the itchiness the bites caused. This is the curse of the north woods. With the coming of warm weather comes the hordes of flesh-biting insects arriving in full force.

Two nights later, Max was in his stand. Dusk was falling when the small bear came into his bait. Max heard a heavy crash not far away, the young bear, sniffed the air, ran directly under Max's stand to disappear into the hemlock cover. A large male bear entered the clearing. When he paused not thirty yards away, Max shot him just under his chin. The heavy bullet from the .38/55 dropped the large bruin in its tracks. It took Max the rest of the night to skin and process the large bear.

Max arrived at Agnes's trailer with the pelt, the meat, the innards Agnes needed to properly tan the hide. He had the meat packed in dry ice. Agnes nodded to him, told him to give her a few weeks to make the pemmican. Max was preparing for winter in the month of April.

Max was anxious for Lucille to meet Ivan and Marie. He proudly drove up to their cottage. He had told Lucille how Ivan and Marie had helped him, even told of his ordeal in the woods where Ivan found him. They were welcomed into Ivan's home, had a pleasant visit. Marie tried to get Max interested in obtaining a high school diploma. Lucille chipped in that she would help him get a GED certificate. Max was embarrassed by all the attention. Ivan was wearing his uniform and that caused Lucille a little angst. Her experience with law enforcement was clouded by what she had seen as a child. She had witnessed sometimes brutal treatment of tribe members by local police. Ivan's sturdy appearance disturbed her. His, French Canadian wife, Marie, hardly came up to his shoulder. She knew of Marie and her grandfather by their visits to the tribal center to buy furs. They were both respected for their treatment of her people. Fort Kent is a small community, everybody knows your business.

Marie knew of Lucille who had won a scholarship to the State College. She was surprised to see the young woman with Max. She thought about her own attraction to Ivan, decided there's no putting any logic to who winds up with who.

The next morning dawned clear and cold. The morning sun was welcome as Ivan hooked up the trailer and his three-wheeler. Amos had told him the dirt road that paralleled the Quebec border was passable to the top of the first long hill he came to. He suggested for Ivan to park his rig at the log landing and use his three-wheeler from there.

Ivan put his Model 54 Winchester into the scabbard on the three-wheeler. He added his thermos, his lunch. After being shot, he went nowhere without being fully armed. When he pulled into the log landing, the foreman directed him to a spot to park his rig. The man told him there were a lot of people traveling the road. The road showed signs of heavy traffic. Ivan knew most of it was recreational, he cared about what was not recreational. He encountered four rigs, checked them for proper registration. The people he encountered so far, had all been polite, courteous. When he observed tracks heading towards a possible border crossing, he made note of it. As the day wore on, the sun had softened the surface of the road, it was tough going to the log landing. When he got back to his truck, he radioed the Border patrol of the possible crossings.

Border patrol agent, Jack Murphy was looking at tracks leading across the border. He noticed the tracks didn't look right. It appeared to him that the three-wheeler was towing, some kind of sled. He could only wonder what was packed on that sled. He carefully made note of the area and the strange tracks for a future stake-out site. Jack and Ivan would return to the site and try to solve the mystery of what sort of contraband was being brought across the border.

Jack enlisted the aid of Ivan and Deputy Mark Schaffer to stake out the crossing. They had a roadblock set up at the log landing. Mark was hidden in the woods one hundred yards below the roadblock, Ivan was manning the truck blocking the road. Thankfully, the nights had not been extremely cold. This was the fourth night they had established the roadblock. Ivan checked out all off-road vehicles passing through. So far, they had caught three drunk operators. About two in the morning, two three-wheelers stopped before the roadblock. Jack motioned for them to come forward. They ignored the order. The man on the rear three-wheeler broke and ran. Deputy Schaffer gave chase, then tackled and cuffed the man in the mud. The remaining man opened fire with his handgun. Jack returned fire with his M1 carbine, killing the felon. The sled being pulled contained 150 pounds of what later turned out to be, Heroin. The man Deputy Schaffer caught claimed to be an innocent bystander. He stated he ran because he was afraid. The man had no record, was given the benefit of a doubt, released from custody. After the ordeal was over, Ivan suffered flashbacks in his mind, of Auschwitz and the violence he had witnessed and experienced there. He complained to Marie that the violence, degradation, that he endured would never leave him. She held him in her arms, kissed him repeatedly.

Ivan was having coffee in the local diner with Deputy Schaffer. Mark was telling him he had to be ready to use the gun on his hip.

"Every person you meet in the woods and on your patrolling is armed. You have to be ready to defend your life. Jack told me you hadn't even drawn your revolver until the felon started shooting. Jack was ready, he returned fire immediately, he did the right thing. He told me to have this talk with you, told me you needed to hear it."

"I don't know that it's in me to take a human life. I just don't know."

Mark stood up, "I don't want to be the one to skid you out of the woods Ivan Petrov. Listen to what I'm telling you."

Ivan watched the tall, lean Deputy walk out. Is everyone, in this life jaded he thought. Most of the people he meets are good, honest, law-abiding people. Even the poachers he meets are usually just trying to feed their families, he can't think of them as bad people. Maybe that's his problem, he just doesn't want to meet bad people. Ivan forced himself to resume his patrol. There were fishermen to be checked, he needed to get on with it, forget about Auschwitz.

The fact that Ivan treated people fairly, always treated people with dignity, went a long way with the local people. Ivan had gained the respect of the people in his community.

Lucille had just gotten back from a trip from deep into the
Allagash with Max. He had shown her where his trapline
was located. Although she had been born less than twenty
minutes from Fort Kent, she had never set foot in the Allagash
before. She had enjoyed the outing right up to the point where Max
got a little too amorous. She had firmly pushed him, away, told him
they were not ready for a relationship. When Max let his anger show,
Lucille decided it was time to cool off. Max did not respond well to
her words.

When school started, all of a sudden, Lucille was too busy to
have any time for him. When Max went to collect his pemmican
from Agnes, he asked the older woman how Lucille was? Agnes
ignored the question as she handed Max his Pemmican. Max said,

"Can you tell her I'm sorry and that I want to see her again?"

"No Max the trapper. I cannot speak for Lucille. I can tell you
that you came to these forests to take what you desire. You cannot
take from a woman that which is hers to give."

Max's face turned red as a feeling of shame washed over him.
He left like a dog with his tail between his legs. On the ride back to
town, he decided to talk to Lucille, apologize for how he had acted.
He waited outside her apartment in town for over two hours before
he saw her walking towards him. When she stopped in front of him,
he apologized, pleaded with her to forgive him.

"You made me afraid Max. My own mother was afraid of my father. I grew up around women that were afraid of the men they married. Fear will never be a part of my life. I had thought you were different. I'm not sure anymore. I only know that fear will not be a part of my life. I am not an object to be used to satisfy you or anyone else. It's best that we don't see one another for a while. Maybe time will heal what happened between us,"

Max did the only thing he knew, he packed up, left for the woods. He hunted for grouse during the warm fall days. He passed the warm afternoons dozing in the sun. His sets had all been made. He was eager to try out some new scent lure he had bought from a supply house. His heart ached at the memory of Lucille's words. His father's admonition came into his mind, "Do the right thing, Max." He was truly ashamed of himself for his actions. He vowed if she ever gave him another chance, he would never let her down again. He had time he thought. Time to return to Fort Kent, ask Lucille to wait for him. Tell her that he needed to say goodbye before the trapping season started. He wasted no time in paddling back to Allagash.

Lucille was surprised to see Max standing by her apartment door.

"Can I buy you a coffee, Lucille? Can I please talk to you?"

Lucille took his hand and together they walked down to the diner. Max told her that he had to say goodbye before he left for the winter. He asked her to give him another chance. He told her he was ashamed of himself for his actions. Lucille touched his hand, told him not to worry, she would see him in the Spring.

Max's spring was back in his step. The sun shone, brighter, the very air was purer. Max checked his traps by day, fleshed and stretched his pelts by night. When he had idle time, he studied the material Lucille had given him. He was determined to get his GED just to please her, show her he was committed to her. A snowstorm buried all his traps. He was in the process of recovery and reset when he broke through the thin ice, fell up to his knees in the freezing water while trying to untangle a drowning trap chain that had hung up on an underwater snag. He didn't panic. He made a roaring fire, warmed his feet, dried his boots and socks. It was a confident Max that knew how to take care of himself that strode through the newly fallen snow to his shelter. Max was growing up, learning from others, doing the right thing.

Lucille had a free week before school started. She chose to spend it with her grandmother. She happily helped Agnes with her canning of fruits and vegetables for the coming winter. Helped her tan hides, put up pemmican, preserve fish. Although Agnes didn't have a thriving business, she had no trouble earning enough money to more than meet her expenses. Trappers stopped by to pick up their pemmican. Others stopped to pick up the leather clothing that Agnes specialized in. A Frenchwoman stopped by to pick up a supply of herbal tea leaves that Agnes made. All were greeted cordially, all treated Agnes with respect. It was respect she had earned over the years. She was an independent woman living an independent life.

The electrician had just finished installing the remote starter for an emergency generator. Agnes thanked him as he was leaving. It was necessary because of the frequent loss of power during the winter storms. The ice storms were pretty severe, could result in loss of power for as long as two weeks. Agnes lived at the end of the line, lost power on a regular basis. The young man took a nice buckskin vest as payment for his labor. Agnes was known as the best barterer in the region. Lucille was sewing the pieces for a pullover buckskin shirt. The customer wanted it fringed across the chest, and down both arms. It was an old design that went back, centuries, but was still in demand. She was using the foot-powered sewing machine that a machinist had made for grandmother years ago. She had been a young girl when grandmother had gotten the machine, was amazed it was still operational. Grandmother was totally prepared for hard times. She had propane gas lights as well as electric ones. She had two good sources of heat, sufficient canned goods to last the long winter. She made her own clothes, moccasins, and anything else she needed.

She had a place for every tool and utensil and woe be unto anyone who didn't put them back in their proper place.

They grilled some nice moose steaks backed up by day-old potato salad that Lucille loved. They drank herbal tea as the sun dipped low in the western sky casting breathtaking colors all along the western horizon. It was a beautiful spot in good weather.

Ivan had just finished checking fishermen when he decided to pull into the home of Midas, Moran. The elderly man was an artist that worked magic on the broad palms of bull moose antlers. Midas traveled thousands of miles collecting shed antlers, was an excellent source about the goings-on in the backcountry. Not much escaped the old man's eye, and he freely passed the information on to Fish and game. Midas stopped his work on a shed. Ivan looked at the scene of a musher and his sled dogs flowing across the broad palm of the shed. Midas poured them coffee told Ivan he had seen tracks of a mountain lion. Ivan listened politely. Maine's official stance was that there were no mountain lions in the State. It was, however, illegal to shoot one. Since Ivan had seen tracks of mountain lions in the Allagash, he had no problem believing him. He told Ivan of an illegal killing of a female moose in a mud wallow alongside a snowmobile trail. Ivan made note of the location, told him he would certainly check it out. Fish and Game depended on good people like Midas for their tips. There were many, many, tips phoned in, relayed to the wardens.

Ivan had been notified by a biologist that collared moose #235, was not moving, hadn't moved in 24 hours. Ivan knew this was the moose Midas had told him about. Ivan arrived at the scene, found the animal's head and the tracking collar laying close to it. Some of the meat had been taken by the poachers. Much of the meat had been eaten by varmints. Bones and moose hair were scattered about the scene. There was little Ivan could do at this point, but he would definitely increase, his patrols in this area. He picked up the tracking collar before he left. Ivan knew that there were a few poachers in his area. Most of the poaching was done to feed their families. He could understand it, but he would try his best to curtail it. Midas had told him that, "Hansen's meadows," was a hot spot for night hunters. Ivan determined he would set up a vigil there.

Ivan was parked on a piece of ledge cap on the edge of the green field. A few deer had entered the field while paying no attention to his pickup. Just after ten, the field was lit up by the lights of a jeep. After a shot was fired, Ivan immediately, drove into the field, blocked the exit with his truck. He radioed for assistance, stood behind his truck with his rifle in hand. A Sheriff's cruiser parked at the entrance. Ivan had him stand by with his blue lights flashing while he drove his pickup down to the parked jeep. He wrote out a citation for the young man and his uncle, confiscated the deer and their rifles. The deputy asked what would happen with the deer? Ivan told him the meat would be given away to the needy. He thanked the young deputy for his help.

Marie woke to the sound of Ivan heating coffee on the stove. She helped him make a sandwich, sat with him while he ate. It was a familiar tale for her now. She had heard this story many times, always worried when Ivan was out at night. Ivan sought the comfort of his wife, fell asleep with her head on his shoulder.

James Devine was a poacher. He was not your ordinary poacher that shot meat for his family. He had a regular route much like a milkman. He had given up jacklighting deer because it was too easy to get caught. He would travel the back roads at the best times deer were on the move. Three in the morning, the roads were deserted, sometimes he would catch deer crossing these dirt roads, shoot them in the light from his headlights with his six-inch .44 Magnum pistol. He would cruise the roads until an hour past dawn. He never put a deer into the back of his pickup while he was armed. He would repeat this procedure the last two hours of daylight. If he spotted a deer in the fields or brush, he would shoot from his truck's windows, immediately leave the area. He was, in effect, a moving target. After he had an animal down, he would return home, get rid of his firearm, grab his tools, and recover the meat from the carcass. At his home, he would neatly package the meat, deliver it to his many customers. If he was ever caught with the meat, he would be found guilty of possessing illegal deer meat, not shooting deer out of season.

Ivan was standing over the remains of a poacher's kill. The animal had been processed in a way that was becoming, very familiar, to him. Picture the animal spread-eagled, laying on its stomach. The poacher would slice the hide open from its neck to its tail. He would then skin the hide down far enough to separate the meat, without ever touching the guts of the animal. He even took pains to cut around the larger bones to make his burden less. Ivan looked down on the head, the four lower legs of the deer, and the undisturbed gut pile. Ivan noted the poacher had even taken the liver and the heart of the animal. This was the fourth time he had responded to farmers' complaints. He knew that there were probably many more remains like this scattered through the bushes surrounding the fields.

There was a faint moonlight shining when James approached the doe he had shot just before sundown. He quickly skinned the hide back from head to tail, peeled it down to expose the meat. Using his bone saw, he separated the lower legs, separated the hams from the spine, cut around the large bone, packed the meat into his backpack. He cut out the backstraps, cut out the usable meat on the shoulders. He added the heart and liver to his backpack. The rest of the animal he left laying where it had fallen. A quarter-mile walk to his hidden truck, and he was on his way home.

This was the strategy that Ivan was faced with. The butchered remains were spread out over two hundred square miles, or more. There was no, hot spot, for him to find. He was faced with catching a poacher that was super cautious. He was having coffee with detective Schaffer telling him about the elusive poacher. Mark told him the man had been doing this for years. He had heard tell of the man's methods years ago. Ivan asked him, "How do we catch someone like this?"

"The only way to catch him is to get to his kill before he does. He obviously shoots and runs only to return later to process the animal. Even if you catch him, he will be guilty only of possessing an illegal deer."

"I have to do something to stop this man. He is stealing from all the honest hunters out there."

Mark laughed. This man figures he's more deserving than your average hunter. His mindset is that the deer belong to the men that spend all their time hunting them. Make no mistake, this man knows the woods, he knows the animals he hunts. Have you thought about what he does with the meat after he poaches them? Ivan shook his head, shrugged his shoulders. This man could be anyone. He could be a logger shooting them as he goes and returns from his job site. He could be the milk man shooting them on his route. If it's not the parish priest, it could be a husky farm girl. Ivan just shook his head at Mark's words.

"You're not helping me, Mark."

"Tell you what, I'll check with all the people that sell meat in the area. Maybe this guy is taking business away from them."

Ivan liked the sound of that.

Marie was gone when Ivan arrived home. He got a chicken diner going, put the bottle of wine he had bought for her in an ice bucket. Marie came in and helped him prepare the yellow beans and toss a salad together. They shared the salad and the wine while the chicken cooked.

"Did you get a chance to talk to Max before he left?"

"No, I've been too busy trying to catch a poacher."

"I heard that Max and Lucille had some kind of a fight."

"People gossip about things that are none of their business. Max is a big boy; he can take care of himself.'

"Max is a baby lost in the woods. He needs a woman to pull him out of his fantasies into the real world."

Ivan did not want to argue with his wife; he just grunted.

9

Ivan had quickly learned that Marie was not only outspoken she was as immovable as a granite boulder in a disagreement. She wouldn't compromise on any issue. She was right and you were wrong. Ivan took the easy way out with his petite, wife, he just wouldn't argue with her. That aside, he loved her dearly. She had changed his life. She had brought back the happiness he had felt in his youth, pushed back the dark memories into the recesses of his mind. Those memories had never diminished in his mind. He had only to see an elderly person walking on the side of the road, or a child sitting in its yard, or a uniformed officer, for the memories of Auschwitz to flood his mind, making him lightheaded before he could gain control of himself. For all his size and strength, despite the fact he was an armed officer of the law, he felt the cold fingers of fear when his memories surfaced. When he was with Marie, his memories didn't haunt him. When he was in the forests, his memories didn't haunt him. Perhaps he felt he should have died as he saw so many others die—men who were shrunken inside their meager clothing; men who worked and starved to death in the freezing cold of the long winters; innocent people being herded into the gas chamber; people that were stripped of their belongings, stripped of the garments they wore, stripped of human dignity. No one that hasn't endured suffering and brutality over a long period of time can understand what happened at the camps. Ivan came back to reality when he heard the distant sound of a rifle shot. He put his truck in gear, drove down the dirt road towards the distant fields. He passed right by the poacher's prey without ever knowing it was there. He continued his patrol which carried him farther away from the poacher he was hunting for.

Mark Schaffer checked on every butcher's shop he knew of. Spoke to merchants, gas station owners, truck drivers, in his desire to help Ivan catch his poacher. Ivan was quite a study, he thought. There was a part of the man you couldn't reach. Part of him that was private, off-limits. One farmer had told him of a green pickup that, he saw parked on his wood road where it didn't belong. That was the most common information he got. People didn't like it when other people trespassed. He doggedly continued talking to people, he made a list of those people that had been previously caught shooting deer at night, or out of season. When his list topped more than thirty people, he abandoned the idea. He switched tactics, decided to enlist the aid of other deputies in looking for the elusive poacher.

Deputies started to report random gunshots just before nightfall. Ivan would respond to the affected areas, try to spot an animal laying in a field. It was frustrating work for Ivan, but he persevered in his effort to catch the poacher. He finally got a break when he spotted part of an antler sticking up out of the short grass. He radioed Schaffer, requested his aid. Schaffer had his cruiser hidden up a logging road waiting for the poacher to arrive. Ivan was in the field fifty yards away laying in the short grass. Night had fallen along with a wet, heavy dew that soon had Ivan getting uncomfortable. Without warning, Ivan saw the shadowy form of the poacher approach the dead buck. Ivan waited until the poacher had made his initial butchering cut on the animal before he keyed his radio three times. When Ivan saw, Mark's cruiser, stop at the entrance to the field, he approached the poacher revolver in hand. James didn't offer any resistance, allowed himself to be taken into custody without saying a word. James had been through this before. He knew he was going to be found guilty of possession, not illegal shooting. He knew he would pay a fine, lose his hunting license for a year, but he wouldn't lose his custom Mauser model 98 in .25-06 caliber.

James pleaded guilty to possession of an illegal deer. His only statement to the court was, "I happen to see the antler sticking up, though I would salvage the meat before it spoiled. He was found guilty of a misdemeanor, assessed a small fine, lost his hunting license for a year. Ivan was satisfied they had caught the man, didn't allow himself to question the law. Mark laughed, told Ivan,

"I told you so."

James continued to poach deer. No license was necessary to poach deer, and he had customers to keep happy.

Ivan had no trouble accepting the meager penalty that the law imposed on James. He would continue to carry out his responsibilities, let the State worry about the laws. Mark continued to harp on the inadequacy of the law, while Ivan chose to concentrate on his responsibilities. He concentrated his efforts on the trappers in his area. These men were professionals, out to make a dollar. He wanted to impress them with the need to follow the laws to protect the very animals they derived their income from. He started a trapping seminar for young people and first-time trappers. His training course was approved by the State and Ivan received a commendation for his efforts.

10

Indian summer was in full force on this beautiful October day. The multi-colored leaves were falling to the ground. It was a day whose beauty was marred by the disappearance of a young woman. Louise Beday was a Native American maiden who painted landscapes of the Allagash. The comely young maidens canoe had been found drifting on the water. Some of her painting supplies were in the canoe as well as a lunch basket and a thermos. Mark had looked over everything and concluded that the young woman had not touched her lunch or drank from the thermos. All he had to go on was her sketch pad found lying in the bottom of the canoe. Four days had gone by with no clue as to what had happened to the young woman. Mark was at his wit's end when he met Ivan, asked him to look at the sketch pad. Ivan thought he recognized a particular scene. He told Mark he thought he could take him to the spot.

The sun was shining brightly when Ivan turned the motor off on his boat, tied off the boat to a handy tree limb. Max had volunteered to come with them. It proved to be the correct spot when they saw an easel set up on the edge of a clearing. The newly fallen leaves had erased any sign that anyone had been there. The easel stood as an eerie sentinel as to what had transpired there. A quick search turned up a woman's hat, one leather glove. Clearly, something had happened here. Mark got as many people as he could to aid in the search. Twenty-odd people were systematically searching the woods. Mark had a grid worked out and he and Ivan were on the wings of each search area.

Late that afternoon, Deputy Johnson found the murdered body of the maiden. No pains had been taken to hide the nude body. A thorough search turned up no forensic evidence. Mark was hopeful the autopsy would shed light on what had transpired. The results of the autopsy revealed that the young woman had been raped and strangled. The victim had been struck in the head, had bruising on many parts of her body. The man who assaulted her had type O blood.

Max and Lucille were visiting Agnes. They talked of the tragedy that had happened to the young woman. Agnes knew the victim, stated that they had the exact same compass. Max quickly saw the significance of the compass, asked Agnes if he could show it to the authorities. Agnes agreed, added, "Louise never goes out in the woods without that compass."

Max brought the compass to Ivan who quickly told Mark of the new information. Marie sat at the table shaking her head at the news of the killing. Mark photographed the compass for the police records, told them, "This could be the evidence that gets this rapist, murderer caught. I don't believe the killer would not keep this."

When Ivan had seen the body of the young woman, he was immediately back to Auschwitz in his mind. Memories of the camp flooded through his mind making him unable to function. Mark had grabbed his arm, told him to sit down and recover his senses. Mark began to realize the abject horror that Ivan lived with. Mark could now begin to understand why Ivan had not drawn his revolver when the drug smuggler had been shot.

The compass was a very old, best-quality one that was not a common item. Mark felt it might just be what he needed if only he could find a suspect. Mark had interviewed everyone he could think of, had not come up with a single clue. Mark decided to visit Agnes to return her compass, perhaps she could shed some light on the life of Louise Beday.

There was no response to Mark's knocking on the trailer door. He walked around the trailer to find Agnes fleshing a deer hide. Various pieces of buckskin were suspended over a smoky fire. At the sound of his voice, Agnes quickly pivoted to face him. He quickly identified himself, apologized for startling her. Agnes wiped her hands on her apron, told him she was just about to make tea, would he like a cup? Mark nodded yes, followed her into her home. Mark noted that it was the cleanest, the best organized trailer he had ever seen. Agnes replied, "I like an organized place."

The tea was strong, hot, flavored with honey, Mark liked the taste.

"Can you tell me anything about Louise?"

"Her mother and I got the same compass from a fur buyer many years ago. Louise got the compass after her mother went to another life. Louise roamed these woods making her paintings. She was desired by many men, chose not to be with them."

"Do you know anyone that was bothering her?"

"No, I don't see her very often anymore. You should talk to her grandfather. If anyone knows of Louise, it's her grandfather."

Mark had already spoken with the local police who had no information to give him. He followed Agnes's directions to a small house where he saw a withered old man sitting in a chair by an old Ford pickup. The old man told him that he didn't interfere with his granddaughter's life. Mark pressed him about any men she might have feared or been afraid of.

"She was afraid of all men. When she was young, she had been attacked by three young men. They were never punished for what they did to her."

Mark thanked the old man, drove back to his office to search the records for the assault on Louise. He had to go down to the basement, check through the old records before he found the report. Two of the men had moved out of the area. Joseph Crouper lived in Fort Kent, a half-mile from the center of town. He had a record of public drunkenness, assault, and battery on a woman, had served time for sexual assault on a woman. Mark got a current photo of the man, drove to Allagash, showed the picture to as many people as he could. He was having coffee with Ivan when he showed the picture to the waitress. She told him the man had been in the diner the morning Louise went missing. She added that the man was, a "creepy bastard", always staring at the women. Mark enlisted Ivan's aid and together they drove to the man's home. Mark noted the pickup and the canoe laying alongside it.

"I think I can get a search warrant based on the man's past and the fact he was in Allagash the day Louise went missing."

Judge Fairbanks read the warrant application, signed the warrant that was valid only for the compass that Louise was said to own. He added that he thought Mark might be legally on a fishing trip. Mark called another deputy, the trio paid a visit to Joseph's house, served the warrant. The Sheriff had warned Mark that he could only search for the compass. Anything else he found that was not in plain view would be excluded.

Joseph was drinking beer, had a bottle in his hand when he opened the door. Two other men were drinking with him. The deputy got their names before ordering them to leave the premises. Before Joseph sat at the table, Mark made him empty his pockets, took the hunting knife on his belt away from him. The man sat at the table getting madder by the minute. Ivan stood a few feet in the back of him, keeping a close eye on the muscular man. Joseph was about 5'10" and solidly built. Mark and the deputy searched for over an hour without finding the compass. Disgusted, Mark went out to search the pickup. The truck was unlocked, and Mark saw a backpack by the passenger seat floor. When he opened the backpack, he saw the compass. He compared it to the picture, it was a perfect match. Mark should have known better, but in his eagerness, he burst into the kitchen with the compass extended towards Joseph. Joseph went completely mad at the sight of the compass in Mark's hand. Ivan grabbed him around his neck, wrestled him to the floor where the deputy cuffed him. Joseph accepted a plea bargain, was sentenced to 25 years to life.

As a result of the case, Mark was offered a job as a detective with the State Police. He was assigned to the north country he dearly loved.

After the burial, a wake was held in the town hall for Louise. The crowd of people was overwhelming. Agnes was there with Max, Lucille, and Louise's grandfather. Many tribal members attended. Ivan, Marie, Mark, Carol, and the Sheriff attended to pay their respects. Murders were scarce in the Allagash. Ivan prayed it would always be so.

Back at home. Marie was telling Ivan that he was a Game Warden, not a policeman. Her feelings were that Ivan should, "steer clear," of police involvement. Ivan sternly told her that he would always offer to help when called on. Who is better able to help the police when the crime happens in the woods? Marie gave up her argument, hugged her man to her. Ivan clearly won that argument.

Marie had agreed to lecture on how to properly handle furs, how to properly finish fleshing and stretching the pelts for maximum value. To her, it was a shame to take a forty-dollar pelt, mishandle it and get little money for it. Marie used an Indian woman to handle those pelts that she bought that had been only skinned, salted, rolled flesh side in. She explained that some furs should be skinned, "cased," versus those skins that are skinned open. Using the proper stretching boards was necessary to avoid overstretching and distortion of the pelt. Cuts, scrapes, bullet holes all lowered the value of the pelt.

Marie had started going with her grandfather when she was twelve years old. She loved handling the furs. Had studied with her grandfather on every aspect of the fur trade. In reality, very few trappers handled their pelts properly. She hoped that her lectures would be of help.

Max had attended three of Marie's lectures. He wanted to get the most from his pelts that he could. Marie had told him that long-haired fur was coming into vogue, and their prices would go up. She recommended that Max should concentrate on lynx, fisher, coyotes, and foxes. Max was maturing. It was evident to Marie that the young man was serious in his desire to become a top trapper. He had the will and the stamina to withstand the harsh winters. He and Lucille had become frequent guests at their home. She would miss their visits over the long trapping season. She was planning a barbeque for their friends on Labor, day. She prayed the weather would co-operate.

Labor, day in the Allagash marked the end of summer and the fervent hope that winter would hold off for two months. The unpredictable weather could bring a sleet storm or heavy snow at any time. Ivan hoped that Indian summer with its cool nights and warm days would win out, but he well knew a kiss from the north winds could bring snow and sleet at any time. All his vehicles had been tuned up ready to reply to the harsh conditions ahead. He was enjoying the warm weather riding his three-wheeler down a logging road. When he topped a rise, ravens took wing below him. He stopped by a deer carcass that had the hind end removed, its antlers removed, and the balance left to the scavengers. There was little he could do except pull the carcass off the trail. Although appreciation for wildlife was on the upswing across America, in the Allagash region, the use of wildlife for food remained strong. Farmers and loggers were independent, often hardheaded people. They would not be easily persuaded to change their views on any subject. It was much the same in Ukraine, Ivan thought. People take care of their needs.

It's hard to put a figure to, the numbers of deer that are poached. The people that engage in this practice are varied. You may think that it's only country folk that poaches; you'd be wrong. In western Penn., a minister who admitted poaching over 200 deer was caught. His explanation to the judge was, "I fed the meat to the poor and the needy." Many people poach for the excitement, the thrill of it. Many are hunters that spend many hours in the woods. Some want trophies, some want meat, some just want excitement.

Ivan knew his chances of catching the farm boy shooting a deer to feed his family, or anyone who occasionally shot a deer out of season, were slim. He concentrated on people who took many, animals on a regular basis. Input from farmers, timber companies, private citizens that were outraged by poachers, was his best source of information. He always followed up these tips which led him to areas that repeat poachers were using.

11

This beautiful Labor, day, with its bright sunshine and a balmy westerly wind, was marred by the disappearance of a young girl from an established camping area in the Allagash. Detective Mark Schaffer, Maine State Police, was in charge of the investigation. Mark immediately assigned two State policemen, two deputies to interview the other campers. Mark was conferring with Sheriff Tower who wanted to get a search party started immediately. Mark cautioned that he wanted Ivan and as many trappers as possible to lead the search. He reasoned that these experienced woodsmen were more apt to find signs of the missing eight-year-old than anyone else. Mark was adamant, would not initiate any search until these men arrived.

By nine that morning, Ivan and eight experienced trappers were ready to start the search. Ivan had proposed a circular search of the campsite, extending out to a two-hundred-yard circle. Mark nodded his assent. Each trapper led at least two law enforcement members. The trappers were tuned in to any disturbance in the woodland as they slowly led out the search. A spry, sixty-eight-year-old trapper found the first sign. The search was halted while Ivan, Mark, and Sheriff Tower Joined Alfred Holmes. He pointed out the faint signs of a struggle. They were in sight of the camping spot of the missing little girl.

The old trapper would not be hurried. Step by step he led the way another one hundred and fifty yards to where the little girl lay naked in the underbrush. No attempt had been made to hide her.

Mark put his ear to her chest, felt for a pulse. The little girl was barely breathing, but she was alive.

Medical personnel were on hand, quickly got the little girl to the hospital. Little, blonde-haired, Julie Jones responded to treatment. She regained consciousness in the ambulance.

Mark ordered the search to continue. Trapper Holmes eventually tracked the suspect back to the campsite. No one had signed out that morning. The child molester was in the campgrounds.

Mark and Sheriff Tower were just outside Julie's hospital room waiting to possibly speak with her. When they entered the room, Julie was in her sobbing mother's arms. Mark waited politely for them to calm down before approaching. Julie had a terrible bruise on her forehead, just above her eye. Julie appeared calm in her mother's arms. The doctor had told them Julie was probably unconscious when she had been assaulted. She described an older boy who she said, "He led me into the woods to show me something."

A State Police artist soon had a sketch of the boy. Armed with the sketch, Mark quickly found and arrested the boy. Under questioning with his lawyer present, the boy admitted his guilt. Everyone involved was relieved by the positive outcome. When the story reached the newspapers, trapper Alfred Holmes became an instant hero. Mark and Ivan were drinking a coffee while Alfred was being interviewed by the press. The old man down-played his part in the search. His only comment was, "Glad I could help."

Mark was highly praised by his superiors for the way he took charge of the scene, initiated a search using experienced people, bringing the case to a quick solution. He was promoted to Detective Sergeant. Ivan was happy for his friend, happy that the trappers had responded to his appeal.

As much as Ivan loved his family, he could not bring himself to want children. It was becoming a sore spot between him and Marie. Marie had almost threatened him with stopping to take her birth control pills, but she reasoned that Ivan must still be suffering from his years in Auschwitz. How do you comprehend what Ivan endured for almost four years? You cannot put yourself in his shoes, or his mind. Marie knew that she brought her man great comfort. Ivan was always peaceful and calm with her, but there were signs that he hadn't fully conquered his fears. From what she read about survivors of the camps, she doubted he would ever be rid of the memories of Auschwitz. Ivan always looked for the best in people. He never had a bad word for those people he cited or arrested. His thought to her was always, "Walk a mile in someone's shoes before you pass judgment."

In Marie's interest in understanding her husband, she started reading books by noted Russian and Jewish authors. When she tried to discuss them with Ivan, he would sometimes become irrational. One book she tried to discuss with him was about one day in a prisoner's life and the hardship he had endured. Ivan soon built up the conversation by going into a rant that he had endured that life for almost four years, he didn't need to be reminded of it. Everything that Marie said, set him off on a new rant. He was almost foaming at the mouth when he saw a book about the German death squads. He started with seeing his entire family herded into a trench, being shot to death, he ended in a hysterical description of a woman holding her infant in front of her just before the both of them were shot. After his rants, he would fall into a depression that might last for days. Marie never brought another book home with her, she read what she wanted in the library in fort Kent, but she vowed she would never stop trying to understand, help her husband.

Ivan never got rid of his demons. Only when he was deep in the woods alone did he not have thoughts of Auschwitz. In towns or cities, his memories would surface at the slightest thing. If he saw a group talking, his mind would see them being herded into the gas chambers. If he saw a man pushing a wheelbarrow, he looked for the body inside it. If he saw a man put his hand on a child's back, he saw the child directed to a trench. The scenarios were endless, without substance or real meaning, but they were real in Ivan's mind. He had seen it over and over for four years. It would never leave him, he would never know what "normal" was.

12

Peter Weber was a simple farm boy in 1936. He was born to parents that had good genes. He grew to be just over six feet in height, had blonde hair, blue eyes, and easy-going nature. He was the perfect candidate for Nordic males. He, and all his classmates, soon fell under the spell of Adolf Hitler. Peter joined the brown shirts, was devoted to the principles put out by Herr Hitler. He was soon selected to join an elite group called the SS. His black uniform attracted the attention of a comely young woman from a neighboring farm. Blonde-haired, blue-eyed Karin Schmidt soon became Frau Karin Weber.

Peter's education started in Warsaw. His, eight-man unit followed behind the Waffen army as they conquered Poland. He soon became used to treating Jews and Poles as human garbage. His unit organized mass transfer of people destined to work as slave labor in the camps that were being built. Peter was not a heavy thinker. He comforted his conscience by thinking, "I'm only obeying orders".

After Germany had conquered Europe, Peter thought the Germans under Hitler, would rule the world. At an assembly, A General asked for volunteers for special units being formed. Without a thought, or a doubt, Peter took a stride forward. Peter was very proud as he was selected, joined a group of fellow robots that had stepped forward. Their Commander was a stern, forceful leader. He preached to them the importance of preparing the occupied lands for the arrival of good German families that would repopulate the conquered lands. In any other culture, the Commander's statement about repopulation would have caused much controversy. In Nazi Germany, it didn't raise a hair.

Peter's unit did very little until the great push to conquer Russia began. His introduction to the new unit was arranging the hanging of eight partisans. Peter had little thought of, the "animals," they hung that day. His unit held a little celebration after the hanging.

His next assignment was a little different. He found himself standing on the edge of a deep trench that had been freshly dug. People filed single file into the trench until it was full. Peter was looking down at a woman holding an infant in her arms. His unit was called to attention. His unit was ordered to get ready to shoot. Peter aimed his rifle at the woman and child in front of him. When the order to fire was given, the woman and her child were still standing. Some understanding of what he had been ordered to do, finally penetrated Peter's brain. It was eerily silent after the volley of shots had been fired. Peter felt his commanding officer prod him in the back. He ordered Peter to shoot the woman and child in front of him. Peter obeyed.

A pep talk was given to the unit, praising them for their actions. They were told it was for the betterment of the German people. Absolutely necessary to achieve Germany's ends. A few of the men felt as Peter did, they were stunned by what they had done. Extra food and drink, was passed out to his squad. They were praised by their commander.

The very next day, another trench, another line of "animals" was placed in front of them. This time, row after row of people were herded into the trench. The living stood on the dead for a time, only to join them in death. Between each volley of shots, their Commander would walk the edge of the trench, his Luger pistol occasionally firing into the trench.

This describes Peter's existence for over a year. This period came to an end when German expansion into Russia came to an end. German forces were in full retreat from a Russian army that matched and exceeded their own brutality. Millions of German soldiers were taken prisoner by the red army, never to be heard of again. Peter and his unit fell back west. This time, they didn't follow the Waffen army, they led it in a full-blown retreat. In the last weeks of the war, Peter shed his black SS uniform, stole the uniform of a Waffen private, deserted the army, fled to his farm.

When Peter arrived at his farm, the Russians had already passed through. Every woman in the house had been raped multiple times. All the furniture, plumbing fixtures, farm equipment, had been confiscated. The farmhouse was as barren as the unplanted fields. Peter accepted the fact that his wife had been impregnated by who knows who? He loved and still respected his wife, vowed he would welcome the coming child as his own.

Peter and his pregnant wife made it through to Switzerland. Using monies his dead parents had hidden in the barn, Peter and his wife emigrated to the U.S.A. They were soon swallowed up in the mass exodus of 1946.

Peter's son was born with a Slavic triangular face, black hair, and a dimple in his chin. Peter not only accepted the child he grew to love the boundless energy of his new son. Karin was relieved that her husband had accepted the boy, relieved that he treated her the same way he had before the war. Peter had met Herr Muller in Boston. Muller had convinced the former SS man to become foreman of his lumber Mill.

Peter had taken to the job like a duck to water. He had no problem with the French Canadiens, the Irish, the Englishmen that worked in the mill. He was easy to get along with, possessed great common sense that bode him well in his new job.

Peter's war experiences didn't seem to bother him. He had shed the uniform of the SS, adopted the woodsman's red wool jacket as foreman of the mill, without a wrinkle on his brow. His wife was ignorant of his role in the war. Peter didn't even own a firearm, never spoke of the war. Germany and the SS were out of his life, out of his mind.

Herr Muller's sister now owned the sawmill. She knew nothing of Peter except that he was a good, reliable workman. She left the operation of the mill strictly in his hands. Peter's only thought of Muller's arrest was, thank God it's not me.

Peter and Karin and their son, Ben were out for an outing in their new, Ford half-ton, four-wheel-drive pickup. A long, scenic drive brought them to a nice restaurant in Fort Kent.

Abraham and Eve Lecenski were seated at an outdoor table in front of the restaurant in Fort Kent. They were enjoying a cup of good, hot coffee after a wonderful meal. Eve pointed out, the brand new, pickup to Abraham as it parked across the road opposite them. I only wish we had enough money to buy a truck like that. As the trio exited the truck, she said to Abraham,

"It's him."

A startled Abraham took his wife's hand, looked at the approaching trio. He was confused as he didn't recognize the people walking towards them. Eve was clutching his hand so hard that it was causing him pain.

"What is it, Eve?"

His wife remained speechless. He gently tried to lift her from her chair, she didn't budge. He looked at her, shook her hand.

"What is it Eve? What's the matter?

"It's him."

Although she remained speechless, Abraham looked at her.

"The truck Abraham, write down the license on the truck."

Abraham dutifully walked across the road, copied the license plate on the shiny new truck. Eve had left her seat, gone into their old truck, was sobbing with her head down as Abraham got in the truck.

"What is it Eve? What's happened?"

"The monster that shot my sister and her baby was driving that truck."

"Are you sure Eve, are you really sure?"

An enraged Eve showed him a face that made him pull back.

"That is the animal that shot my sister and her baby. Do you think I would ever forget the face of evil that took my family away from me?"

Eve was getting hysterical.

"If I had a gun, I would kill him right now. That animal doesn't deserve to live." Abraham continued to try and calm Eve down. She screamed at him,

"Take me away from this place, take me away right now."

Abraham started to drive to their farm. He pulled the truck off the road, turned to Eve.

"We have to tell the authorities."

"The police don't care, don't care about my family. No one cares about my family."

Eve started to cry uncontrollably. Abraham turned the truck around, drove to the one person he knew that did care, Ivan Petrov.

Marie opened her door to the sight of Eve almost comatose in the arms of Abraham. She led the couple to the kitchen table, wordlessly put the coffee pot on, waited patiently for them to speak.

"I saw the animal that shot my family. I saw the animal that shot my sister while she was holding her newborn baby. Nobody cares what happened to us. We are just worthless Jews that the world refuses to acknowledge what happened to us. The courts don't care, the worthless laws don't care, nobody cares."

Marie served them hot coffee, phoned the police, requested that they notify Ivan he's needed at home. The time passed slowly in silence while they awaited the arrival of Ivan.

When Ivan received the message, he turned his pickup towards home, drove as fast as he safely could with his blue lights flashing from the grill. When he entered his house, he saw Marie standing by the kitchen counter with her hands folded under her breasts. He sat down opposite Eve, accepted the cup of coffee Marie placed in front of him. The very air seemed supercharged as Eve told her story. Ivan had witnessed first-hand the murderous German death squads. Her story was not unfamiliar to him. Old memories came to the surface, his face felt flushed as he tried to bring his own emotions under control.

Ivan called dispatch, had them notify Detective Mark Schaffer to call him at home. He called Marie's father, asked him to contact the Jewish Embassy. Ivan had barely hung up the phone when Mark and Sheriff Tower knocked on his door. While Eve recanted her story, Mark had the license plate run, got the name and address of Peter Weber. Marie perked another pot of coffee, made sandwiches for the group.

Eve finally calmed down but was in a state of shock. Ivan told the couple they would do everything they could to find out the truth. Ivan watched the broken couple drive away from his home.

Mark asked Ivan if he thought he could identify the man.

"The Germans had many death squads, it would be a miracle if I could identify him, but I do know the name Peter Weber, he is the foreman for Herr Muller's sawmill. I've spoken with him a few times. He is a tall, Germanic-looking man with a good, friendly attitude. I would never think that he was a member of a death squad."

Mark let out a small laugh.

"If we could tell a criminal by looking at him, our jobs would be simple indeed. We need to talk to this man, confront him with the accusation that has been formerly made."

"Let me call Marie's father, give him Peter Weber's name, he's going to contact the embassy."

Ivan and Mark drove to the home of Peter Weber. His pretty blonde wife, Karin ushered them into the kitchen. Ivan bluntly asked Peter if he had been a member of a Nazi death squad? Peter was slow to respond. He sat heavily in a kitchen chair, admitted he had been a soldier in the Waffen army, denied being a member of the SS. His wife Karin blanched at his, words, she knew full well he wore the uniform of the SS when he married her.

Mark told Peter that a complaint against him had been filed which claimed he was a member of a death squad. The complaint claimed that his act of murder had been witnessed. Peter seemed to diminish in size as he repeated his denial.

Mark told him they would find out the truth. "The Nazis kept excellent records. It's just a matter of time before we get to the bottom of this. You are advised not to leave the area."

Mark nodded to Ivan. They left Peter sitting at his table, his wife standing behind him.

In Ivan's pickup. Mark spoke softly to an agitated Ivan. "Did you know that the Russian soldiers murdered the guards when they liberated the camps? In some cases, they let the inmates kill the guards. I have read many books about the camps and what happened there. Did you know that at the Battle of the bulge, American soldiers murdered captured Nazi soldiers in retaliation for what they did to captured American soldiers? Of course, you know that the Japs murdered so many people it's beyond counting. American Marines fighting in the pacific murdered Jap soldiers. The fact is Ivan that Peter is not a monster. He followed orders given by a superior officer. If you think that any culture would not commit murders as the Nazis did, you are as naive as a newborn baby. If America had been conquered, their own people would have acted just as the Nazis did, given the same circumstances. In every occupied country, the local people turned against the Jews; the Nazis murdered for them. No country is exempt from the brutality brought on by Hitler and those like him. I'll finish my spiel by telling you that the Nazis had to disband the death squads because the morale of their soldiers fell, so low."

Ivan finally came back to himself. "People like Muller must be punished for what they did. If I am given an illegal order, I would refuse to carry it out"

"There are many like you Ivan, but there are many, from every culture, that would obey an illegal order. Genocide is not new or restricted to Germany. It had been practiced all over the world and will continue given what people are."

"It is so easy for people who have never suffered to think that they have all the answers. Do you think Peter Weber should be given the death penalty for what he did?"

"Men like Peter are just a little cog on an enormous wheel. I believe in the rule of law. I think people like Peter should be held accountable for what they did. I'll leave the punishment up to the courts."

"Eve Lecenski would shoot Peter dead without a moment's hesitation."

"Would you Ivan? Would you take your revolver and shoot Peter dead?"

Ivan looked steadily at Mark. "No."

"Always remember, Ivan, when it comes to people, there is no black or white, only gray."

It was a subdued Ivan that waved goodbye to Mark. He entered his home to be embraced by Marie. She fussed over him, made him a meal, sat with him. Ivan brought her up to date, told her about Mark's comments to him. Marie told him that Mark was a friend, that in his own way, he was trying to make him heal, come to grips with the reality of life today.

Ivan had enough talk for one day. He drove his truck to an abandoned farmhouse, parked hidden from the entrance to the lush fields. It would be a dark, moonless night that would encourage the deer to come out early to feed in the field. Ivan was mulling over Mark's words when the three deer entered the field, began to feed. Ivan felt a sense of calm come over him as he watched the animals feeding. Traffic rolled down the dusty road without stopping. The deer had eaten their way to the top of the rise in the field where they would be visible from the road. Dusk was rapidly darkening the sky when a pickup stopped to look at the deer. As darkness became complete, the truck pulled away down the gravel road. Ivan enjoyed the peace and quiet for another hour before driving home. By the time he finished cleaning up, had a snack, Marie was sound asleep in bed. He gathered his wife in his strong arms, fell asleep, never moved a muscle until the dawning woke him.

The month of October is a busy month for a game warden. Although the fishing season is winding down, many die-hard anglers are still at it. The small game season opens in October sending hordes of hunters into the woods. A popular, illegal, practice in the north country is riding the back roads, shooting grouse, partridge, that come to the gravel roads to fill their crop as an aid in digestion. People that had access to the many, private dirt roads in the timber company holdings traveled these roads with the express thought of shooting grouse. The only way a warden can catch these people is by the use of decoys placed in an appropriate place. With the aid of fellow warden Jake Fellows, Ivan caught many people shooting from their vehicles. Almost every citation Ivan wrote resulted in the loss of a hunting license for a year. Ivan and Jake made a lot of people unhappy in October.

Ivan accepted that he alienated people by his very job. He could live with it. Once trapping season opened along with deer season, Ivan usually worked at least seventy hours per week. Marie was busy with her fur business, was gone as often as Ivan. Ivan had no trouble being alone. Ivan appreciated every moment he could spend in the outdoors. The isolation only brought him peace and calm.

Abraham could not get his wife out of her bitterness. She had become a different person after seeing Peter Weber. When he came in from the fields, she would be found sitting at the kitchen table, smoking her cigarettes, staring into space. She didn't rant and rave. She didn't respond to his attentions. She had isolated herself just as surely as if she was all alone on a deserted island in the middle of the ocean. After a breakfast he made for himself, he left the house to work the fields. Eve didn't even know he had left.

Eve took Abraham's rifle out of the closet. The .44-40 Winchester lever-action was familiar to her. Abraham had taught her to shoot using this rifle. She filled the magazine with the blunt, stubby, bullets, left the farm in their old pickup. The old truck should have broken down before it reached her destination, it didn't.

Peter had been worried sick since the accusation had been made against him. He had tried to stop his wife from sobbing, tried to stop her from questioning him about his activities during the War. He had hope, hope that the records had been lost. It was his word against whoever filed the complaint. He thought it was a good sign that weeks, had passed, and no more mention of Nazi death squads had arisen. Peter couldn't take responsibility for what he had done. In his mind, he had obeyed orders. If he had refused to shoot, he himself would have been shot. He kissed Karin goodbye, picked up his lunch pail, went out onto the porch.

Eve's mind was gone. It was full of memories of her family, full of the memories of being separated from her family that day, full of the memory of seeing her family marched into the open trench, full of the memory of her sister and her newborn baby being the only ones left standing in the trench after the volley of shots. In her mind, she saw the face of the tall, blonde, German soldier turn his head to look at his Commander. Saw the blonde-haired German shoot her sister and her baby.

She had parked the old pickup right behind the shiny new Ford pickup in Peter Weber's driveway. She was seated on the passenger side of her old truck with the barrel of her rifle sticking out the window. Peter had just started to descend the steps when he noticed the old pickup truck parked behind him. He stopped on the last step, looked at the woman framed by the window in the old truck.

"Do you know who I am Peter Weber?"

Peter looked hard, did not recognize the angry face of the woman.

"Do you remember shooting my sister and her baby," screamed the woman.

Karin appeared on the porch, looked at her husband. Peter turned to address her when the bullet struck his chest. He grabbed onto the railing, turned his face towards his wife. He tried to speak, but the blood pouring from his mouth prevented it. As he struggled to breathe, another bullet slammed into his chest. He fell to the ground, rolled on his back, saw the clear blue sky above him. His vision was blocked by the face of a strange woman. The last thing Peter Weber saw was a smile on the face of Eve Lecenski.

Karin stood frozen on the porch. Eve turned her attention to Peter's wife. She yelled,

"The Nazi scum is dead."

Eve's face lost all expression as she sat on the bottom step with the rifle laying on her legs.

Ivan must have been the closest officer to the scene of the shooting as he arrived first. Ivan stood behind his pickup door, took in the scene in front of him. Peter's wife was crumpled on the porch holding onto her son. Eve was staring into space sitting on the bottom step by Peter's body. Ivan was frozen behind his truck door.

Mark stopped behind Ivan's truck. He quickly took in the scene. With revolver in hand, he walked past Ivan, disarmed Eve, handcuffed her. He hollered to Ivan, call an ambulance. Eve had not said a word. It appeared to Mark that she had completely lost her sanity. Mark put Eve in his cruiser, approached Ivan.

"Go comfort the wife and her son. Stay with them until I can talk to them. Ivan nodded, dutifully walked up the porch. Mark looked at Eve who had not moved a muscle. As Mark reached for his thermos, he thought, Ivan never even reached for his revolver. He decided he would leave that out of his report. He offered Eve a sip of coffee. When she nodded yes, he removed her cuffs, gave her the cup. He stood by Eve until the ambulance arrived. He instructed the attendant to place a blanket over Peter, take Eve to the hospital. He cuffed Eve's hands in front before turning her over to the ambulance attendant.

Karin was distraught, claiming that her husband was a good man, not a murderer. Mark took her statement, left to await the forensic unit and the coroner. The death of Peter Weber was greeted with great joy by some; by others, it was greeted as cold-blooded murder, totally gray, thought Mark.

Eve was judged mentally unfit to stand trial. Abraham had great hopes that she would be treated, someday released from custody.

Mark and his longtime girlfriend, Carol were seated at Ivan's kitchen table. Mark had decided not to mention that Ivan had frozen at the scene. He had decided that Ivan was beyond help when it came to his memories of Auschwitz. Auschwitz, he thought with disgust. What a dirty, filthy name to be imposed upon the world to its everlasting shame.

Coming back from a fur buying trip, Marie decided to visit Abraham. The crop of potatoes had been, harvested, the fields were barren as the wind-swept snow blew across them. One lone house set back from the road in the middle of three hundred acres of fields. How the wind must howl, she thought, as she parked behind Abraham's old truck. Abraham told her the crop was good, he might even buy a new truck. Marie laughed at his comment, asked him about Eve as she sipped the strong coffee.

"Eve just couldn't deal with it. She's never been right since she saw Peter. Your father said he would keep me updated on Eve's status. He told me she might be released in just a few years."

"Do you visit her?"

"I visit her every week. She's finally starting to talk with me. She even laughed. I miss her, so much, my life seems so empty without her."

On the drive home, Marie was happy that Eve was making progress, glad that her family had helped Abraham. She entered her home, joined Mark, Carol, and Ivan at the kitchen table. Mark pushed a folder across the table to her. She saw it was a report on Peter Weber from the Israeli Embassy. The report verified that Peter Weber had been a SS member, had been assigned to one of the very first death squads. The report also verified Peter had been one of the murderers of Eve's family. Marie put the report down, asked Mark if a copy had gone to Eve's doctor?

"Everyone connected with the case had received a copy."

"Did peter's wife get a copy?"

Mark nodded. Ivan said,

"He was a farm boy just like me."

Peter's wife had read the report on her husband. No matter Peter's past, he had been a true, faithful husband and father to her son. Karin had suffered greatly at the end of the war. She had been raped so often she had lost track of how many she had endured. She would never forget Peter and the love she had for him, but she had learned, when one door closes, another opens.

Agnes waved goodbye to Marie. She had just bought ten deer hides and one moose hide from her. She would use the heavy hide of the moose for the soles of the moccasins she would make this year. Lucille had undertaken the tough job of tanning the moose hide. Lucille was very adept at tanning, was a great help to Agnes. The trapping season had ended, and Lucille was telling Agnes that Max had a very good season. Marie had told her Max needed to do a better job of fleshing his pelts before he received top money for them. Agnes hoped the tanning solution would do its job before the temperature dropped and the hide froze. It was a minor thing as the solution would continue working when it thawed out. She was just getting ready to go inside and make tea, when Max pulled into her driveway. Lucille greeted him with a kiss, Agnes waved the couple inside. Max had many stories to tell of his time in the woods. He had seen many moose and deer along his trapline, gave Agnes a salted piece of moosehide he had cut from a moose he found dead. Agnes fed the couple a good meal before Max put Lucille's bicycle into the trunk of his car and the couple left. Agnes had time to walk out back of her home, check the small game snares she set for hares and grouse. It was illegal to use snares, but Agnes had used them all her life. A nice grouse would make a good meal.

Ivan knew it would be a long day as he turned onto the dirt road that was the western boundary of his assigned territory. He felt a pang of guilt at his own pleasure in the solitude of the long ride along the Saint John River. Scattered farmland broke the heavily forested lands. He stopped his truck in front of Peter Weber's home. The house was deserted, with no sign of life. When he passed Muller's sawmill, it was in full operation. He checked a few hunters, checked a couple on a three-wheeler. Late that afternoon, he drank the last of his thermos, turned onto the paved road, and set a long ride home.

Ivan's thoughts turned to Marie as he drove. She had finished the fur year, had resumed her domestic duties. Before he had left that morning, she had been folding clean clothes from the dryer. She was humming to herself as she worked, giving each folded article a tender pat as she placed them in piles. Marie showed Ivan that same tenderness. She could go from a stern businesswoman to a tender woman with the same ease she used in putting on an apron. Ivan smiled as the light from his kitchen window came into view, it had been a good day.

— ❧ **14** ❧ —

Jacob Miller had been born in a double-wide trailer halfway between Fort Kent and Allagash off Route 161. His father was a successful, frugal timberman who had run a successful firewood business. He had a doting mother that intervened between her sensitive son, and his abrasive father. Jacob had attended local schools, graduated from high school, and was immediately put to work cutting and splitting firewood. The fact that he hated the work meant little to his father. If the young man had not been introduced to alcohol by his friends, he might have lived a long, miserable life cutting wood for his father.

Fate intervened one miserable night on the icy roads. His father's pickup had skidded on a sharp corner directly into the path of a fully loaded logging truck pulling two trailers. His parents had died in the crash or in the resulting fire that engulfed both vehicles. The police investigation had cleared the truck driver from any fault in the accident.

Jacob was now a rather wealthy young man thanks to the insurance money and the savings of his parents. Jacob went from alcohol to hard drugs. He paid no attention to the business his father had worked so hard to establish. Two years of drinking and drugs had turned the young man into a man who was unstable, to say the least. Never, really-sober, Jacob was falling apart faster than his neglected double wide. Jacob had not run afoul of the law. He was careful to do his drinking and drugs in the privacy of his double-wide.

Mrs. Kay Wilson was washing dishes when she saw Jacob shoot a deer in the back of his trailer. Mrs. Wilson had no love or understanding for Jacob, she called the Sheriff's department, reported the shooting.

Ivan met up with Deputy Johnson, both men drove to Jacob's trailer. Ivan was getting out of his truck, preparing to walk around the front of it and walk up to the front door. The Sheriff's deputy was ten yards to his left. The front door flew open, Jacob shot the deputy. Ivan saw the deputy fall, crouched behind his pickup hood, drew his revolver, held it in both hands over the hood of his truck. Jacob stood in the doorway staring at Ivan.

"Get off my property, you don't belong here."

Ivan hollered in a loud voice, "Drop the rifle, drop the rifle."

Mrs. Wilson was standing outside. She yelled very loudly. "Drop the rifle, Jacob, drop the rifle."

A bleary-eyed Jacob worked the bolt, slammed another cartridge into the chamber. Ivan again hollered for him to drop the rifle. As Jacob started to slowly raise the rifle at Ivan, Ivan started the long double-action pull on his revolver. In his mind, Ivan never heard the sound of the shot, he never felt the revolver recoil into his hands. In horror, he watched Jacob drop the rifle, fall down the few steps to the ground. Ivan was in a state of shock when Mark arrived on the scene. Jacob and the deputy were dead. Mark took the revolver from Ivan's hands, started to gently talk to him. Ivan came back to himself enough to answer Mark's questions. Mark put Ivan in his cruiser, told him to talk to no one. Mark talked to Mrs. Wilson who had called 911 immediately after yelling at Jacob. She testified she and Ivan had given vocal warnings for Jacob to drop his weapon. It was a good hour before the order had been restored. Ivan was in Mark's custody. Mark spent another hour telling Ivan what to expect. He talked to Ivan until he felt sure Ivan had fully recovered.

As was customary, Ivan was put on paid leave until after the investigation by the State police was done. Marie tried to take Ivan out of his funk. She was scared that Ivan would never accept what he did, that his mind would go back to the holocaust. Ivan had left her, gone back to the dark forests of the Allagash. Marie was determined to find him, go to him in his time of need.

Mark and Max responded to Marie's plea for help. Max told them if they could find his canoe, he could find him. Marie placed her knapsack midship, held on as Mark and Max paddled the canoe. The dark water was swiftly passing as the sun was rising with the promise of a beautiful day. Max steered the canoe to the sandy shoal, pointed out the drag marks in the sand.

"This is where Ivan found me when I was starving."

Max led them through the maze of the swampy territory. When they approached the shelter, Marie ran to the entrance, Ivan was sitting cross-legged over a small fire. Marie took over by pouring the hot coffee from her thermos, putting it in Ivan's hands.

Marie said, "You can't do this Ivan. You can't run away from the people that love you, to run away from your responsibilities."

Mark touched Ivan's arm, "You need to report in two days. You've been cleared, you have to resume your duties."

"I wasn't running away. I just needed to be by myself to think this out. I've been over the shooting a thousand times in my mind. There was no other choice, I had to shoot."

Marie took his arm. "Let's go home." Before their canoe had touched the shore, Ivan had come to the realization that he had done what he had to. He thought, *'Ivan Petrov is no Nazi.'*

Ivan was finally becoming able to cope with his memories. Although they still made him light-headed at times, they did not paralyze him. Ivan's friendship with Mark went a long way to accomplish this. Mark was someone he could talk to confide in, trust.

Marie was pleased to see the improvement in Ivan, got closer to Carol, did her part to nurture the friendship between the two couples.

It was spring and Amos carrier's thoughts turned to romance as it did every Spring. He had long admired the Native American woman Agnes that he had met many years ago. He had been alone five years since the death of his wife. He found the long nights lonely now that he had turned his business over to his granddaughter, Marie. He had a nice collection of weasel and ermine pelts that weren't worth very much money but were desired by Agnes for trim on some of her leather garments. He was wearing the buckskin coat Agnes had made for him when he pulled into her driveway. He could see a plume of smoke coming out of her stove pipe as he knocked on the trailer door. Agnes welcomed Amos in. He showed her the tanned pelts, asked her if she could use them. Agnes inspected them carefully.

"How much?"

"The price is you'll have to let me take you out for a good meal in town."

Agnes gave a light laugh.

"What are you after old man, you should be dried up by now."

"There's still a little fire left in this old man."

"I think you have lost your mind since your wife died."

"Maybe, but I'm old enough to know what I want."

Agnes ran her hand over the almost pure white ermine pelt, remained silent.

"What do you say, Agnes, are you afraid to be seen with an old man?"

"I can bear your company in exchange for these fine pelts, but I warn you, you will only get a bare smile as your reward."

"That's more than enough pay for this old man."

Marie came out of the bank to see her grandfather and Agnes go into the best restaurant in town. She tried to put it out of her mind, but by the time she arrived home, she was consumed with what she had seen. When Ivan came home, she told him what she had seen, was visibly agitated. Ivan argued that Amos had a right to see anyone he wanted, added that a man needs the company of a woman on occasion. On occasion, she yelled. Is that what a woman means to you? Be reasonable Marie, we're not talking about me. Ivan, my grandfather has no business taking a woman to a restaurant. Ivan decided he would not win this argument, went into silent mode.

As the night went on, Marie got madder and madder, she fumed in her chair, didn't go to bed with her husband. Two days later, she drove her car to Agnes's trailer, was dumbfounded to see her grandfather's truck in her driveway. She immediately drove home, unloaded on Ivan. Ivan had decided to stay non-committal. Marie would not let it go, it totally consumed her. Ivan finally agreed to drive her to Agnes's trailer.

Amos was sitting on Agnes's couch puffing on his pipe when the knock on the door came. Agnes opened the door, let Marie and Ivan into her home. For once, Marie was speechless as she sat at the table; an embarrassed Ivan sat beside her. Agnes told Marie, "Your crazy grandfather has decided to court me, I can't make him stop."

Amos tapped the ash out of his pipe, said, "We should all go out for supper; it's still early, and we haven't eaten."

The best Marie could come up with was a nod of acceptance. They followed Amos and Agnes back to the restaurant in Fort Kent. Marie was polite, but not very talkative during the meal. Amos appeared in a very good mood, kept the conversation going. When they parted, Marie was subdued on the ride home.

"They both looked very happy Marie, maybe you should butt out."

Marie was wiping the tears from her eyes when they reached home. Ivan could not understand what the problem was, but he kept to his decision to keep quiet. Marie reached out to her parents, told them of Amos's apparent romantic connections with Agnes. Her father sounded pleased that his dad had found someone, her mother didn't see the problem.

Agnes was making a pair of moccasins for Amos.

"If we marry, I am not going to change my life. I won't move from my home. I won't stop my work."

"After we're married, we will add a bedroom and a new bathroom, and a new heating system. I'm too damn old to keep chopping wood."

"Come over here, old man. Put your foot in here."

Amos complied, stroked her hair as she made the adjustments to the moccasins.

Amos owned a timber acreage that completely enclosed a pond he called, "Eagle Pond." It held bass, yellow perch, and Northern Pike. Many years ago, he had built a log cabin on it. This is where he planned to take Agnes on their honeymoon. Agnes fell in love with the cabin the first time she saw it. They spent two days catching fish, laughing, and getting to know one another better.

When Marie read the wedding invitation, she had to sit down. A wedding was planned at Amos's cabin on the pond. Amos wanted Marie to stand up for him, Agnes wanted Lucille to stand up for her. The civil ceremony went off without a hitch. Family and a few close friends attended. When Marie cried, Amos put his arm around her.

"I hope those are tears of happiness."

"I love you grandfather."

Ivan drove home from the wedding with a smile on his face. Marie was happy and smiling again.

Amos and Agnes spent most of the summer at the cabin while work was ongoing on Agnes's trailer. Amos spent most of the day puffing on his pipe, running back and forth to the trailer picking up whatever Agnes needed to keep her happy. He derived great pleasure in the morning watching his new wife braid her hair. Lucille and Max were the most frequent visitors to the little pond. Max learned to put up fish for the winter months, even helped Agnes make his pemmican for the fast-approaching winter. Warm days and cool nights made for perfect conditions.

Agnes did not recognize her trailer when they moved back in late August. The whole of the trailer had been encased by a gable roof. The emergency generator was in a utility room that held a new washer-drier combo. A new bathroom, and a spacious bedroom. Agnes was amazed at the transformation of her trailer. Amos had the water system upgraded with a new pump and a hot water heater. A neat, covered, concrete slab went the length of the trailer. The bedroom had been paneled in knotty-pine, looked fabulous. Agnes gave Amos a rare smile and a fierce hug in their new bedroom. Agnes continued to work as she had done before marrying Amos. The difference was her work was made much easier by her new equipment. She found that what used to take her three or four days, only took her a day now. She still wore her moccasins, her leather dresses, and braided her hair. She was determined not to lose her identity. She made a beautiful Indian buckskin dress for Marie. The dress was decorated with blue and yellow beading, trimmed with ermine fur. Marie wore it proudly.

Lucille was amazed at the work done, was very happy for Agnes. For a housewarming gift, Amos bought his wife a new leather sewing machine. Whenever he saw a way to ease and modernize Agnes's work, he quickly filled it. Marie was a frequent visitor, became good friends with Agnes and Lucille.

$$\text{\textbf{15}}$$

Ivan started his patrol with a calmer, more settled attitude. He had come to grips with the shooting, felt he was better able to handle his responsibilities. Mark had gone a long way in settling his mind. Mark had proven to be a good friend. Ivan felt the time he had spent in the camps would no longer hound him. He found himself better able to put in context the war, the camps, his role in life. For the first time, he contemplated the idea of children. He was proud of his position as a game warden. He realized his position enabled him to grow as a human being. As he turned on to a long, winding dirt road, a brilliant sun had risen in the east. The promise of a beautiful day made him smile.

Max was fully outfitted, ready to face another long trapping season. He had branched out, got permission from the timber companies to trap problem beaver. Beaver, were scarce, and the State wanted to build the population back up. Max didn't think he'd get many permits, but he looked at it like a foot-in-the-door proposition. Lucille had accompanied him while he prepared. They spent many days deep in the Allagash enjoying its natural beauty. Max had gotten his GED, asked Lucille to marry him. She accepted his engagement ring with the understanding they would wait two years before they married.

Lucille woke up early in Agnes's trailer. Amos was already awake, greeted her with a smile and the offer of coffee. Agnes was already up, was working on her new sewing machine. Amos told the women he was going trout fishing. Agnes told him there was plenty of room in the new freezer he had bought for them. Amos laughed. Told her they needed to fill it up as he left them.

Lucille told Agnes that she was engaged to Max. Agnes joined her with a fresh coffee, told her Max was a decent young man, she hoped it would work out for them. Marie joined them with fresh donuts she had made that morning. She had kissed her grandfather before he left, was looking forward to a gabfest with the girls.

Mark was having breakfast in the diner with Carol. Carol was pushing him about their relationship. Her position was they had been going together for five years, it was time to make a commitment. Mark's position was that he liked their relationship just as it was.

When she delivered her ultimatum, Mark remained no-committal. Carol was feeling anger as well as frustration at Mark. She definitely felt that they had dated long enough. It was time for Mark to make a decision one way or the other. She left a stoic Mark nursing a coffee.

The sticking point for Mark was, he didn't want the responsibility of a family. In his own mind, he was not ready for fatherhood. He didn't desire any other woman, he felt he wanted to maintain his single life. In his work as an officer, he had definitely seen the worst in people. He had seen many couples with children beat down by life. He didn't really know what caused so much strife among these people, but the fact was, it was rife in the area. He always thought that the children were the losers in these families. Many times, they were torn away from the life they had known, tossed into foster care as well as State institutions. He felt really bad about Carol's declaration. Doubted he would change his mind. He sighed inwardly as he left to investigate a burglary just outside Fort Kent. He had come to love Carol very, deeply, this was going to hurt.

Agnes was surprised she had adapted to Amos so well. She found she enjoyed not only his company, but enjoyed the smell of the man. Pipe tobacco mixed with the male smell of him. She enjoyed his caresses, enjoyed his presence in her bed. The man was attentive to her every need, aware of her every need. His quiet demeanor suited her to a tee, try as she might, she could find little fault with the man. Marie was a surprise to her. She had thought the young woman stiff and aloof, was surprised to find a caring thoughtful woman that loved her grandfather, accepted her with good grace and a smile. Life does have its twists and turns. She turned her attention back to the vest she was sewing, had to finish it today for a customer.

At the end of the trapping season, Max was in the private timberlands picking up his beaver traps. He had received four permits from the State to trap the large rodents. When he was stopped for ongoing roadwork, he met Morris Hamel. Morris had a CJ Jeep with an air compressor in the rear which he used to drill holes in the ledge cap. Max explained the problem his family had with water freezing up, and Morris told him it was an easy fix for him. Max told him the details of the ledge, Morris told him he could blast a trench through the ledge for about two hundred and fifty bucks.

As Max was picking up his traps, he thought he wanted to help his mother and father with their water problem. He knew it was his mother that would wind up lugging water all through the winter, felt it was not something he wanted her to continue doing. He phoned his mother, told her he would be coming down with his fiancé Lucille, and the man who'll blast the ledge. His mother told him Orla's husband Peter, had been a great help in easing her burden over the long winter.

When Max and Lucille arrived, his dad had bought a new inch and a half copper line to replace the old lead pipe. By two that afternoon, Morris had drilled his holes, packed them with dynamite, was ready to blow about fifty feet of trench through it. Morris had warned them he couldn't guarantee that the house foundation wouldn't crack from the explosion. Max's dad told him he accepted the responsibility, "Blow the damn thing."

When Morris touched it off, a huge explosion resulted in the air filling with granite stone dust. After Morris left, the whole family turned out to clear the trench. Max's dad took charge of the new line, made the connection that enabled water to run into the house gravity feed. Mom now had a constant source of water for the first time in her married life.

Max's dad had recovered his good humor, went out of his way to make Lucille feel at home. Orla's husband, Peter had proven to be a great help in the work. Max was happy to see his sister happily married, living at home with mom and dad.

Max and Lucille left the next morning. Lucille had enjoyed the outing very much. She felt good that Max had thought to help his family out, happy that Max was more than content to abide by her wishes. They had a nice meal in Rangeley Maine before driving north to Fort Kent.

Agnes and Lucille showed Max how to properly flesh and stretch his beaver pelts. He received top money from Marie for the circular pelts, and he had learned a new skill. Max had received permission from the timber companies to trap huge drainage between three interconnected ponds. It was virgin ground that hadn't been trapped in over fifty years. The only requirement they made was that Max would handle problem trapping for them. Max was ecstatic over the new, virgin grounds, planned to waste no time in setting up the new site.

16

Ivan was totally relaxed as he drove down the long gravel road. He felt like he was better able to leave the past behind him. His old station wagon was full of lumber he would need to build a new addition onto his house. They had a baby coming and he wanted to make two new bedrooms in the house. Marie seemed to glow since she had become pregnant. She had a little morning sickness, but it did nothing to interfere with her happy disposition. Her whole family was thrilled with the news. Her mother insisted on staying with them after the baby was born until Marie got back on her feet.

The Sunday papers had a big expose on the Nazis in South America. Ivan sipped his coffee as Marie read the article to him. Ivan stayed non-committal, didn't want to offer an opinion. Ivan tried to tell himself that every German wasn't responsible for the holocaust.

Mark and Max arrived to help him with the construction. Max happily spoke of his new trapping area, Mark was quiet, non-talkative. Mark was feeling the effects of Carol ending their relationship. Ivan wouldn't touch the subject with a ten-foot pole. Marie told Mark,

"For Christ sakes, marry the girl."

Marie made a nice moose meat stew for everyone before she left to visit with Agnes and her grandfather. Although Mark wouldn't speak of it, he was devastated by Carol leaving him. He decided his next stop was Carol's house and a proposal for marriage. He hoped he hadn't ruined their love for one another. At the end of the day, Ivan lay down on the couch, fell into a dreamless, refreshing sleep.

When Marie came in, she covered Ivan with a blanket, went to her bed alone.

Mark was seated in his cruiser awaiting the arrival of Carol from her Job. Carol was the owner of an insurance business that was popular in the north country. She had worked hard to build her business, had a good reputation for fairness in her dealings. Her car was in the driveway, his knock on the door had gone unanswered. Mark knew she often jogged home from her office to her home. He was debating whether or not to search for her when he saw her figure approaching him. She slowed to a walk as she approached Mark who was leaning against his cruiser smoking a cigarette.

She produced a handkerchief, wiped her face carefully as she waited for Mark to speak.

"I know this is not the time or the place, but will you Marry me?"

Carol continued to wipe the perspiration from her face. A slow smile appeared on her face before she leaped into his arms, kissed him with passion. Mark hugged her fiercely, and they both went into her home. Carol's mother was delighted with the news, gave Mark a quick hug and a peck on his cheek. Her father passed out cold beers, shook Mark's hand. Their next stop was Mark's parent's house. Mark's dad, Philip, had forty pounds on his son, was in excellent shape for his sixty-two years. He was an inch shorter than his son, heavily muscled from his years in the logging industry. His mother was getting a little rotund as the years passed. She gave Carol a brilliant smile and a hug. Philip congratulated them, told them he would inform Mark's brother and sister of the good news.

His parents' living room was decorated with mounts of bucks, bears, a beautiful full mount of an eastern coyote with a grouse between his jaws. Mounts of brook trout, lake trout, and largemouth bass, testified to the abilities of his father. Philip had been a rabid sportsman all his life. It had been a disappointment to him that his sons hadn't followed in his footsteps. Oddly enough, it was Mark's sister Jean, that turned out to be her father's constant companion. If anything, she was, more avid than her father to hunt the abundant local game.

The families got together for a big barbeque to celebrate the coming wedding. Problem was, Carol was Jewish, Mark was Roman Catholic. It didn't take long before the arguments started. Mark's brother Paul stated that the life of Christ was a historical fact, as was the fact he had arisen after being crucified by the Romans at the bidding of a prominent Jewish Rabbi.

Carol's father agreed that Christ had been born a Jew, was crucified by the Romans. He stated that in the Jewish faith, Jesus was considered as a false prophet, not the one true God. Therefore, Jesus is incidental to the Jewish faith that believes in only one true God who has not returned to earth as yet.

When the conversation turned to, what Church or Synagogue will the couple be married in and how will the children be raised, Carol butted in.

"We will be married in a Civil ceremony in Mark's field surrounded by the woods and the people we love. We will expose our children to both faiths, let them make their own decisions. Mark and I believe in one true God who created heaven and earth. The Catholics say Jesus is the son of God, died for our sins, arose from the dead to ascend to heaven. The Jews believe God will arrive in a golden chariot pulled by winged horses. The Muslims believe their God ascended to heaven on the back of a winged horse. I don't know what all the other religions believe, but they all believe in one God. Strive to live a decent life without harm to other people, have, no hate in your heart, respect and honor your parents. What more could any God want?"

After Carol's statement, children began to play together, people started eating and drinking. Laughter could be heard all around her, her parents and Mark's parents were happy and smiling. Mark thought to himself, everything is totally gray. As the daylight faded and the guests began to leave, the northern lights began showing on the horizon. Carol took Mark's hand, told him, "God is smiling on our coming union."

17

van traveled all through his large district discharging his duties. He couldn't help but notice a new breed of people were moving into his district. Potato farms were being subdivided, sold to rich people from down-country. They put up elaborate very scenic homes. Large homes with multiple bathrooms and bedrooms. Most of these people were unable, or unwilling to cope with the local animals. If the deer browsed their shrubbery, they complained to fish and Game. If skunks, foxes, or coyotes, appeared by their homes, they called Fish and Game. In frustration, Ivan gave all the nuisance calls to Max. Max became a part-time member of the Fish and Game Department. Max soon developed a style of dealing with these people. He customarily live-trapped the species, causing the disturbance. When a black bear persisted in tearing one residence's garbage shed apart, Max and Ivan put out a baited barrel trap to capture and move the offending bear to a new area. The bear returned within a month, tore the shed apart. Under orders from Fish and Game, Max shot the problem bear, brought it to Agnes to make pemmican for him. He had Agnes make him a winter coat from the large bear's hide. Change in the north country was coming. It was coming slowly, but it was definitely coming. Increased demand for services led to escalating taxes. Land values soared timber value soared. Middle-class America was beginning to suffer the increased cost of goods. Middle-class America was beginning to feel the effects of inflation. Middle-class America was in danger of disappearing.

Abraham did not let the dawning catch him in bed. He had arisen in the pitch-black darkness, made his breakfast, was drinking his second cup of coffee when the weak rays of the sun crested the horizon. After he had harvested his potato crop in the fall, he had plowed using a moldboard plow, harrowed four rows at a time, added fertilizer, added pesticides to control insects in the soil, awaited the arrival of spring. His seed potatoes were due to arrive any day now and he had to hook up his implement that made four rows at a time. The resulting rows would form hills to accept the seed. He would spend every hour of daylight forming the rows. He figured at least three days to complete the job. Abraham was a simple man. He had a love for the earth and the produce it delivers that help him earn his living.

Abraham read only two books. His Bible was always handy on the small table by his easy chair. Next to the bible was a book devoted to the raising of potatoes. This book was his second bible. Abraham tested his soil frequently, took the advice of the Agricultural department as Gospel. Everything had to be done in the proper order if you wanted a decent crop. Eve was not here to help him, he had to hire a neighboring boy to assist him. The farm boy could drive a truck, operate a tractor, was able to understand and follow his directions.

He planned to have the young man operate the planter while he would keep him supplied with seed. Abraham would be able to handle the rest of the operations by himself. When the flowery plants started to appear, he would have to make the decision of, whether or not, to irrigate, fumigate the plants to control bugs.

A potato plant can be very pretty with its white flowers, its green tomato-like orbs that look like green tomatoes, but are inedible. While the plant is green and flowery above ground, below ground, a special stem called a stolon, is growing to produce the tubers. Oddly enough, the longer the vine above ground stays flowery and green, the better is the tuber underground.

Abraham was worried the lower part of his field might be too wet to plant. The samples he had were borderline. If no more rain came before planting, he felt it would be okay. After planting, the rain would be welcome, cut down on his irrigating.

Three days late, the neighbor boy. Steven Lange, was on the tractor with the planter attached, idling at the start of the first four rows to be planted. Abraham loaded the hopper on the planter, held his breath as he watched Steven start planting. The planter was old, but operated the way it was designed. Abraham, walked behind, it until he was satisfied everything was working properly. Abraham hurried back to his seed bin to fill his loader to replenish the hopper at the end of every row.

Abraham constantly looked after the young man by making sure he was well-hydrated and well-fed during the long days of planting. Abrahams long day was not finished as dusk approached. He would walk the planted rows making sure there were no "skips" in the rows. He only found a few skips which pleased him no end.

After his supper, Abraham would pray for his wife, thank God for the safe day's work. Pray for the souls of all the departed. Abraham held no hate in his heart. His belief in his God was strong enough to let the memory of the holocaust shrivel and die in his mind.

Eve locked away in her room (cell), did not plan to ever let the memory of what the Nazis did ever fade from her mind. She was very careful to tell the doctors exactly what they wanted to hear. She was very careful to allow herself to become more open to the suggestions pushed upon her by the doctors and her therapy. She never let herself get too emotional. Never made herself stand out. She expressed great regret at the act of murder she had committed. Time and time again, she expressed sorrow at the act she had committed. Abraham had told her she was correct in her identification of Peter Weber as the Nazi that had killed her sister and her baby. The doctors never gave her that information. She had few visitors except for Abraham, John Carrier, and his daughter Marie. Marie was especially kind to her, seemed to be a good friend.

In her heart, Eve knew she would kill that Nazi again without a second thought. She would happily kill every Nazi scum left on the earth if only she had the chance. All the therapy and the doctors in the world would never cure her of that. Abraham and his God. The God who abandoned them to the Nazi scum. There is no God. He is a myth to give desperate people hope when there is none. But she would never let on how she truly felt. She would smile, show regret when she should. Her only regret was that she couldn't kill more of the Nazi scum of the earth.

Abraham was hopeful that Eve might be released soon. Her doctor had sounded very optimistic that she might be released soon. He would rototill her garden spot in anticipation of her release. He would pray to God that she be released to plant in her garden, to enjoy and be thankful for the harvest of the earth. In another two weeks, the potato plants would flower and blossom, he prayed Eve would be with him to enjoy the beauty and abundance delivered by God.

18

Mark put down the book he was reading on the slaughter of the Jews in the gas chambers of the camps. He was going to meet Ivan at the local diner. He would not discuss his interest in the war with Ivan. The man was slowly emerging from his time at Auschwitz. Ivan had become more confident, more settled within himself since the shooting. No one could say why the event changed him, no one can get into the mind of another.

Mark told Ivan that Eve Licenski was going to be released. Ivan nodded at the information, said, "It is good that she will be going home. She has experienced enough horror in her life. How are you enjoying married life?"

"I don't find it much different than our dating. Carol has always been the one I love."

Ivan nodded, continued to drink his coffee. After Mark left him, Ivan left for a planned week and a half checking on boaters and anglers in the half dozen Lakes and Ponds within the Allagash.

The small town of Dexter, located west of Allagash, become newsworthy when a mother of four children was found badly beaten in front of her home. A neighbor who had witnessed the assault on the woman by her husband told authorities that her husband had fled into the woods after the assault. It was reported he was seen carrying a rifle as he entered the woods. Mark Schaffer was put in charge of the investigation, quickly radioed for Ivan to report to him.

Ivan was on the waters of the Allagash River when the call came. It took him over three hours to rendezvous with Mark. Ivan could contribute little except that the man was not noted as a woodsman or hunter. Mark did not know where to start the search for the man. He didn't want to flood the woods with armed men just to capture a wife beater. His feelings were someone could get seriously hurt or killed while engaging in fruitless searching.

Ivan suggested that the man couldn't hold out long in the bug-infested woods this time of year. Food in the deep conifer forest was very scarce, potable water was non-existent. Mark decided they would wait the felon out. He ordered that four travel trailers normally used by lumbermen be placed on the outskirts of town. The small town was encircled by the trailers. Mark ordered that each trailer broadcast music and news from local stations. He assigned law-men to watch over every trailer, 24/7. Ivan told Mark he thought it was a sensible plan. Mark, the Sheriff, and Ivan would stay in Town during the vigil.

Irwin Sheldon was about as miserable as a human being can get. He had caught his wife in the arms of his brother-in-law, knocked him to the ground, kicked him repeatedly in his side as he lay at his feet. He struck his wife. Slapped her again and again until she collapsed at his feet. With his wide-eyed children huddling together in fear, he had grabbed his rifle, ran into the woods behind his home. He hadn't even thought to even put on a long sleeve shirt before he fled. Darkness was falling, the bugs were viscously biting him with no mercy. He had no food or water, had a hangover that made his head pound, felt about as low as a human being can get.

It was just past midnight when Irwin started walking towards the sound of radio he could hear in the distance. When he finally reached the dirt road, started to walk towards the source of the music, headlights, blue flashing- lights, appeared in the road ahead of him. He dropped his rifle to the ground, placed his hands atop his head. Turned away from the flashing lights.

Deputy John Howard approached the suspect with his hand on his unstrapped revolver. He quickly cuffed the un-resisting man, led him to his cruiser where he gave him water, notified the Sheriff he had the suspect in custody. Mark told Ivan that he had given exactly the right advice, said, "He was happy that no one had been injured in the arrest. We have a lot of domestic abuse calls in this area. Men get to drinking, come home, slap the wife or kids, damn shame."

Abraham was thrilled to pick up Eve. Although she was quiet on the ride home, Abraham was encouraged when she started a conversation about the planting, told him she looked forward to planting in her garden. Abraham filled her in about the planting, told her about the neighbor boy he had hired. Abraham was very careful to act as normally as possible. If Eve sensed he was ill at ease with her, she didn't show it.

It was awkward at home. Eve cooked a nice meal, they cleaned up together, watched the TV. Eve did not join him in his evening prayers. When he questioned her, she replied, "I'm done praying to a God that doesn't listen. He doesn't care about my family. He doesn't care about the Jews."

"You can't mean that Eve. Don't turn away from God."

Eve turned her back to him in bed, did not reply to his plea. When Abraham awoke during the blackness of the night, Eve had left their bed. He found her asleep in another bedroom. He stroked her hair, kissed her cheek, left her, sadly returned to their bed.

The next few weeks set a new pattern for Abraham. Eve continued to sleep apart from him, would not offer him the comfort of her affections. She would cook his meals, clean the house, work diligently in her garden. She would not talk with, would not even touch him. Abraham continued to pray to his God. He asked God to return his wife to him. She would not go to Town, would not go to the dealership to buy a new truck, would not leave the house with him. She had abandoned any semblance of a wife to him. Abraham was determined to give her all the time she needed, all the time she needed to regain her senses.

When Abraham came home for lunch the next day, Eve and the new truck were gone. There was no note on the table, nothing to indicate where she had gone. Abraham waited until dusk before he called the Police. Mark was told by a deputy about Eve's disappearance, decided to investigate. Abraham's truck was parked in the bus depot's parking lot. The keys were still in the ignition. Eve had bought a one-way ticket to New York City.

Mark and a deputy returned the truck to Abraham, gave him the news of his wife. Abraham listened with no visible reaction, but inside he was shaking, couldn't believe that Eve had left him. Abraham prayed fervently to his God for the return of his wife. Less than a week later, Mark and Ivan knocked on Abraham's door. They told him that Eve had shot and killed a former SS Captain that had been identified as being the leader of a death squad during the War. Abraham took the message with no visible reaction. When the two men left, Abraham was standing in his open doorway staring at his flowery fields.

The memory of Eve stayed alive for a few days in the north country she called her home. Articles appeared in the local papers causing people to keep her story alive. Ivan took it all in with a great deal of sadness. It was apparent that Eve's suffering on earth was to continue.

Mark spent as much time with Ivan as he could. When he wasn't busy on cases, he rode with Ivan, made him talk it out. Mark was glad to see that Ivan was handling the news in a calm manner. He and Carol made sure to visit with Ivan and Marie. Marie was but a few weeks away from giving birth. Marie had great sympathy for Eve, great sympathy for Abraham. Ivan thought there was little that could be done to help Abraham in his time of need. He thought it was a great pity that they couldn't help the man.

Ivan drove in his yard to see Marie standing on the steps, bent over as far as her extended belly would allow. He ran to her side, supported her.

"My water just broke. We need to get to the hospital. I called the doctor's office, told them I'm on the way."

Every time Marie would moan, Ivan would press the gas pedal down harder. Marie told him to slow down before they had an accident. At the hospital, Marie insisted Ivan wait in the waiting room. When Mark and Carol arrived, Ivan was pacing in the small waiting room. It took about three hours before a nurse came in, announced that Ivan had a healthy baby daughter. Ivan was led to his wife's bed to see his daughter nursing at her breast. Ivan felt his chest swell at the sight. He kissed Marie, softly stroked the baby's light-colored hair. Mark and Carol came in, oohed and crooned over the newborn baby. Marie gave them a weak smile as she closed her eyes, drifted off to sleep.

Ivan was overwhelmed by the birth of his daughter. He happily greeted Marie's parents, her brother, and his wife. Everyone thought the baby had Ivan's eyes, Marie's nose. They all agreed she was a beautiful baby. Duty calls when Mark's radio goes off, prompting the two men to leave the hospital.

When Marie returned home, she was fussed over by her mother who didn't allow her to do a thing except feed the baby. They named the baby Katya after Ivan's mother. After Marie's mother left, a new order returned to their home, dominated by the needs of the new baby.

Ivan was sitting on the couch with baby Katya in his arm. The baby was warm, occasionally waving her arms, kicking her legs up towards her face. Ivan was amazed that Katya could almost touch her nose with her feet. Marie laughed at the baby's antics, put her arms around Ivan's neck, kissed and nipped at his neck playfully. Ivan told her Mark and Carol were expecting a child. Marie was pleased with the news told him she would talk to Carol about child care. Marie hadn't found anyone for daycare and her busy time fur buying was fast approaching.

Amos and Agnes had offered to watch the baby, but Marie was a bit reluctant to put that burden on them. She was hoping she could find a local, young, mother to care for her daughter.

While Ivan was enjoying his daughter, his mind was full of the alert he had gotten from headquarters about the number of black bears that had been found with their gallbladders missing and the carcasses left to rot. Ivan knew that his area was a prime country for the poachers. Nobody paid any attention to gunshots in his area. Nobody paid any attention to vehicles parked at the entrances of wood roads. Thousands of miles of dirt roads made the area very appealing to poachers.

His first thought was to get the aid of Mark. Mark had vastly more experience than he did in dealing with felonies. He knew State and local Police were also notified about the ongoing poaching.

19

Herbert Hormel was born in Milan N.H. on a small farm. His dad worked full-time at the paper mill, tried to keep the farm going. Herbert learned all manner of things growing up on a small farm. He learned to make the most delicious baked beans from his mother. He learned how to hunt, fish, trap, from his uncle. As a young boy, he shot deer for his family on a regular basis. He had a special liking for bear hunting and by age 22, he had shot over a dozen bears. An Asian gentleman he knew from Berlin had offered to buy the bears gall bladder for the unheard price of two hundred and fifty dollars. That represented more than a month's pay for his, hard-working father.

When Herbert compared working in the woods cutting timber to the easy money selling a gall bladder, there just wasn't any comparison. As a young man, Herb set up a business selling baked beans from a roadside pull-off close to the Berlin ski jump. He had developed quite a repeat business for his beans.

He also developed contacts for the sale of venison. Herb used his experience in hunting and trapping to make his way in the hard life of the north country. Herb's one big failure in life was alcohol. Herb was not a daily, drinker, he never drank until he felt he was successful in whatever enterprise he was currently involved with.

When Herb drank, it was, "Balls, to the wall." He would spend every dollar he had, stay drunk for as long as he had a dollar to spend. Herb was a mean drunk. Mean to his family and anyone within arms' reach of him. Herb was over six feet, a well-muscled build, a face that was serene as the flat water on a protected pond. He developed into quite the lady's man, spent lavishly on them. The drunker he got, the less choosy he became.

Herb had saved enough money when he was sober to open a mom-and-pop grocery store in West Berlin. He worked like a dog for two years until the business became successful. It took him a month and a half of drunkenness to lose it all. With his tail between his legs, he fled to Rangeley Maine to escape his creditors.

In Rangeley, he went back to earning real money the easy way. Wardens and law enforcement were scarce, Herb poached his way into another drunken stupor. Even in his cups, he managed to assault and beat to the ground, the husband of the woman he was currently with. This little escapade cost him six months in a county lock-up.

When Herb got out, he traveled north in his quest for bear gall bladders. He left behind him a string of bloated, stinking, carcasses that drew the attention of the Wardens Service. This bright sunny day, Herb headed towards the Allagash with a hangover, his 1894 Winchester .32 special strapped to the side of his motorcycle, and a few clothes in his saddlebags. Herb intended to make a small fortune before the cold set in, return to Berlin in triumph.

In an area between Telos Lake and Round Pond, farmer Joe Fontaine was just finishing up in his fields when he heard the gunshot. This was the third shot he had heard from the same area in less than a week and a half. Each time he heard the shot, he would drive his tractor down his wood road two and a half miles to the end of it without seeing anything suspicious. He did notice a rotten smell in the air, the obnoxious odor seemed worse every time he drove down the road. On his way out this time, his eye caught the glint of something metal off the wood road. The angle of the western sun was just right for him to catch the reflection off, what turned out to be, a motorcycle hidden in the woods.

Joe drove back to his home, notified the authorities of the situation. An alert deputy relayed the message to Fish and Game.

Fish and Game notified Ivan Petrov, ordered him to immediately investigate. When Ivan told, Mark he was going to the southern end of his territory to investigate, Mark told him he had nothing going on, would accompany him. Ivan was more than happy to have the help of his friend Mark.

Walking down the wood road, the smell was very evident in the air. The two men searched for over three hours to find the source without any luck. It was getting dusk when the sound of a shot alerted both men that they were not alone. As they walked down the wood road, they heard the sound of a motorcycle coming towards them. When the cycle came into sight, Mark held up his hand to stop the man.

Herb saw the two officers in the roadway, he slowed as he approached them, accelerated rapidly between them. Neither man would shoot a man under these conditions, they watched their target flee.

First thing in the morning, they found the remains of five bears. Ivan verified they were all missing their gallbladders. They visited the farmer to see what he could tell them of his encounter. Joe's wife and infant daughter greeted them, got a hand-held radio, called her husband to come home. She served the men fresh, strong, coffee as they waited. In a rush of air, Joe came in, greeted the two officers. When Mark asked him about his encounter, he produced a slip of paper with the license number of the motorcycle. Mark wasted no time in alerting pertinent law enforcement. In a matter of a few hours, they had the name, Herbert Hormel from Berlin N.H. Mark thanked the alert farmer, told Ivan he didn't think they had enough evidence for an arrest warrant. Both men checked out the area until they found the tourist cabin that Herbert had stayed in. Ivan took testimony from the landlord and his family, took testimony from the owner of a small diner in the area. They all described Herbert Hormel to a tee. Mark called in a forensic unit, which soon had evidence that the cabin had been occupied by Herbert Hormel.

A warrant was issued, Herbert was arrested in Berlin, extradited to Fort Kent. Under questioning, Herbert gave up his employer for a reduced sentence. The law went a lot harder on the employer than it did on Herbert. Herbert would be sober for at least two years unable to drink his prison sentence away.

A letter was sent to all licensed trappers to be on the lookout for bear poachers, newspapers printed stories of the arrests, and the need to notify authorities. Sportsmen all over Maine were on the alert. Penalties were increased, raised to felony convictions. Although Ivan received praise and a commendation for the arrest, he gave full credit to Mark for the arrest.

Ivan was offered a promotion that would require him to move his residence to another district, he turned it down. He would not leave the Allagash that had healed and sustained him. His memory of Auschwitz never diminished, but now, was controllable. When Ivan returned home, both Marie and Katya greeted him with big smiles. Ivan was a happy and content man. The love of Marie had saved him from his terrible dreams, Katya gave him hope for the future.

Amos was fishing on Lake Allagash when the sun rose in the East. He was marveling at the dawning, would welcome the heat from the giver of all life on earth, the sun. His lure was running deep as he trolled slowly southward. The strike on his line was not unexpected, the strength of the fish was. He increased the drag on his reel, but the strong fish was still taking line. He turned his boat to lessen the pull of the fish. The fish held its own for over a half-hour. When the fish stopped overcoming the drag on his reel, Amos killed the motor, started to recover the line. Twenty minutes later, he caught sight of the monster lake trout just before it dived for the bottom overcoming the drag as it dove. Twenty minutes later, the huge fish was barely moving on the surface.

His net slid easily over the huge fish. He struggled but succeeded in landing the biggest lake trout he had ever seen. As soon as he saw the huge fish lying on the bottom of his boat, he knew he had to release it back to the depths from which it came. As gently as he could, he returned the fish to the water, held it by its tail, gently moved it back and forth to keep water moving over its gills. Just when he had the thought that the huge fish wouldn't recover, it made a powerful thrust for freedom. Amos watched as the fish disappeared into the depths.

Amos drifted on the surface of the lake as he lit his pipe, enjoyed the powerful sun rising to warm his old bones. As he drifted, he reflected on his life in the north country. Although he had run a successful fur business, he owed his wealth to the investments he had made in the U.S. stock market starting over forty-five years ago. His marriage to Agnes had pleased him no end. She was a remarkable woman. She had come to show him genuine affection. She had been true to her words. She never faltered in running her life exactly as she had before she married him. She never asked for anything, still wore her buckskin dresses and her moccasins, still braided her hair every morning. He would lie in bed, marvel at her lithe figure as she braided her hair before her mirror. The angle of the mirror was such that he could see part of her upper body reflected in the mirror while he gazed at the beauty of her spine merging with her hips. When she slipped her buckskin dress over her head, the spell was broken and he would arise.

When Amos became aware of the sound of an approaching boat, he started his motor, decided to call it a day. He gave a friendly wave to the passing boat as he headed towards the landing.

❦ 20 ❦

This cold November morning, Agnes and Amos were working pre-cut pieces of moose hide through a special machine that would soften and finish the leather to make it suitable for moccasin soles. The temperature had risen to just above freezing, but a stiff wind from the north made it seem much colder. Amos was grumbling about going inside to warm up when a single gunshot broke the silence of the deep woods. It was the start of deer season and nobody reacted to a shot from the woods.

After finishing a hot cup of coffee, Amos left to buy Agnes some oil she needed to finish the soles she was making. He noticed four vehicles parked at the entrance to an old, grown-up woods road. He paid them no mind as he headed to Fort Kent.

That evening, Ken Johnson, a camp owner from Portland, reported to Police that James, fuller had not gotten out of the woods. Ivan and Sheriff Tower instigated a search for the lost hunter. It was not uncommon for a hunter to be lost in the woods. The searchers marched down the logging road using a siren to try and guide the hunter out of the woods. Ivan and a deputy stayed the entire night periodically using the siren to no avail.

Agnes was not happy to hear the siren going off, waking her from her sleep. She and Amos were sitting at their kitchen table when Ivan knocked on their door. Amos told Ivan of the shot they had heard early that morning, told him of the vehicles parked at the old wood road they were searching. Agnes poured the weary Ivan a steaming cup of coffee, gave him some relief from the long night.

Sheriff tower had interviewed camp owner Ken Johnson, got a list of names of the hunters from his camp. Ivan scanned the list, did not recognize anyone on the list. Ivan got a search party organized consisting of four seasoned trappers, eight law enforcement personnel. At seven in the morning, Ivan started the systematic search for the lost hunter.

Ivan was hopeful that the trappers would spot the scarce sign that the hunters left. At eleven thirty that morning, trapper John Ingalls found the body of James Fuller. When the coroner determined the death to be from a gunshot wound, Sergeant Mark Schafer took over the investigation.

There was virtually no sign left in or around the body. Ivan was completely stumped as to how the investigation would continue. Mark took the only avenue available to him, an autopsy. The coroner determined that the bullet had broken the right arm of the victim, passed through both lungs, recovered a bullet against the rib cage on the victim's left side. He determined from the amount of blood that had congealed against the ribs, that the victim never moved after falling to the ground. Mark did not hesitate to send the bullet to the FBI's ballistic lab to be tested.

Mark began an intensive questioning of all the people at Ken Johnson's camp. He got a vague description of the three other vehicles that were in the area that morning. An appeal was made in the local papers for information on the hunting party, very few responses were called in.

George Harrison reported that he and his brother-in-law were in the area that morning in separate vehicles. He reported that he heard the gunshot about nine thirty that morning. He added it was the only shot fired that morning. Mark thanked him for coming in, was glad that they at least had a vague timeline for the shooting. George gave Mark the names of two other hunters in the area that day.

Mark's list of hunters in the area that morning had grown to nineteen people, fourteen adults, five minors. Mark was sitting in the Sheriff's office when the report came in from the FBI. They had determined that the bullet was a .30 caliber, 150 grain Remington round-nosed bullet. The rifling on the bullet matched the twist for a .30-30 caliber bullet. Mark knew that the bullet in question was designed for maximum performance at .30-30 Win. Velocities. The chance that it had been handloaded into a faster cartridge was almost nil. He was looking for a hunter using a .30-30 rifle, one of the most common rifles in the north woods.

Mark got a search warrant for the camp of Ken Johnson. He and Ivan had to force the door as the camp was locked, empty. It was a disappointment for him as no weapons were found in the camp. Mark sighed as he wrote out a warrant for Ken Johnson's residence in Portland. Mark requested Fish and Game for the services of Ivan for his investigation. It was approved.

Mark had no need of the warrant as Ken Johnson opened his gun cabinet, told Mark to take whatever he wished. Mark got two Winchester .30-30 carbines from Ken, addresses for four other hunters in his party. Mark collected three more .30-30's from the other houses with no need for a warrant.

A Savage model 219 single-shot .30-30 owned by Ken's sister's son proved to be the rifle that fired the killing shot.

Henry Miller was just thirteen years of age. Ivan sat across from the young boy and his parents. The boy was petrified. He reminded Ivan of an animal in a trap who knows the end is nigh.

The boy's mother was softly sobbing, his father had a hopeless look on his face as Ivan turned the recorder on. Ivan knew that the victim had been dressed in, "Maine green," not a bit of safety orange in his attire. Ivan said to the boy, "It's best you tell us in your own words what happened,"

The boy was hesitant to speak. Ivan waited patiently. His dad touched his son's arm, "Tell the truth son."

The boy was sobbing, barely in control of himself as he recounted the events of that morning.

"I saw a deer running away from me. I know it was a deer, I saw its horns. I followed after it, saw a flash of white through the trees, fired my gun at it. When I saw it was a man, I ran out of the woods. I was afraid to say anything."

Mark talked to the parents, gently took the boy into custody. Ivan felt a degree of sadness both for the victim, for the young boy who made such a tragic mistake.

Sitting in Ivan's kitchen, Ivan told Mark.

"My father taught me never to raise a gun unless you knew absolutely what you were going to shoot. He told me no power on earth calls back a bullet after it has been fired."

Mark nodded soberly, "I got the same advice from my father. Every year someone's enthusiasm overrides their common sense resulting in an untimely, totally unnecessary death."

Ivan added that hunters should wear safety orange at all times while hunting. Marie held baby Katya, kept her silence. She strongly felt there was no excuse for shooting another human being under any circumstances. Baby Katya squirmed in her arms. Down on the floor, the baby crawled to Ivan, pulled herself erect. Ivan caressed the hair on her head, marveled at his infant daughter. As he caressed her, no thought of what he had endured, seen, at the camps came into his mind. The love of Marie, the friendship of Mark, the dark forests of the Allagash were healing his mind and body.

The young boy was convicted of leaving the scene of a killing, was remanded to the Juvenile system until the age of 18 when his case would be reviewed. His family was financially ruined by the civil suit brought by the victim's wife. Ivan had the thought that there were many victims in this sad case. Marie had the thought that the State should make hunter orange mandatory. Ivan, as usual, chose not to argue with Marie.

Amos had allowed Max to stay at his cabin on Eagle Pond in exchange for his cutting the brush that had grown up over the years and doing some repairs on the porch steps. Max thought it was a great deal. Lucille would stay with him over the weekends, happily helped him with the work. Their upcoming wedding was planned for the coming June. Lucille had asked her grandmother to make a traditional wedding dress for her, asked Marie to stand up for her, Max had asked Ivan to stand up for him.

Max was fully prepared for the trapping season. He had made his sets, was anxious for the general trapping season to open. Long hair pelts were predicted to be the most in-demand this season and he had planned accordingly. He had rented a cabin from the timber companies, looked forward to visits from Lucille over the long trapping season. He had bought new snow, machine, felt he could cover a lot more territory with it. He had high hopes for the season.

21

Max left his cabin just as the sun made its appearance on the eastern skyline. The temperature was just barely above zero, the wind was very slight. He was well dressed against the cold, had a sled behind his snow machine to hold all he would need for the day. He had taken to wearing an orange toque as a safety measure against careless hunters. He stopped his sled at the first set of the morning, collected a prime coyote from it. After resetting, he drank a hot coffee from his thermos, enjoyed the quiet stillness of the woods. He was concentrating on coyotes this season and was having a good season so far. He turned his head as he caught the sound of an approaching snow machine. Ivan came into view on his old machine.

Ivan was pleased to see Max. Max offered Ivan hot coffee, but Ivan broke out his own thermos. Ivan was pleased to see that Max was having a good season, patted him on the back before resuming his patrol.

The trail Max was riding on was not an established trail. It meandered over thirty miles before merging with the main trail. He had worked hard to create this trail, was surprised to hear other sleds approaching him. He pulled to the right as far as he could, but a portion of the sled he was pulling was partially blocking the trail.

The two approaching snow machines were just going too fast for existing conditions. They had to know they were on a private trail as it was clearly marked on the main, recreational trail. When they came around the bend in the trail, it was too late to avoid a collision. The lead sled tried to avoid the obstruction, went off the trail, down the embankment, crashed into a cluster of small spruce trees. The second sled crashed into Max's sled knocking Max off his machine. The second sled veered away from the trail, down the embankment, crashed into the first sled, and overturned on its side.

Max was not hurt as he got to his feet, saw two people sprawled in the snow. He went down to render aid, pulled a young woman to safety, checked on the two injured riders. The woman on the first sled was unharmed, quickly tried to help Max. Max had his handkerchief pressed against a young man's forehead to stem the bleeding. He told the unharmed woman to get his first aid kit from his sled. When she returned with the kit, Max had her apply a pressure bandage to the man he was holding. The driver of the first sled had a broken arm or shoulder was in considerable pain. Max did what he could before he unhooked his towed sled, took off down the trail to catch up to Ivan.

A good twenty minutes later, Max caught up to Ivan, told him of the accident. They hustled back to the scene where they managed to load everyone on the two sleds and Max's slightly damaged towing sled. Ivan had radioed ahead for an ambulance that was waiting for them on the timber company's main road.

Ivan wrote out citations for both operators for excessive speed, trespassing on a private trail, causing an accident incurring personal damage. Ivan had their snow machines impounded, hauled to a private storage company.

The damage to Max's tow sled was minimal, he continued on his trapline. Ivan thought it was a hell of a price to pay for a little joyriding.

Baby Katya was standing in the middle of the kitchen when Ivan entered. She toddled to her father's arms, pushed her small arms against his shoulder. Marie kissed him soundly, hugged them both before pouring Ivan a coffee. Ivan recanted the events of the day to her. Marie shrugged her shoulders and said, "People should know better, but some people seem to lose their good sense on these machines."

"It's the love of speed Marie. People love the thrill of speed. Doesn't matter the vehicle, people would race on snails if they could."

Ivan had little time to himself during the busy month of November. Tomorrow, he would ready himself for whatever came up. Sure, as the sun will rise, he will get called out at least three times on a coming day. It's just not possible for a Game Warden to keep up with all the calls during the hectic month of November. Ivan would have to, pick and choose, which calls to respond to.

Mark had been out riding the back roads when the call for an ambulance went out. He had no doubt Ivan had the situation under control. Mark was having an off day, just relaxing, listening to the radio calls, thinking about the upcoming birth of his child. He really wasn't settled in his mind about the baby and the ensuing responsibility of raising a child. He wasn't sure how it would affect his relationship with Carol, but he knew things would be very different after the birth of the baby. It would be easy for him to avoid responsibility by using work as an excuse. He vowed he wouldn't do that no matter how much he was tempted. He finally came to the realization that he was afraid of the coming baby.

Carol's water broke while she was washing dishes. She called the doctor, called dispatch, called her mother and Marie before getting in her car, drove herself to the hospital. When she arrived, she was met by Marie with Katya in her arms. Before the nurses had her settled, her husband and her mother were by her bedside. She was in labor six hours before her son was born. 7 pounds, two ounces of a perfectly formed boy was presented to her breast. She counted his fingers and toes, tried to see the face pressed against her breast. She stroked the baby as he, fed. She ran her hand over every part of his body. Rubbed the soft hair of his head, kissed him repeatedly. Mark received a radio call telling him to report to the station. He kissed Carol before he left.

�֎ **22** ֎

Sheriff Tower notified Mark that a gas station in Ashland had been robbed and the attendant and a customer had been shot. Two men in an older, black chevy sedan had fled north on Route 11. Mark quickly took charge, ordered a roadblock to be set up just south of Portage. Given the time frame since the robbery and shooting, it was highly probable the felons were contained between Ashland and Portage.

Mark hurried to the roadblock with four deputies in two vehicles. An update on the radio advised that the two victims would survive their wounds. Mark pressed the accelerator to the floor. With his blue lights flashing, the men sped towards Portage.

Just as he cleared the town of Portage, he was advised that the suspects had crashed through the roadblock, were headed North towards him. Mark quickly ordered the deputies to block the road. Mark and another cruiser had the road completely blocked. Mark stood behind his cruiser with deputy Johnson. Both men were armed with 12-gauge shotguns loaded with slugs and double-ought buckshot.

The radio announced the felons had ditched their vehicle, had been seen running into the woods on the westerly side of the road. Back in his cruiser, Mark ordered dispatch to advise that Warden Ivan Petrov and at least two good trackers report to him ASAP.

Mark stopped by the three cruisers with their lights flashing, quickly talked with the pursuing officers. They reported that the felons had fired at them during the pursuit. Officer Jenkins advised the felon's car had been damaged enough to cause the two men to abandon it. He further advised a flurry of shots had been fired at the felons as they ran into the woods.

Mark ordered two officers to set up in Portage in case the suspects fled in that direction. Mark ordered another deputy to drive to Portage, return with coffee and sandwiches. Mark strode up and down the road, glanced at his watch, figured they had just four hours of light left, where the hell was Ivan?

Mark assigned five officers to take part in the search. All officers would have flashlights, medical kits, body armor, sidearms plus long guns. He wanted two officers to accompany each tracker. Mark radioed the headquarters and said that the search was about to get underway; he requested officers to be sent to Portage and await further instructions.

Ivan finally arrived with Max and Alfred Holmes. Mark readied the search party, advised everyone that the felons were armed and dangerous, had shot two civilians, shot at pursuing officers. Mark was worried about the elderly trapper Alfred Holmes. The man must be in his seventies Mark thought. He would stay with the old tracker.

Trapper Homes told Mark that the men had entered into an area of over 1600 square miles with only one main timber company road through it. He advised there were endless amounts of woods roads through the maze of spruce, hemlock, balsam, and pine trees. Mark warned the search party to travel at the rate the trackers set, keep a close eye on them, protect them.

Holmes found the first sign. He pointed out a small amount of blood on the side of a small birch tree. He told Mark that from the height of the blood, one of the felons was hit in the leg. Mark nodded, told the search party of the injured felon. The progress was slow as Holmes slowly followed the sign. The wind picked up causing the smaller trees to sway. Every movement caught Mark's attention. He cautioned the party, "Let the trappers work, stay alert for sight of the felons."

Two hours later, Holmes told Mark the pair had separated. He said,

"The wounded man has turned north, the other one is heading west towards the forest road. Mark radioed for officers to cover the woods road inside the restricted travel site. Mark's eye caught the gleam of sunlight off a metal object just before a shot rang out. The radio came to life. The call of an officer down went out. Mark let loose with five shotgun blasts into the dense conifers he had seen the gleam from. Mark put Holmes behind him as he advanced into the conifers. Mark saw a man on the ground trying to crawl away from them. The man had been hit in the head and neck area with a load of buckshot. He died before Mark could put the cuffs on him. Mark radioed that one felon was down, asked about the officer that had been hit.

Mark was advised that Ivan had been hit in his upper right shoulder. Mark left officer Jenkins and Holmes by the dead felon made his way to Ivan who was on the ground with his back against a large black birch tree. Ivan was in considerable pain from the wound. Mark talked with an ambulance attendant, told him the bullet had not exited. He was advised not to try and move Ivan, but to wait for help to arrive. Officer Jenkins advised that the injured felon was still free, Holmes had found his trail. After Ivan was safely on his way to the ambulance, Mark ordered everyone out of the woods except for two officers he wanted to stay with him in searching for the other, wounded Felon.

Mark ordered one officer to stay with the dead felon, resumed the trail with Holmes and two other officers. The blood trail was becoming spotty, hard for Holmes to follow. Mark asked Holmes how he was holding up. The old man answered he was fine, wanted to continue tracking the felon. As night started to fall, Mark heard the welcome news that a copter was en route to them with provisions. Mark halted the search, had a fire made, ordered the men to make a shelter using their space blankets. The copter arrived just as the snow started to fall, lowered provisions to them, made a hasty retreat. The snow was falling lightly as darkness descended upon them. Holmes had banked the fire to throw its heat into the shelter. Mark was grateful for the hot coffee, the food, and the fire.

They spent a long uncomfortable night before the light of a gray dawn arrived. Scattered snow flurries were in the air as Holmes started the search. They hadn't gone three hundred yards when they came upon the campsite the felon had made. There was evidence of a small fire, considerable blood where the man had lain. Mark received a radio call telling him that Ivan was in the hospital, resting comfortably after surgery to remove the bullet, cleanse his wound. Mark advised he would be out of radio contact as they were closing in on the felon.

When they came to a good size stream, Holmes advised they were less than two miles from a forest road he was familiar with. Mark called on the radio. Had officers cover the road in question. Mark had barely turned his attention back to the trail when Holmes pointed, "There he is."

The felon was laying behind a log with a pistol in his hand. Mark got in front of Holmes, ordered the felon to drop his weapon. Other officers hollered for the man to drop his weapon. When the felon raised up with his revolver pointing at them, everyone opened fire. The felon lay dead over the log he had hidden behind. Mark felt no sympathy for the man.

Mark ordered the helicopter to come, pick up the dead felon. After the pickup, they had a short walk to a forest road where they were picked up.

Mark was sitting by Ivan's bedside drinking a hot coffee, digesting the excellent meal he had at the diner before coming to the hospital. Ivan was sleeping soundly when Marie entered the room with Katya in her arms. Marie was somewhat resentful that Mark kept involving Ivan in these criminal matters. Ivan was a Game Warden, not a cop. Why does Mark keep involving him?

Mark quickly guessed what Marie's thoughts were, told her, "When the crime involves the woods, or searching the woods, Ivan and his trappers are invaluable to Law Enforcement. He reminded Eve that Ivan was in fact, a law enforcement officer."

All the commotion woke Ivan up. His first thought was to ask Mark about Alfred Holmes's condition.

"The old man looked better than any of us. I think the old man is made of oak. He's the hardiest man I've ever known. I hear that he's going to get a commendation for all his help to law enforcement, he well deserves it."

That was welcome news to Ivan, he worried about the old man.

Ivan told them the doctor said he could expect a full recovery, no loss of use in his arm. It would take at least a month to heal properly. Marie smiled at that news. Baby Katya wanted to go to her father. Marie set her on the bed near Ivan. Ivan rubbed her shoulder, talked quietly to her. Marie hugged Ivan, left her tears on his shoulder.

Mark was hesitant to open his door. He entered as quietly as he could. When he walked into the living room, Carol was nursing his son. He approached her, kissed her gently on her lips, lightly rubbed his son's hair. The baby paid him no mind as he nursed. Carol's mother came out of the guest bedroom asked Mark if he was hungry. Mark thanked her for the offer, told her he had already eaten.

When Carol joined him in bed, he sighed as he held her to his chest, told her it was good to be home. Carol told him she had decided to take a year off from work to take care of the baby. Mark answered that whatever she decided, he was in agreement with. She offered that she might watch baby Katya for Marie and Ivan at the same time. Mark nodded his understanding, pulled her closer to his chest. Mark couldn't help but notice that Carol smelled just like the baby. Carol snuggled as close as she could to Mark, fell into a dreamless sleep.

Infection had set in to Ivan's shoulder. As his fever mounted, the dream of his happy smiling parents and siblings was in his mind. As his dream turned towards the killing of his family, he felt a touch on his shoulder, awoke to hear the doctor tell him they had to operate on him again. They felt that they must have missed a piece of cloth pushed into his flesh by the bullet. Cold sweat was on Ivan's face as they wheeled him to the operating room. Ivan feared the dream more than he did the infection.

Marie dropped Katya off with Agnes and her grandfather, hurried to the hospital to be with Ivan. Terrible thoughts were going through her mind as she drove. She blamed the incompetent medical staff for Ivan's infection. "How could they not see a foreign body inside the wound?"

By the time she arrived at the hospital, she had calmed down. She reasoned that there must be a good reason for them to miss something. Everything in life is not so simple, she mused.

She was worried about Ivan. She had left in such, haste, she hadn't noticed her breasts were leaking milk. She decided she had to see Ivan before taking care of the problem. In his room, she removed her coat, was instantly noticed by a nurse who supplied her with a breast pump. While Ivan slept, Marie emptied her breasts, tried her best to hurry the process.

Ivan was just waking up when she sat by his head. She put her hand on his forehead, found it warm and dry to her touch. She was kissing his cheek and neck when he came back to himself. He put his good arm around her shoulder, told her he loved her. Marie cried on his shoulder, clung to him.

Ivan was tired, but he was now healing. When he awoke, clear-headed, the following morning, he wanted nothing but out of the hospital. His doctor told him if he had no fever by late afternoon, he would release him.

23

Mark was sitting at Ivan's kitchen table drinking coffee, reading the articles in the newspaper about the capture of the felons that had robbed a store, shot two people. Although there was much praise for law enforcement, one article was criticizing Mark's use of non-law enforcement people. The article noted other instances when Mark had used trappers to catch felons. Max stated that perhaps law enforcement could utilize people with the necessary skills. Mark nodded his agreement, said, "Until law enforcement has people with the trapper's skills, I will continue to use them."

Ivan told Max he ought to apply at the Sheriff's office for a job as a deputy. "They certainly could use your skills."

Mark thought to himself that Max's short stature might work against him in a job as a deputy. It was hard for him to envision Max wrestling with drunks and people under the influence of drugs. Mark put his doubts aside, told Max, "If you're interested, I will talk to the Sheriff about taking you on."

Max was a little stunned by Mark's statement. He hesitated before telling Mark he would talk it over with Lucille, let him know.

At Amos's camp on Eagle Pond, Max and Lucille were sitting on the porch catching the last rays of sunshine.

"I'm not against you becoming a deputy Max. Are you sure you want to put yourself in such a dangerous position?"

"It's a good career, Lucille. I'm not afraid. They will give me the training to help overcome the fact I'm not that big. Many women become police officers, why not me?"

Lucille sat in his lap, kissed him soundly. Max responded with a fierce hug, feeling elated that Lucille would support him.

Mark, Ivan, and Sheriff Tower were in the local diner. Mark had presented his case to Tower as to why he should hire Max as a deputy. Sheriff Tower grinned at them. Tower was a big man, 230 pounds on his big frame. "Any one of my deputies could pick up Max with one hand and shake the life out of him. Do you honestly think he's suitable for law enforcement?"

"He brings a set of skills that your department seriously lacks. He is a tracker of note. He possesses great common sense, would be a good addition to your force."

Tower stood up, told them, "Send the young man by, I'll at least talk to him, size him up."

Ivan shook the Sheriff's hand. "I think Max would be a good fit, he's a quick learner."

Mark told Ivan he thought the Sheriff was, "on the fence", about Max, had hope that the Sheriff would at least consider him.

When Max stood in front of Tower's desk, Tower thought, he does have a sturdy frame at least. Tower spent twenty minutes talking with Max. He decided he would take a chance with Max, told him, "If you can pass the police academy, I'll hire you.

When Max left the Sheriff's office, he was elated. He notified Lucille, Ivan and Marie, Mark and Carol that the Sheriff was going to send him to the academy. He drove to Amos and Agnes's house to give them the good news. When he called his parents, gave them the news, he was proud when his father told him, "I know you'll do the right thing Max."

Lucille decided she wanted to marry Max before he was due to leave for the academy. She was finding it harder and harder not to wind up in bed with Max. She wasn't sure if her passion was overriding her good sense, but she knew it was time to marry him.

Lucille and Max could think of no better place to get married than the camp at Eagle Pond. Agnes threw herself into making all the preparations. Amos happily helped move and set up the tables and chairs necessary for the expected crowd of people. Although Lucille had planned for a small, private wedding, the list of people soon grew beyond her expectations. Besides his family, Max wanted Mark and Carol to attend. Besides Agnes and Amos, Lucille's mother, three sisters, and two brothers were going to attend. What started out as a wedding involving six people, grew to a crowd of over thirty people.

Marie, Agnes, Carol, threw themselves into food preparation, flowers, getting a small band to provide music for, dancing in the grass, as Agnes put it. Max was a helpless bystander during the preparations.

A brilliant sun dawned the day of the wedding. The temperature was mild for September, the air was fresh, the smell of conifers was heavy in the air. Marie and Agnes wore traditional Mic-Mac dresses. Amos and Ivan wore blue suits. Max looked resplendent in his new blue suit as he awaited the appearance of his bride-to-be. Agnes preceded her granddaughter down the aisle. Lucille was dressed in a leather dress decorated with beading, quills, the fur of ermine. Her hair was braided, beaded moccasins upon her feet. Max had bought a pair of Wellington boots with heels that brought him up to Lucille's height. Agnes stood by her granddaughter. Ivan stood by Max.

After the ceremony, the festivities began in earnest. The many different cultures blended together without a hitch. The food and drink were abundant, the dancing proved to be a great success. Max was pleased to dance with his mother and his sisters. He watched as his father danced with his bride, felt his breast swell at the beauty of his bride. When he danced with Marie, she whispered to him, "I told you a woman would drag you out of the woods." Max laughed at her comment.

Amos and Agnes were the last to leave. Lucille hugged her grandmother, thanked her for all she had done.

Finally, they were alone. Max watched as Lucille unbraided her hair, rose to stand face to face with him. After a deep kiss, Max pulled her wedding dress over her head to find her completely naked under the garment. Lucille stood proudly in front of him before surrendering to his strong arms. Max finally found out what it was to love a woman. Max had done the right thing.

At the Academy, Max was struggling with a man a head taller than him, about fifty pounds heavier. He managed to hold his own, finally tripped the man, forced his arm behind his back, applied the cuffs. The instructor touched his shoulder, motioned for him to release the man.

Max found the Academy very hard. He seemed to struggle with everything except the shooting. Shooting was second nature to him; he excelled in that aspect of the training. Lucille helped him with the academics, kept at him to learn it well.

After making love the second time that night, he groaned, "I have to wrestle a 200 pounder tomorrow and you've got me wore out." Lucille patted his chest. "You've got no one to blame but yourself."

Max threw himself into the training with all he had. The instructors gave little indication of what your status was in the group. It was only when you convened in the morning that you would notice, someone was missing. Max was praying it wouldn't happen to him. Max kept his mouth shut whenever possible, did a lot more listening than talking.

The morning of the final exams, Max was quiet but confident he had tried his absolute best. He finished rather quickly, placed his test face down on the instructor's desk, calmly walked outside to join other cadets. By noon that day, he was informed that he had met all requirements, would graduate on Friday.

Max was the shortest man in the group of graduates. He stood proudly, his head facing forward, erect. His eyes scanned the crowd, his eyes moistened when he saw Lucille with his parents, Agnes and Amos. Ivan and Marie were in the back of them. Dressed in his deputy's uniform, he accepted the degree with pride. Mark was one of the first to congratulate him. "Well done, Max, welcome to the club."

The training officer, Jules Jenkins, was the most experienced deputy Sheriff Tower had. He was a tough, but fair man, the Sheriff trusted him to properly educate Max in a responsible and timely manner. He chose to train Max on the second shift, by far the busiest of the three shifts. He gave Max maps that must be memorized by him ASAP. Radio communication was another area that Max needed to learn intimately as soon as possible.

One of the most important facts he gave Max was the need for an officer to listen to what people say to him. This ability is vital when an officer is in a crowd situation. Jenkins told him, "Never go off half-cocked. Listen, make your decision, act with authority, only use the amount of force necessary to make the arrest. Never pull your weapon unless it is the last resort." Jenkins was very skillful in constantly reminding Max of how to act in certain situations, constantly telling him of situations that demanded he pull his weapon and be ready to use it if vitally necessary.

Max's head was swimming with all the directives given him by Jenkins. Lucille helped him greatly by her constant repetition of what he needed to learn. She taught max a method of recall that used keywords to trigger his memory. Max was mentally exhausted when the days of learning finally ended.

Max's first real test came when he turned the cruiser onto the tarred road and saw a blue pickup weave across the yellow line. He immediately put on his flashers, pulled a u-turn, fell in behind the weaving truck. Max keyed the mike, notified dispatch, carefully pulled up alongside the truck. He kept a safe distance, held the front of his cruiser even with the pickups driver's door. He hit the siren a few times, the pickup kept going. Max called for assistance, fell back behind the pickup. Jenkins was observing, didn't utter a word. The radio cackled advising assistance was five minutes out. When Max saw the cruiser blocking the road ahead, he closed up to the bumper of the pickup, and hit the siren.

The blue pickup braked, pulled slightly off the road when its front wheels, settled into the soft shoulder. Max was out of the cruiser, revolver in hand as he approached the driver's door. As he reached for the door handle, he saw the driver laying against the steering wheel. He pulled the door open, ordered the driver to raise his hands, get out of the vehicle. When the driver failed to respond, he told Jenkins to cover him, holstered his weapon, pulled the driver out of the vehicle down onto the roadway, cuffed him.

It turned out that the driver was medically impaired. The driver was taken to the hospital, cited by Max for unfit driving due to a medical condition. As he cleared the scene, Jenkins told him he had handled the situation correctly. He listed the things that Max did correctly, told him he was correct in drawing his weapon.

Sheriff Tower was pleased to see that Max had passed his first real test, praised Jenkins for his dedication as a training officer. Max proved to be a quick learner, was assigned third shift duty on his own.

Ivan was almost completely healed. The doctor told him to start the light exercise with his healing shoulder. Ivan tried a few pullups, a few pushups before the pain flared in his shoulder. He relaxed a bit, tried again until the pain stopped him. He kept this up for a week before he was certified to return to duty. Ivan spent a lot of time with Marie and baby, Katya. Mark and Carol made frequent visits, Max and Lucille encouraged him in his healing. Mark chided him by telling him he needed to wear a suit of armor when he was on duty. Marie saw no humor in the statement, was a bit resentful that Ivan kept being drawn into Police activities. Ultimately, she came to the realization that Ivan was a law enforcement officer, live with it.

Ivan slowly pulled out of the field he had been watching. Four deer feeding in the field ran across his headlights in their dash for the safety of the woods. He grinned to himself as he turned towards home. The radio came to life announcing that an officer needs assistance, Town line Bar and Grill. Ivan was but a few minutes east of the bar, turned his flashers on as he sped towards the bar. When he pulled into the parking lot, he could see a Sheriff's cruiser stopped with its blue lights flashing. He stopped with his headlights illuminating a crowd of people. He ran to the crowd, saw a deputy on the ground being pummeled by two men. Ivan struck one man rendering him senseless. He grabbed the other man, twisted him to the ground, cuffed him. He took the deputy's cuffs, cuffed the senseless man. Deputy Max was trying to sit up. His face was bloody, one eye was rapidly closing, blood was flowing from the deputy's nose. Ivan called for an ambulance, aided Max the best he could. Max had a knife wound on his side he hadn't noticed at first. Ivan held Max until the ambulance attendants took over his care. Reinforcements arrived, started to interview the crowd. The two assailants were taken away by another deputy.

Max's wounds turned out to be relatively mild, but his face would look like a rainbow of color in the morning. Ivan drove Max home after he was released from the emergency room.

Max told the Sheriff that he had done the right thing. When he broke up the fight, a person behind him stabbed him in the side. Another man grabbed him from behind, pulled him to the ground.

"Next time, wait until assistance arrives before approaching a crowd. Officer safety is the most important thing, wait for backup."

Max recovered from the incident, had learned an important lesson. He thanked Ivan for his assistance. Ivan told him his bent nose would remind him to be more careful.

Mark was sitting at his kitchen table opposite Carol and his son. Carol was breastfeeding the infant while Mark was trying to break the news to her. He decided to wait until she finished with the baby before he gave her the news.

"I've been ordered to take over the investigation of a missing Police chief down in Upton Maine. I tried to get out of it, but my superiors are up in arms about this case, insist that I'm the man to solve it.

Carol told him she understood the pressure he was under, told him she was able to handle everything at home, had plenty of help from friends and family if need be. Mark was relieved that his wife was with him.

PART II

1

Turner Brook Road, Upton Maine.

From his perch against a large bull pine tree, he could see the sharp curve in the road slowly giving way to a straightaway about 200 yards long. A harsh yellow sign advised, "Caution, steep grade." Any vehicle rounding that curve would slow down gradually to prepare for the descent, pass 75 yards from his position. Less than fifty yards behind him was a logging road that numerous off-road vehicles traveled. The muddy road was full of potholes holding water trapped by the clay-like soil. This logging road had many other roads and trails connected to it. Most were dead-ends, but three of them led to well-paved roads. Dusk was falling and the light was starting to fade. It was getting close to that eerie time of day that raised the fears born of ancient man into many people. Shadows started to lengthen on the roadway. The air was changing from mild to a damp chill as the night air started to fall. There would be frost on the ground in the morning.

He had come prepared. He removed a plastic bag from his coveralls, dumped the contents on the pine needles in front of him. With his gloved hand, he brushed the pine needles away to make a smooth impression in the soil. Into this hollow, he placed three partially smoked filter cigarettes. He carefully pressed them into the ground as if they had been snuffed out there. He threw a fired .30-06 case about two feet slightly to his right. Taking a piece of a red sweater from the bag, he rubbed it against the rough bark of the bull pine. He didn't stop rubbing until he could plainly see the fibers clinging to the rough bark. Satisfied with his layout, he sat down with his back against the tree, spread his legs apart a bit, pushed the heel of his boots forcefully into the soil, twisting and turning his feet until it was plain to make out the size 12 boots he was wearing. From his pocket, he took a single 180 grain .300 win. magnum cartridge and bolted it home in his rifle. The view through the crosshairs clearly showed the yellow warning sign.

With dusk approaching, his prey should be approaching. It didn't matter to him that he had nothing against this officer. It was the uniform he wore, the Deputy Sheriff's cruiser he drove that mattered. The U.S. was turning into a Police State, and that had to be halted. He hoped that by the example he would set, others would copy him, let America know that the loss of personnel freedoms would not be allowed to continue. He was in agreement with some western groups that openly opposed the government and its high-handed policies. It was time to put the Government on notice that it would no longer be tolerated. He kept his thoughts to himself. No one could be trusted to share his beliefs. One thing he knew for sure: if more than one person knows, the whole world knows.

Deputy Sheriff Peterson wasn't in any hurry. After you hit sixty, life doesn't have the same urgency it used to. He was looking forward to getting home, completing the model airplane he was building. He had built a large collection of them and they were a great source of pleasure for him and his grandchildren. He drove slowly and carefully down the straightaway, mindful of the caution sign and the steep grade it warned of. Deputy Peterson never saw the hole appear in his windshield, never felt any pain from the bullet smashing into his chest, severing his spine as it passed through his body. The hydrostatic shock from the impact totally shut down his nervous system. He died instantly.

As the shooter raised his head from the stock, he saw the cruiser slow down, drift to the right, roll about 40 yards before being stopped by a cluster of saplings, small trees. From his elevated position, he couldn't tell if the cruiser had cleared the road enough to be hidden from sight. He pocketed the fired cartridge, walked the few yards to the logging road behind him, mounted his three-wheeler, began the nine-mile journey to his truck. He wouldn't allow himself to panic, kept his speed moderate, forced himself to relax. After turning onto the trail that led to his truck, he stopped by a small marsh, walked to a hole he had previously dug. Shedding his coveralls, gloves, and his oversized boots, carefully buried them. From his day pack he had hidden there, he put on fresh clothing, continued to his truck without passing anyone.

Three years after the murder of Deputy Peterson, the police had failed, to come up with a suspect. Although they had checked out almost all the people who owned .30-06 rifles, tested them for comparison with the fired case found at the scene, they had made no match.

The shooter knew the Police would not match the shell casing. He had picked it up in a gravel bank outside Bangor two years ago. Two days after the shooting, he drove to his shooting range, fired five rounds of oversized lead bullets through his .300 win. magnum. The oversized bullets coated with lapping compound would change the ballistic characteristics of his rifle. The Police had never given out any details as to what was found at the crime scene, but if you owned a .30-06, smoked Winstons, wore size twelve boots, liked to wear a red wool sweater, you definitely had a lot of explaining to do.

2

Ray Chance and his boss, Don Boer, were framing up the walls of a new house off Route 10 when Ray looked up, saw Jim Sawyer and his wife coming down Route 10 towards Newport. Behind them, a State Trooper had his blues on. Jim pulled his pickup to the side of the road, the officer pulled in behind him, turned his cruiser slightly into the travel lane. Fucking cops, Ray thought, stop a guy and his wife for a traffic offense, act like it's a major felony bust. The Officer had Jim and his wife out of the truck, standing in front of it while he searched the truck. The Officer had found an empty beer bottle which he held in his left hand as he approached Jim and his wife. When Ray looked up again, the Officer was conducting a field sobriety check on Jim. The whole affair was turning into a slight confrontation as Jim's wife was upset, alternating crying and yelling at the Officer. The Officer completed his field check, retreated back to his cruiser. A Newport cruiser was approaching from the opposite direction, put his blue lights on, crossed the center line, parked in front of Jim's truck. Two officers got out, stood behind the cruiser's doors. One of the Officers approached Jim and his wife. Here we go, Ray thought, ready to put this guy in jail because he has a dead soldier in his truck. You're dammed if you throw it out, dammed if you keep it in the truck. Ray looked up again as the party was breaking up. Jim and his wife were leaving and the State Trooper was back in his cruiser ready to bag another Al Capone coming down Route 10.

The Newport cruiser pulled over, stopped by the boss's truck. Don walked past him to greet the Officer who was a friend of his. Ray couldn't understand this friendship Boss had with a Police officer. Boss used to be the biggest deer poacher in Sullivan County, yet he could laugh and joke with this cop. It wasn't like the old days when the fine for shooting a deer out of season was sixty-five dollars. Today a guy would pay a thousand-dollar fine, possible jail time. You were penalized less time and money for running over some guy crossing the road. Fucking laws don't make any sense. Boss calls it "ripple justice." Nobody cares about the splash, anymore, just pass more laws to cover all the ripples. Ray could hear them talking about property taxes, the boss's favorite subject, and how unfair he thought they were. Ray had listened to these arguments for years, was bored to death hearing the same, old, rational. Fucking State would never change. Need more money? Raise property taxes. Screw the retired fixed income homeowner, screw the guy who loved his home, chose to improve it rather than buy lottery tickets with his extra money. Screw the young couple with three or four kids, let the wife work to pay the taxes.

Boss had changed a lot in ten years. No more, grab the gun after work, go out to shoot a few deer. No more hounds to run all night coon and cat hunting. No more trips to the fur buyer or meat house for some extra money. Ray didn't miss the money as much as he missed the excitement of it all. Ray tried it on his own, but it was no good. No one to share it with, no one to talk to. For boss, it was all about the money. No money for hides, no money for meat, no reason to keep doing it.

For all that he liked boss, he was a hard man in many ways, could be narrow in his thinking. Boss expected you to work hard, do good work. He was a dying breed. A man who wanted to do everything on a house, not hire out a thing. Boss bought a piece of land, subdivided it, built speculation. Boss didn't like interacting with people and spec building was a way to maintain his independence. But times are changing and Boss is not changing. He's working longer and harder for the same money. It's getting harder and harder to get approval from the town for lot size, septic tank approvals, road requirements, and subdivision approval. Boss kept running out of land, was constantly worried about the rising cost of buying new land. There was a market for the homes they built. Three-bedroom ranches on half-acre to one-acre lots. Workers bought these houses. The houses were not fancy or ornate but were a good solid home priced to sell.

The last time the road agent was out to check on the road and driveway requirements, he remarked that the town didn't want any more of these simple houses. The town wanted larger, more expensive housing. It cost too much in services to the town compared to what they got back in property taxes. Boss called the road agent a communist motherfucker and a few other names he could think of. Boss can be mouthy for a little guy. Boss always sticks up for the workman, says the workingman gets none of the financial breaks that low-income people get from the government.

Boss talks like a workingman; looks like a workingman in jeans and tank top tee shirt. Boss likes it best when the sweat is running off us and the framing is going up, but Boss doesn't live like a working man. Nice cape house on 16 acres, two-car garage, fucking horse barn complete with that damn quarter horse he's fallen in love with. Why in hell would a man, forty-one-year-old, fall in love with a horse is beyond Ray. Boss had that horse three weeks and she's never been ridden or even handled very much. Had to fight just to get a halter on her, lead her around the pasture. Next thing, Boss has a bridle and a saddle on her. Next thing she bucks him off against a tree and he comes up pretty hard against it. Ignorance doesn't stop him though, back up he goes and he's bucked off again. He's learning now. He ties the reins back to the saddle horn so she can't drop her head to buck, climbs on. The horse doesn't move, just stands there shaking all over stiff-legged as can be. Satisfied, he dismounts, takes the tack off, and in the house, he goes for a beer.

Boss doesn't look so good, lots of pain in his back. After about an hour, he can't move without pain. Just about this time, Boss's wife walks in, takes one look at him, hollers, "What did you do?" Boss's wife is a very pretty woman. Short with dark hair to her shoulders, still looks good after having three children. She's one of those women you rarely meet, pretty on the outside, absolutely beautiful on the inside. Why she married Boss was a mystery to everyone who knew them, especially Ray's father-in-law who had a hard-on for Boss's wife.

Boss can't stand without pain, wife takes him to hospital emergency room where they confirm, three cracked ribs.

B oss is getting pissed. He can't work on the framing, is too impatient to watch Ray work. He storms around the work site, trying to find something to do that doesn't hurt him.

"Fuck this," he says as he throws down his hammer. "Let's go up north, do some hunting. Let's go to Errol where there's a chance we might get a crack at a bear."

"I don't know, I'll have to check with the wife,"

"Fuck that, call her at work and we'll get the hell out of here. Come over to the house when you're ready and we'll take off."

Ray pulls up to his house, heads to his apartment. Boss owns the house let's Ray use the two-bedroom apartment rent-free as part of his pay. Boss ain't cheap, pays good, treats him fair.

His wife, Pam, is sitting on the couch and damn. George Disnard is sitting next to her. Ray doesn't even stop to think before he grabs George by his throat, picks him up, punches him in the face all in one move. George crumples against the couch, half on the floor, moaning and holding onto his face. Pam tries to help George, but Ray pulls her back, raises his hand to strike her. Don't, Pam yells, stop it. Ray grabs George, half drags him to the door, pushes him out.

"What the fuck is this? Are you fucking George?"

"No, he just gave me a ride home and I asked him in for a drink."

"Don't be asking a guy in for a drink when I'm not home. What kind of woman are you?"

Pam doesn't answer, turns, and goes into the bathroom. Ray knows what kind of woman she is. Before they got married, they couldn't do it enough. In the car, on the ground, or against the side of a building. Anywhere, anytime. Married five years, and he has to beg for it.

Ray starts packing a bag as Pam comes out of the bathroom.

"Where are you going?"

"Hunting with Boss."

"I don't want you to go, stay here with me. We're supposed to spend the weekend with my parents."

"I'll be back in five or six days, try to keep your legs closed while I'm gone."

"I won't be here when you get back."

Ray feels the anger rising in him, doesn't answer her, picks up his backpack and his rifle, goes out the door.

Standing by Ray's truck are George and Officer Little. Little turns away from George and asks Ray, "What happened here?"

"Ask George."

Officer Little glances at George, but George has nothing to say to him.

"I'm leaving on a hunting trip if we're done here."

Little nods at Ray, "We're done."

Officer Little doesn't quite know what to think of Ray. Over the past ten years since high school, he's come in contact with the results of Ray's actions. The usual scenario is one or two guys holding their bleeding heads while Ray is massaging his sore knuckles. Ray had always been big with the local girls before and after he had married Pam. Little thought marriage had barely slowed him down.

Larry and Pam had attended high school together. Larry knew her father who owned the local hardware shop, was a selectman. Pam had always been known to be on the wild side, had raised the blood pressure of many a schoolboy. Although Larry didn't know Ray very well, he knew him to be a loner and a fighter. Ray wasn't really a big man. He was about 5'10", 165 pounds, but he was really quick with his hands, extremely strong for his size. Larry thought back to the night of his senior prom when four of the local boys were giving Ray a hard time. Ray had been seeing two of their girlfriends and the boys were going to set him straight.

It appeared to be a harmless event at first. Four boys standing outside the gym entrance talking and waving their hands in excitement. Larry remembered that Ray hadn't seemed excited or angry, he was just standing there turning his lighter over and over in his hand with no expression on his face. The boys started to push in closer, then Steve Arnold put his arm out to push Ray backward. What Steve got was a kick to the groin and a knee, that mercifully missed hitting him full in the face, but still put him down on the macadam. One of the other boys grabbed Ray in a headlock of sorts, and the other boys started punching at Ray's head and body. Breaking free, Ray punched two of them, and the third boy backed off. One of the teachers had witnessed the scuffle, came out of the gym, ordered the boys to stop. Turning to another teacher, he asked him to call the Police.

Thinking back, Larry remembered how entirely calm Ray had been. You couldn't tell from looking at him that he had been involved in a serious fight. There was a little blood on Ray's cheek, but he hadn't moved to wipe it off. If he hadn't known better, he would have thought that Ray was a witness, not the main focus of the fight. For all that he was aloof, apart, Ray possessed a social side that belied his nature. In a group, he was quiet but attentive. He had an easy rapport with the group never drawing attention to himself but seems to fit in and be a part of it.

Ever since high school, Larry had a feeling of uneasiness whenever he saw Ray. On the night of the fight, Larry had approached him, offered his handkerchief. Ray hadn't even glanced at him, just said, "No thanks". Larry had never tried to approach him again. He was an enigma that Larry was afraid of and fascinated by at the same time.

LT. Bob Harris responded to the call from the high school. Technically he was the Juvenile officer, new to the department, with eight years, experience in Derry, Mass. He had left Derry because of the increase in crime in the area. It seemed like the whole world was breaking the law, and they all lived in Derry. He was tired of the attitude of the cops he had worked with. They had room in their lives only for other cops. Their attitude was, if you didn't wear a uniform, carry a badge, you were part of the problem, you just hadn't been caught yet. When the Juvenile position had opened up, he had applied for it with little expectation that he would get it. To his surprise, he was hired. After a year on the job, he had settled in, became content. There really weren't enough Juvenile cases to keep him busy, so he served as a training officer, assistant shift commander. He had hopes of being promoted to Deputy Chief as Chief Hanely wanted to slow down, but still hold control.

As Lt. Harris approached the teacher standing outside the gym, he was aware of the sudden silence that greeted his arrival. Most people, even kids, had a degree of respect for Police officers that made their job easier to perform. This was a far different scene than would have greeted him in Derry where a single officer never responded to a complaint. This was a benefit of living in a small town. Big city thinking hadn't caught up yet.

As he took in the scene, he noticed the selectman's son sitting on the ground holding a towel to his head. Thanking Mr. Warren for his input, he walked over to the group to hear their side of the fight. Steve Arnold hollered out that Ray had started it and they had tried to stop him. Steve wasn't a very likable kid. His parents had money and position in town and he tried to take full advantage of it. Bob knew that Steve was a bully who never acted alone, always had some cronies to back him up, intimidate other kids. Bob knew Ray through one of his new friends, Ray's boss.

Ray's only comment was that he defended himself. After two groups of kids gathered around, Bob repeatedly was told that the four boys had attacked Ray. Bob asked Ray if he wanted to file charges?

Ray responded that it was all over as far as he was concerned, felt no need to file any charges. Bob told the boys that the prom supervisor would not allow them back in to the dance. Ray responded that he wanted to talk to his girlfriend who was inside the gym. Bob asked Larry Little if he would contact the young lady, give her the message? After delivering the message, Larry asked Bob if he could give him a ride home? Bob knew Larry wanted to be a police officer, he nodded yes. Bob had spoken with Larry's family, encouraged them to support Larry in his quest.

On the ride home, Bob remarked that Ray was a little old to be hanging with high schoolers. Larry let out a light laugh, "He only cares for the girls, as many as he can get."

Bob asked Larry to keep his eyes open, let him know if he sees anyone using drugs, or selling drugs around the high school. Larry replied that he didn't hang with that crowd, but would let him know if he saw anything. Nice quiet night, Bob thought, just the kind I like.

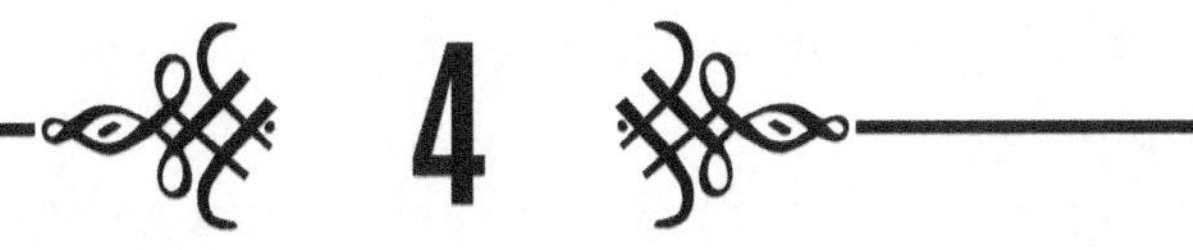

B oss is ready to go when Ray arrives.

"Toss your shit in the back, let's go."

Boss's wife gives him a bag of sandwiches, a cold six-pack, his medication, a hug and a kiss. She tells them to be careful as they leave the house.

Boss tells him to drive as he pops a pill, gets into the truck. Boss's truck is just about a new ¾ ton GMC four-wheel-drive pickup. Ready for anything in this powerful rig. Boss swaps trucks every two years always buying either a GMC or a Ford, he'll only buy American vehicles. Ray thinks one of the nicest things about a hunting trip is the drive-up. Time to relax, anticipate what lies ahead. Boss doesn't like driving the interstate, so they head north on Route 10 through Hanover, Lyme, along the Connecticut River. Two and a half hours later, they leave Berlin on Route 2. Glancing at Boss, Ray sees the medication has gotten to him as he is sleeping, very close to hitting his head on the dashboard. Ray pulls off as they enter Maine just past the white birch area. Stopping the truck has awoken Boss, they both get out, share a sandwich and a beer side the roadway.

Ray asks if they should head for Errol.

"Nah, let's head to Bethel tonight, check with the local boys in the pool hall, see if they'll tell us what's a good area this year."

Ray doesn't care about billiards, but Boss is really good at it. Boss plays in a lot of tournaments, more than holds his own, enjoys gambling on the side as well. The place is pretty crowded for a

Monday night. Only six tables in the place and they're all occupied. Boss heads over to talk to the owner who he's known for quite a few years, Ray buys a beer, settles down at a table.

The owner tells Boss the hunting has been pretty good just west of Upton.

"Been running my bear hounds, seen a lot of deer in the area. The place was clear cut years ago, grown back with a lot of feed. Lots of logging roads crisscross the area giving you good access. Jim's brother shot a six-pointer yesterday. Not much horn, but close to 200 pounds, good deer."

"Doesn't that area go back into Umbagog?"

"Yeah, sure. You can get to it off Route 26 about a mile and a half out of Errol. Be careful though, you'll be hunting right along the border with Maine."

"Any chance of getting a game tonight?"

"I'll make a few calls."

Boss says he's hurting a little, doesn't want to take another pill.

After Ray finished his second beer, three guys walk in, announce, "Who wants a game?"

Boss stands up, stretches to his full 5'6", tells the guys, "That'd be me."

They agree on nine-ball, twenty dollars a set, race to three. The first game, Boss gets him on three fouls, the guy says, "No way, we ain't pros, we don't play that game." Boss says, "Okay," takes the cue ball in hand, and proceeds to run out.

About an hour and a half later, the guy is down three sets, is getting pissed. Boss offers to give the guy two games in a race to five, double or nothing. Guy agrees. As Ray is finishing his fifth beer, Boss has finished the set, and the jerk hands over his money. Boss tells the guy he'll pay the table time, goes over to the owner, pays up, and thanks him for the help he's given us. Winning puts Boss in a good mood, he says, "I'll drive Ray, you've had too many beers."

The next morning, it's snowing softly as they leave the Errol diner, head out to the area recommended to them. Pulling the truck over by one of the numerous logging roads, they get out, get ready to hit the woods. After walking in about twenty minutes, they cut some tracks crossing the logging road, heading into the dense pine and hemlock. Boss says," Tracks can't be too old," decides to follow them. Ray doesn't think much of that idea, all you usually get is a long walk and running tracks. Tells him to give him an hour to go up the road, cut up in. Deer should stay with the wind in their faces, circle before bedding down. I'll keep circling up ahead, until I cut their tracks, try to push them back to you.

Boss figures that's a good idea, lights up a Camel. Ray takes out his compass, sees the logging road runs north, south, so the main road is westerly, should be safe to head out south, southeast if he doesn't go too far north. As Ray walks up the road, he cuts two more tracks, so there's at least four deer in the area he's going to circle. Pretty good sign so far, he thinks. Walking up the road another half mile, he decides to cut in, start to make a large circle back towards Boss. The dense conifers gave way to a nice clear cut that had grown back with a lot of blackberry bushes, small trees that have been grazed on by the deer.

The Ruger .300 win. mag feels good in his hands as he feels the glow of anticipation while slowly walking along the edge of the cutover area. Although it's snowing softly, there's not enough snow to dampen the sound of his footsteps. Coming to a fairly open hardwood ridge, he stops, lights up a cowboy killer. It's good to be deep in the woods. Quiet and surreal, it's like your own existence doesn't matter out here. You're an interloper in a place where life ebbs and flows without you. Ray starts to feel the cold slowly, insidiously, work its way through his boots. Cold feet first, then that uncomfortable feeling that tells you, it's time to move. Looking across the cut, he sees another hunter working his way through the slash. He thought the hunter must have passed their truck, gone in above them. He didn't think the main road curved that much to allow this hunter to be in this position so quickly.

Snow is starting to accumulate on the ground. About two inches has fallen and it's still coming down softly, steadily. Crossing over a brushy ravine, he sees a pair of tracks heading northeast. Deer are walking so it's hard to tell if Boss had jumped them. Woods are too thick to follow them. He turned southwest to start heading back towards Boss. It's about eleven when he crests a ridge, jumps a bunch of deer. He catches sight of gray bodies, white flashing tails running, bounding through the thick cover. Walking quickly now, he tries to push them towards Boss.

Don has been sitting by a fallen pine for about an hour. He's just about ready to head back to the road when he sees glimpses of deer coming towards him. They'll pass within 75 yards from him if they continue on their present line. They're walking fast. Three does skirt the opening. The fourth is a buck as he sees the flash of ivory antlers. He raises his 742 Remington to his shoulder, aims at an opening the buck will have to cross. The buck looks small through his peep sight as he approaches the opening. The buck's shoulders appear in the peep sight and he fires almost instantaneously. After the jolt of the recoil, he sees the buck almost fall, recovers himself, bound sharply to his right. No time for another shot as the buck disappears into the thick cover. Putting the rifle down, he lights up a smoke, winces at the pain in his back. Wait an hour before I follow the buck he thinks.

Ray hears the shot, hopes it is Boss that has fired. Walking faster now he heads down the ridge towards the sound of the shot. He's in the footsteps of a group of deer headed towards the shot he had heard. He sees tracks in the snow where two deer separated, went easterly away from him. He tops a knoll, sees Boss sitting on a fallen pine tree. He lights up a smoke, sits next to Boss.

"Came right by me by that small opening. Shot at a small buck. He's hit and I want to wait another half hour before we follow him up." The snow has stopped falling, Ray is warmed up from walking. They follow up the tracks together, find a blood trail at the edge of the opening.

"Punched right through both lungs," Ray tells Boss.

Pushing through the dense hemlock, they see the buck splayed out in death. The fallen snow had just started to stick to the hide. Boss looks him over, running his hand down the buck's neck and back. Ray grabs the six-pointer by the horns, pulls him in position for Boss to gut him. Boss does the honors, gets the buck ready to travel.

Nice deer, Ray thinks. Nice, neat six-pointer, about 150 pounds. Just the right size for good eating. Boss ties his drag rope on, affixes his tag to the antlers. Ray takes ahold of the drag rope, starts out for the truck.

Ray says, "I think there was another buck in the bunch that turned south."

"Let's get this one out, we'll come back, try to pick that bunch up after they settle down."

After hanging up the buck, they returned to the area, hunted until dark, never saw another deer. Ray was disappointed that they hadn't made contact with the maker of the big tracks in the snow.

The next morning dawns clear and cold. Yesterday's snow has frozen and a noisy crust has made quiet walking all but impossible. Boss suggests they scout with the truck, see if they can find some fresh tracks crossing the logging road. Travel is slow up the road, but they manage a few miles before Boss pulls into a turn-off.

"Roads getting really bad, we better hoof it from here."

Walking a few hundred feet up the road, they come across a small bear track made when the snow had been melting.

Boss studies the track. "Small bear, doesn't have enough sense to den up."

Ray sees the track is heading east, decides to follow off to the side of the tracks in hopes of spotting the small bear. Ray tells Boss the country is too open to hunting. Ray decides he's going to head east to the top of the ridge. Boss offers to circle around to the ridge in hopes of pushing something to him. Ray nods as he heads east.

Around ten in the morning, the sun is up, and coupled with a mild southerly wind, the crust is disappearing slowly. Ray has worked his way further away from the boss while following the ridgeline.

When Ray crests the ridge, he sees a small brook about three hundred yards below him. He notes that the brook is running east. He thinks it must turn west at some point if it flows into Umbagog. He follows the brook about a mile through the beeches. The brook has gotten wider, slower, it's still flowing east down the mountain. Just as he's getting ready to turn back, he sees two deer feeding in the beeches below him. Turning his scope up to the tenth power, he sees its two small bucks. He takes a solid position, tries to see a good opening to take the long, downhill shot. The deer have turned away from him, head further away from him. He can't see the lead buck clear enough to take a shot. He focuses on the following buck, tries a shot between the intervening branches. After touching off the Magnum, he can't see the results of the long shot. Both deer are gone, but he tries to keep his focus on where they were when he shot. As he walks towards the spot, he thinks, it always looks different after you shoot.

He picks up the tracks in the melting snow. He sees where one deer has skidded in the snow. A few gray hairs, some spotty blood tell him he's made a hit. He comes onto a bed with bloodstained snow, tracks leading down the hill. The deer sign shows the animal is hunched up, unable to travel normally. Hoping to run the deer down, he follows the tracks as quickly as he can. Coming through some rocks, he sees the injured deer below him, hunched up, trying its best to run. He pulls up, fires off-hand at the running deer, sees it go down, only to get back up, continue down the mountain. Ray ejects his fired round into the snow, hurries to where the deer had fallen. He doesn't notice the markings on the tree as he continues the chase. Lots of blood in the trail now, must have hit him the hind end, he thinks. At the bottom of the ridge, he crosses a paved road. He follows across the road into a thick pine grove. Following much slower now, he tries to peer through the thick pine. He hears the brook running in front of him, sees the small buck standing with, its head down, nose touching the snow. Taking careful aim, he fires, and the buck is finally down for good.

If it weren't for the snow, I'd never have gotten this buck, he thinks. The buck had been hit too far back. The first shot had gone through the paunch, through the guts, stopped against the far shoulder. The second shot had hit a ham causing massive blood loss. The finishing shot was through the neck. Ray put down his rifle, knelt to gut the deer.

"What you got there?"

The voice comes from behind Ray. From his position, crouched over the deer Ray turns, sees a cop. The cop is a big guy about forty, looks comical in his uniform of a uniform jacket, hat, green work pants below. He's wearing work pants, but there's no wear on them. No shiny material on the knees, no wear evident on them. Got a brand new, big pistol on his duty belt. Looks to Ray like another hick cop playing the role.

"Now you put down the knife, step to the side away from the rifle."

Ray asks, "What's the problem officer?"

"Do you have a hunting license?"

Ray looks over his shoulder, answers, yes.

"Well, put it down on the deer, step further away."

Ray complies with the order, steps away about six feet.

"Step back further," orders the cop, his hand on the butt of his semi-auto.

As Ray steps back, he notices that the retaining strap is still secured on the holster.

"This here's a New Hampshire license."

Ray doesn't respond, just looks at the cop as he takes a smoke out of his pack, lights up, turns the lighter over and over in his hand.

"Do you know you're in Maine?"

"I shot that deer in N.H. up on the ridge across the road."

"Didn't you see the paint line on the trees coming down that ridge?"

Ray shakes his head no.

"Well, you're in Maine now, that's an illegal deer, you're under arrest for possession of an illegal deer."

"But I—"

"Tell it to the judge. Now turn around, put your hands on top of your head," as he drops his hand back to the butt of his handgun.

As Ray starts to turn, he drops the lighter from his hand, reaches inside his jacket grasping the butt of his Model 29 .44 Magnum, turning slightly he goes into a crouch as he brings the Magnum to bear on the cop's chest.

There is a look of bewilderment on the cop's face as he stumbles a little, starts to draw his handgun. As his semi-auto starts to clear the holster, the first bullet strikes him in the chest. As his legs start to buckle, his handgun drops into the snow, the second bullet strikes his chest an inch from the first round. He falls forward onto the ground. He is dead before he hits the snow.

Ray is stunned. His body feels like a fire from hell is rushing to his head. When he had shot the deputy, years ago, he hadn't felt a thing. This time, he had to stop himself from blindly rushing from the scene. Fighting hard to overcome his desire to run, he slowly regains control of his mind and body. Looking quickly around, his mind is making every bush and tree a witness to what he's done. There's no one in sight, just him and the dead cop. Suddenly, he's aware of the revolver clutched in his two hands. His first instinct is to drop it. Regaining some control, he re-holsters the weapon. Think, think, he tells himself. The cop must have seen him cross the road while he was tracking the deer. It was just like Boss always told him when they were poaching deer.

"Some simple thing is going to get us caught. The more times you spin the wheel, the greater the chance your number will come up."

Leave it to Boss to come up with some simple shit, he thinks. Why did that cop have to push? Couldn't he plainly see what had happened? No, Ray thought. The prick knew what happened, decided to push it because he was the law. The cop didn't look arrogant now.

He looked almost peaceful, like he'd laid down to rest. His cruiser must be up on the road, Ray thought. Ray had to force himself to approach the cop's body, go through his pants pockets looking for keys. No keys. Rolling the body over, he sees the keys clipped to his duty belt. After unclipping the keys, he takes his handkerchief out, wipes the cop's pistol, replaces it in its holster.

The snow is melting faster now, brown patches are appearing all around him making the forest floor look dirty, dingy. He's hotter than hell as he fights the impulse to shed his jacket, tear off his shirt. The dead cop is one big guy, can't leave the body here. If anyone has seen the cruiser parked on the road, this is the first area they'll search. Damn, even if I move the body, they'll search here. Ray doesn't want to trust in luck, luck is what got him where he is. Ray starts to walk down the stream. He can see that it narrows up. The banks are getting steeper, the channel narrower. Backtracking, he walks upstream past the dead cop, to a big pool of water close against the bank. Through the trees, he can see a highway sign that must mark the bridge that this stream runs under. "Christ," Ray says. It's only about two hundred yards to that bridge. Looking at the pool again, it's full of tree limbs, brush, and debris. Lots of wood in there, he thinks.

It's the best chance I have. Even if the water level goes down, the brush will conceal the body. Walking with more purpose now, he pulls a branch about twelve feet long out of the pool. Reaching for his knife, he realizes it's back on the deer carcass. He drags the branch to the carcass. Trims the branch up so he has a pole, to which he attaches his drag rope. Grabbing hold of the dead cop, he struggles to drag the heavy body to the edge of the brushy pool. Tying his rope around the cop's neck, he retrieves the cop's hat, gloves, forces them into the cop's jacket, pushes the body out into the steam, uses the pole to slowly pull the body to the pool. He tries using the pole to push the body underwater but soon realizes he can't get enough leverage to do it. He strips his clothing off, glides into the pool. "Christ," he thinks. The water is ice-cold, he feels his muscles tightening up in protest.

Feeling with his hands, he realizes it's a treetop with branches below, as well as above the water. Pushing and shoving, he finally succeeds in wedging the corpse among the branches below him. Half standing on the corpse and a tree limb, he forces the body down further into the branches. Cold, shivering, he emerges from the water, dresses, goes back to the deer carcass where he retrieves his license, his lighter. Grabbing the buck, he drags it under some brushy hemlocks, hides it as best he can. The snow has melted, the warm air signaling a change in the weather. Satisfied he's left nothing behind, he backtracks to the paved road, walks to the cop's cruiser.

The cruiser is a Chevy Blazer, almost new from the look of it. Driving north, he sees a pickup truck coming towards him. As they pass, he returns the wave from the driver, continues north. He sees a logging road to his left, pulls into it. The road only goes about three hundred yards to a log landing. He gets out of the cruiser, looks to his left, recognizes the ridge he had followed the deer down. Back in the cruiser, he engaged the four-wheel drive, forced it into a cluster of low hemlocks. The cruiser is partially hidden, at least off the road.

It's getting late in the afternoon. He realizes he's got to get back with Boss before he's missed. Boss won't panic, knows Ray likes to stay on a good stand until the last light is available. Not quite satisfied with the hidden Blazer, he wipes it down, makes sure he's left nothing behind, makes for the ridge and Boss.

Now if he can only get back to Boss without being spotted traversing the ridge. Once he's on the logging road leading to Boss's truck, he'll be safe. Starting up the ridge, he knows what a deer feels like, he feels the panic of the hunted. Stopping behind a large hemlock, he surveys the open hardwood going up the ridge. If he's lucky, there's no other hunter to spot him. He waits for the shadows to lengthen, darken the ridge. He removes his fluorescent vest, stows it in his pack. Feeling calmer now, he makes a hard push up the ridge. After twenty minutes of walking, he has crested the ridge, is back to the brook that leads to the logging road. It had been dark about half an hour when he reaches Boss's truck.

"Any luck?" Boss says as he gets in the truck. Ray shakes his head no, calmly lights up a smoke. The drive back to the Errol motel was uneventful, Ray breathed a sigh of relief.

"We better head back in the morning before my deer starts to spoil in the warm weather."

"Yeah, no sense in wasting a deer."

Radio dispatch from Bethel has been trying to contact Upton Police Chief Alan Hayward since four in the afternoon. The Chief hadn't called in his 10-20, hasn't responded to his hourly checks. The dispatcher wasn't too concerned as the radio reception in the mountains is sometimes intermittent. After no response from the chief at the six o'clock check, dispatch advised Maine State Police that they are unable to raise the chief. A quick check by trooper Wilson turned up nothing, plans are laid for an extensive search in the morning.

The dawn breaks ugly the next morning. Rain, fog, gusting winds hamper the search effort. The next day, the weather has cleared up, turns much colder. Two small planes, a helicopter take part in the search. Almost immediately, the air searchers spot the chief's Blazer in a small hemlock grove, dispatch ground forces to the scene.

After confirming it is the chief's cruiser, a systematic search of the immediate area fails to turn up anything. The pine grove below the bridge was part of the search. The searchers failed to see any sign of the chief, the rain had washed away the blood on the ground, the searchers did not notice the dead deer under the hemlock bushes. The pine grove represented a small area, was quickly dismissed by the searchers.

Maine winter started in earnest overnight depositing ten inches of heavy, wet snow, and a Police Chief still among the missing. Even though the weather had made ground search next to impossible, small groups of law enforcement officers continued to search likely areas on their own time. Police had checked with all motels, hotels, cabins, hunting camps, compiled a list of Maine hunters, non-resident hunters who were in the area the day of the chief's disappearance.

Lead investigator Sergeant Mark Schaffer arrived on the scene, immediately took charge. After talking with Trooper Wilson, he decided that under the present conditions it was impossible to conduct a proper search. Mark uses all the resources at his disposal to get the names of all the hunters in the area that day. He's decided to go public, appeal for any information available regarding the disappearance of Chief Hayward. He orders part-time officer Susan Mitzven to take charge of all the paperwork, handle the phones, the radio. Trooper Wilson has been assigned to him, has proved competent and helpful so far. Rewards have been offered for information by civic groups as well as police agencies.

Mark feels it's of primary importance to learn all he can about chief Hayward. Reading over all the police records, he comes up with all the normal contacts a small-town cop has. Officer Mitz, as she likes to be called, seems very hesitant to tell him anything about the chief. Mark holds back on pressuring her decides he has to learn more about the chief from other sources before interviewing her. Trooper Wilson offers that the chief was often curt, stand-offish in his dealings with him. He added that he didn't care for the man, thought he was a poor officer.

Turner Brook Road was one of the chief's favorite areas to ticket speeders for the past two years. The name, Albert Smith, comes up four times in a year and a half. He notes other names that come up more than once on his reports.

After talking with the selectman, he starts to form an opinion of the chief. The Chief's citations seem to come in spurts of a week or two of activity, then a week or two of little activity. While questioning the selectmen about the seeming lack of activity, the selectmen respond that the chief had set his own hours and they were generally satisfied with his performance.

Mark thinks the lack of any details about the disappearance of the chief leaves the door wide open. Hunters are only one of the possible reasons for the chief's disappearance. It could be anyone. Without a definite direction to go in, he feels like he's awash in a sea of emptiness.

Susan Mitzven is a very pretty woman, dark hair falling to her shoulders, alert blue eyes, comely features. She is in her, mid-twenties, she is studying to get a degree in Criminal Justice. Mark approaches her at her desk, says, "I need to know exactly what you think of the chief." In obvious discomfort, she sighs, plays with the pens and pencils on her desk.

"He makes inappropriate comments. He brushes by me when there is no need to. In short, I think he is a sexual predator. Other women have filed complaints against him, but never strong enough to warrant action against him. He's never actually touched me with his hands, but his intent is plain to see. If I didn't need this job, I would leave in a heartbeat."

Her statement has opened up another avenue of investigation he needs to consider. He tries to get more information, but Mitz says that outside of the office, she has no knowledge of the chief. He tells Mitz to get a list of complaints filed against the chief. Mark is very disturbed by Mitz's statement. If the press got wind of this, it would look very bad for law enforcement. The press loves nothing more than a "black sheep" to harp on.

Two reports he reads claiming conduct unbecoming, abusive mannerisms, are not on file with the State Police. The complaint from Mrs. Albert Smith immediately draws his attention. She had filed a complaint with the selectmen who had neglected to inform him about it, or any other complaints on file. The selectman claimed that she had not wished to file a formal complaint, just wanted the selectman to know that the chief was a "dirty cop."

He took the list from Mitz, decided to drive to Turner Brook Road. About a mile and a half down the road, he sees a small pull-off on the left side of the road. Pulling his cruiser into this pull-off, he could see about an eighth of a mile down this straightaway to a highway sign denoting a bridge. Sitting there, he tried to picture Chief Hayward sitting there waiting for speeders. He wished the snow was gone so they could do an extensive search.

Driving over the bridge, past the logging road where the cruiser had been found, he continued down the road until he came to a mailbox marked, A. Smith. He turned into the driveway he walked to the front door of a small ranch house.

In response to his knock, he was greeted by a very beautiful woman who asked to see his credentials before allowing him inside. Mrs. Smith was a stunning woman, very tiny just over five feet, dark hair falling to her shoulders, about ninety pounds.

"I need to ask you about the complaint you filed against Chief Hayward."

"He's dead, isn't he?"

"We don't know that for sure. Would you tell me what led up to you filing the complaint?"

"You have to promise you won't tell my husband."

"I won't tell him, but before this is over, he may find out."

"He followed me home, pulled in behind me. I got out of my car to talk with him, he asked me if I had just smoked a joint. I told him I didn't smoke that stuff, just plain cigarettes. He asked me if he could search my car, I told him I didn't want him to. He never even asked for license and registration like they always do, I was getting scared. He's such a big man and he was standing real, close to me. I tried to back up, hit my car door, couldn't go any farther. He said if I didn't let him search me and the car, he could arrest me. I was so scared I was just about to let him search when my husband pulled into the driveway. He left me, walked over to Al. Al asked him what the problem was? Chief told him I had thrown a cigarette out the window, he was telling me not to start a forest fire. He got back in his cruiser, left."

"So, then you went to the selectmen?"

"Yes, because I was so scared. They told me they would have a talk with him, not to worry. They just wanted me gone. As I was leaving, I heard Mr. Garnett say to the others, I'd like to search her too. They all laughed. I know I wasn't supposed to hear that, but it made me more scared than before I came in."

"Mrs. Smith, I need your husband to come down to see me at the Police station tonight. I'll be there by seven. You can come if you like, but I'd rather speak to him alone." He thanked her, took his leave.

At precisely seven, Albert Smith entered the office, shook Mark's hand. Mark asked him whether he liked to be called Albert, or Al? He responded Al is fine, took a seat opposite the desk.

"You were stopped four times by the chief, given three speeding tickets, how do you feel about that?"

"The guys an asshole. Stops you for going five miles over the limit. He enjoyed writing those tickets, always acting extra polite, always asking how the Mrs. is doing."

"I take it you didn't like him very much."

"I didn't like him at all."

"Do you own any firearms?"

"I have three guns that I hunt with."

"Can you tell me where you were last Wednesday from noon until six in the evening?"

"I was cutting wood in Mexico right up until dark, got home about six thirty that night."

"Can anyone verify that?"

"I was working by myself cutting cordwood."

"Are you willing to take a lie detector test?"

Al hesitated before saying, "I will if I have to, but I don't want to."

Mark lights up a smoke, advises Al that under the law, he doesn't have to, but it would be in his best interest to do so. Al lit up a smoke, didn't respond.

"If you do decide to take it, it will go a long way to clear you of this mess we're in."

Al remains unresponsive. Mark decides the interview is over for now and tells Al he's free to leave.

Mark leans back in the chair, thinks, the guy doesn't seem dumb enough to stash the cruiser less than a mile from his front door, but love and anger can be a powerful force that makes people do dumb things, better check out Al thoroughly. Mark lit up a smoke, poured himself the last cup of coffee from his thermos. He phoned his wife, Carol, asked about his infant son who he could hear wailing in the background. Carol told him the baby was fussy, but okay. She told him that Marie was being very helpful, Ivan had even done the grocery shopping for her. They chatted for a few more minutes before Mark told her he loved her, ended the call. As he left for his lodgings, he thought that he was stuck with a really difficult case. Unless something popped pretty soon, he'd have no reason to stay here until the snow was gone.

While Mitz was doing background checks, Mark phoned the second person on his list who had filed a complaint against the chief. Talking to Mr. Robert Drake from Westfield Mass, he hears that Drake complained that the chief had acted in a bullying manner while he searched his vehicle. He had complained to the selectmen. After two hours on the phone, it was apparent to him that all the complaints against the chief were very similar. It appeared to him that the chief had taken full advantage of his position of power.

Mark asked Mitz to accompany him to the chief's residence. He wanted a witness to whatever the search turned up, someone to document their findings. The Chief owned a small cottage on a local pond. When they forced the front door, the aroma of dirty laundry, cat shit filled the air. Mitz observed the chief was not very neat. The entire cabin was in a general state of neglect. It was the mess of a single man not even doing minimal cleanup. The small living room was dominated by a large screen TV. Mitz noticed that the TV was not connected to any outside source. Bookcases on either side of the

TV were filled with video cassettes. They discovered the majority of the tapes were porn, other mostly sexual films. After searching the entire cabin, they agreed that there was no sign of another person ever being present in the cabin. They talked to a few of the other camp owners in the area who stated that the chief was a solitary man who had very few, if any, visitors. Mark called in the forensics team, had little hope they would turn up anything of value, but he would cover all the bases.

After Mark had finished his investigation of the chief, he felt he had to inform his superiors of the possibility that disturbing things might come out of the 247 requests for information he was going to send out. He wanted permission to have all the statements notarized. Mark stressed the need to get this information while it was fresh in people's minds. Mark felt he had no choice but to await the return of the statements being sent out, decided to return home, await further developments. He authorized Trooper Wilson as O.I.C. while he was absent, and Officer Mitz to keep up with the paperwork as well as keep in contact with him.

Mark had been told by his superiors not to release any detrimental information on the chief without direct clearance from them. They strongly felt the investigation was turning up evidence that would further complicate the case. Mark felt they should, "Let the chips fall where they may," but he would obey his orders.

The affidavits were pouring in. Mark ordered Mitz to read them, tell him of anything she thought vague or nonsensical. He tried to read as many of them as he could when he had the time.

He turned to Mitz. "What happens in Upton at three in the afternoon?"

Mitz looked up from her reading. "The mill changes shifts, school gets let out, can't think of anything else of note." Mark sent her out to get details of school bus routes, who transports the children on Turner Brook Road.

Mark tells Mitz they need to interview the Newly's daughter, Emily. Mitz tells him the Newlys work second shift, will need to call them immediately. Mark thinks back to his initial visit with them. He remembers their small farm with a nice barn housing two Belgian horses. Mr. Newly told him he logged with them in the winter to earn money towards his daughter's college costs.

The couple had told him they didn't know the chief, but had seen the cruiser parked before the bridge many times. Mrs. Newly stated they always slowed down on that straightaway because the chief often parked there. Mark's thoughts had turned in a direction he didn't like. The other children riding on the bus were all under twelve years of age, he hoped they had no involvement in the case. They needed to talk to the long-time bus driver, Alphonse Howard.

Mitz reported that Mr. Howard is a tall, bearded dairy farmer who seemingly has a bad attitude about everything but his herd of Jersey cows. Most of the children are afraid of him because of his curt manner. Mark nods, tell her they have time to visit him before the afternoon bus run.

On the ten-minute drive to the farm, Mitz admits she was afraid of him when she rode the bus. "He's a creepy bastard who lives alone on that run-down farm of his." Howard was there to meet them when they parked.

"You're here about that town cop, ain't you?"

Mark studied the tall, spare older man.

"Well, I just drive the bus you know. I'm not a townie, don't give a damn what them townies do."

"Did you see the chief often while on your route?"

"Well, I could say no except for Turner Brook Road. Guess he likes to sit there now and then,"

"Did you see him on Wednesday, the day he disappeared?"

"Wednesday you say. Can't remember one day from another."

"It snowed that day just about noon, turned to sleet, and then rain in the evening. Does that help you remember?"

"Was slippery that day. Yeah, I saw the town cop, no I saw the cop car stopped side of the road, but he weren't in it."

"Are you sure he was not in his cruiser?"

"He weren't in it I tell you. He was parked on the wrong side of the road like he always done."

"You mean that little pull off before the bridge?"

"There's only one damn pull off before the bridge."

"What time would that have been?"

"Three-ten, give or take a minute or two."

"Are you sure about the time?"

"Just as sure as I'm standing here, been driving that bus twenty-two years."

Back in the cruiser, Mark mulled over this new bit of information. Mitz asked, "Who was driving the cruiser when the man and his son saw him later?"

"Damn good question Mitz. They both stated they saw the chief at a later time."

Back at the office, Mark phoned the Newlys, told them they were on the way to visit them. Mitz told them she would call the, mill, tell them you might be a little late for work. A phone call advised Mark that Al Smith had refused to take a lie detector test. Mark lit up a smoke, tried to calm himself. On the drive over, Mark told Mitz to be very calm and laid back when they interviewed Emily Newly. He wanted them to be very, "laid back", when they met with the family. He wanted to conduct this interview with as much sensitivity as possible. We need to hear what Emily's role in this is.

The Newlys looked very concerned when they entered the house. Mark explained they had a to wait a bit for their daughter to arrive. Just about ten past three, Emily entered the kitchen. It was plain to see she was very nervous. She stood in the kitchen holding her books against her chest. She looked steadily down at the floor. Susan said, "Emily, I think you know why we're here, tell us about your involvement with Chief Hayward." Emily's shoulders were shaking with the effort she was making to muffle her sobs. Mrs. Newly started to rise from her seat to go to her daughter. Mark put his hand on her shoulder to stop her. Mr. Newly didn't seem angry, just resigned as he waited for his daughter to speak.

Emily took a seat at the table, kept her eyes downcast. Mitz asked, "Can you tell us how you met the chief?"

"He asked me if I wanted to go for a ride in the cruiser with him." Mrs. Newly started softly crying. Mr. Newly took her hands firmly in his own hands.

"How old were you when you met the chief?"

"I had just turned sixteen."

"Did you—"

Emily interrupted, "Alan was always nice to me. We just drove around, talked a little, then he would bring me back home. Alan would pick me up two or three times a week, just drive around, talk with me. He cared about me."

Mitz asked softly, "Did you have sexual relations with the chief?"

"Yes."

"When did the relations start?"

"Only about three months ago. We loved each other. Alan was going to Marry me after I graduate."

"Did you see the chief on the day he went missing?"

"No."

"What did you do after school the day the chief went missing?"

6

Mark was having breakfast at the local diner. He was telling Ivan and Max about the strange case he had been sent out on. Ivan asked the question that had been bothering Mark from the onset.

"Why did he get out of his cruiser?"

Max added, "Someone had to be with him."

Both men continued to ask questions about what was found at the scene? Why was there no forensic evidence in and around the cruiser? Mark knew both men were trying to be helpful, but he preferred to let the questions rattle around in his own brain until he could put them in some useful order. As he sipped his coffee, his thoughts turned to the forensics data on the cruiser to, perhaps, give him some solid clues. He thanked both men for the help they had given his wife and son while he had been away.

Back in his apartment, Ray read in the morning paper about the disappearance of the chief in Maine. The story was still on page one, but it was a simple recap of the events. It was becoming, "old news," as the articles were diminishing.

"No leads on the missing police officer," and a short recap of the details. Ray was busy rolling some oversize soft lead bullets in a black mess of lapping compound. He couldn't deny he owned a .44 mag. pistol, but he could change the ballistic profile of his revolver by firing these treated bullets through it. Setting up his reloading press to excessively bell the mouths of six empty cartridges, he loaded up six rounds.

Pam had flown the coop while he was off hunting with Boss. She had cleaned out her things, taken most of the furniture they had bought together after they got married. He had the thought that he should be missing Pam, but the reality was, he didn't miss her. The registered letter from her lawyer was sitting on the table. He didn't care to read it. His mind was full of the *what ifs* that would surely arise once the police officer's body was found. He thought, hopefully, it wouldn't be found until Spring, and I'll be long gone. He felt he had to stay until after his divorce, which would give him a good reason to leave. He was in hopes the investigation would not intensify until then. He was well aware that leaving, might well point the finger of blame at him, that wouldn't do he concluded. He picked up his revolver, reloads, headed out to a local gravel bank to take care of that problem. Always think, he reminded himself, always think.

Back in Upton after a weekend with his wife had refreshed him. He was eager to get back on the case. Mark had finished interviewing all the residents on Turner Brook Road. A father and son had been headed into town that Wednesday, had passed the chief on the road. Both men stated that the chief had returned their wave in passing. That statement led him to believe that whatever happened, happened at the log landing.

Had the chief deliberately driven to that landing? Did he have a passenger? Why didn't the two men state that the chief was alone in the cruiser? He pulled into the log landing, started to read the forensic report on the cruiser. Forensics had determined that a number of people had been in the back seat of the cruiser. Hair samples indicated at least one female had been in the rear of the cruiser since the last cleaning.

Knowing the chief's messy habits, Mark decided there was no telling when, if ever, the rear of the cruiser had been vacuumed. Semen samples taken from the rear seat had matched samples taken from the chief's bed. It could explain why the chief drove his cruiser into the landing. Mark noticed that there had been no fingerprints found on the steering wheel, the door handle, the window buttons, or the driver's visor. Perhaps someone other than the chief had wiped the cruiser clean of prints? Why would the chief wipe down his own cruiser? Forensics finds had included, a small amount of blood on the back seat type O, dirt ground into the passenger side door panel. Mark thought that strongly showed the chief socialized in the rear of the cruiser. It was becoming a certainty that a woman was involved in this mess. That fact opened up countless avenues to be investigated.

Mark let a sigh escape him, opened a detailed map of the Upton area. He was surprised at the number of dirt roads lacing the area. A wealth of roads twisting and turning through three ponds in the area. Two paved roads added to the confusion of the road system. Why did the chief spend so much of his time on Turner Brook Road? To further frustrate him, most of these dirt roads were passable in a two-wheel-drive car. The more he tried to narrow things down, the wider the search pattern became. His mind kept coming back to the same thought. Why did the chief spend so much time on Turner Brook Road?

Mark radioed for Trooper Wilson, Officer Mitz, to meet him at the chief's office. Mark told them it was imperative to find out whom the chief was socializing with. He further asked Mitz to get him the dispatch records for the previous three months. Wilson left to talk with local people, Mitz joined him in reading through the dispatch records. Mitz asked, "What am I looking for?"

"Anything that doesn't make sense, or strikes you as odd."

After reading a few months' worth of logs, Mark was becoming annoyed with himself for not consulting them sooner. Mitz came to the same conclusion he did when she told him, "He almost always signs off between three to three twenty in the afternoon, and he never includes his 10-20 He often signed back on about five twenty, gave his 10-20 as the Police Station." Mitz added that the only time Turner Brook Road appeared on the dispatch records was when he was sent there.

"Good work, keep at it."

Wilson radioed in the name, Daisy Miller as an acquaintance of the chief. Motioning for Mitz to come with him, they drove to the cottage on a pond belonging to Mrs. Miller. She invited them in, Mark accepted the offer of coffee. Mrs. Miller had divorced her husband three years ago, told them she had indeed dated the chief. By the time he drank his coffee, he was told in no uncertain terms that the chief was a sexual predator. Mrs. Miller didn't have a single good thing to say about him. Said he was aggressive, wouldn't take no for an answer. On their last date, she had to physically push him away.

Forensics had indicated that most of the videotapes found at the chief's house depicted women who appeared very young, almost too young they noted. Mitz was disgusted with the report, commented, "It fits the chief alright."

Mark was busy reading more dispatch logs, grunted at her comment. If word of the chief's cinema habits got out, Lord help them. He sent Mitz out to interview two other women that had contact with the chief, told her sternly, "Do not say anything to anyone about the porn that was found." Mitz seemed offended as she left the station.

Mark had been told by his superiors not to release any detrimental information on the chief without direct clearance from them. They strongly felt the investigation was turning up evidence that could further complicate the case. Mark felt they should, "let the chips fall where they may," but he would obey his orders.

The affidavits were pouring in. Mark ordered Mitz to read them, advise him of anything she thought vague, or nonsensical. He tried to read as many as he could when he had spare time.

He turned to Mitz, "So what happens in Upton at three in the afternoon?" Mitz looked up from her reading.

"The Mill changes shifts, school lets out, can't think of anything else of note."

He sends her out to find out the details of the Mills shifts, decides to review his visits to the residents on Turner Brook Road. Six of the residents, work at the Mill. Eight are self-employed loggers. One resident owns the local garage and gas station.

Mitz advises Mr. and Mrs. Newly to work the second shift; the four others work the first shift. Mark thinks back to his initial visit with the Newley's. He remembers their small farm with a nice barn housing two, Belgian workhorses. Mr. Newly had told him he logged with the horses in the winter for extra income to send their daughter to college. He hadn't met their daughter as she was still at school when he visited them. When he showed interest in the horses, Mr. Newly explained many people liked the neat operation of logging with horses. Minimal damage to the land, no muddy roads left to contend with. The couple told him they didn't know the chief, but had seen the cruiser parked before the bridge many times. Mrs. Newley stated that they always slowed down on that straightaway because the chief often parked there.

His thoughts turned in a direction he didn't like. He radioed Mitz, told her to get all the data on the school bus routes. When she returned to the station, she advised that one teenage female lived on Turner Brook Road. The other children were all under twelve years of age. The long-time bus driver was Alphonse Howard.

Mitz reports that Howard is a tall, thin, bearded, dairy farmer who seemingly has a bad attitude about everything but his herd of Jersey cows. Most of the children are afraid of him because of his curt manner. Mark nods, looks at his watch, tells her they have time to visit him before the afternoon school bus run.

On the half-hour drive to his farm, Mitz tells him she was afraid of the man when she rode the school bus. She adds, "He's a creepy bastard who lives alone on that run-down farm of his."

Their knock on his door was answered by a scowling bearded face.

"You're here about the town cop, ain't you?"

"That's right, Mr. Howard," Mark says.

"Well, I just drive the bus you know. I'm not a townie, don't give a damn about what them townies do."

"Did you see the chief's cruiser very often while driving your route?"

"Well, I could say no, except for Turner Brook Road. Guess he likes to sit there every now and then."

"Did you see him on Wednesday the day he disappeared?"

"Wednesday, you say, can't remember one day from the next.?"

"It snowed that day just about noon, turned to sleet, and then rain in the evening. Do you remember now?"

"Was slippery that day. Yeah, I saw the town cop, no, I saw the cop car stopped side the road, but he wasn't in it."

"Are you sure he wasn't in it?"

"He wasn't in it, I tell you. He was stopped on the wrong side of the road like he has always done."

"You mean that little pull-off before the bridge?"

"There's only one pull-off before the bridge."

"What time would that have been?"

"Three ten, give or take a few minutes."

"Are you sure about the time?"

"Just as sure as I'm standing here, been driving that school bus 22 years."

Back in the cruiser, Mark mulled over this new bit of information. Mitz told him the time, doesn't agree with the time given by the father and son. Mark nods, we'll have to talk to them again because they had stated they saw the chief at a later time.

He turned to Mitz, "We have to talk to Mr. and Mrs. Newly about their seventeen-year-old daughter's knowledge about the chief."

The other children on the bus were all under 12 years of age. Mark did not want to go there. He hoped they were not involved. He turned into a pull-off, called the Newlys, requested they meet with them. He assured them he would contact the Mill tell them they might be late going to work. He called headquarters, was informed Albert Smith had refused to take a lie detector test. He hung up, lit up a smoke to calm himself, told Mitz that he wanted them to be very, "laid back," when they met with the Newlys. He wanted to conduct the interview with as much sensitivity as he could, make every effort to let their daughter do the talking.

When they were let into the house, the Newlys looked very concerned. Mark explained they had to wait for their daughter to arrive from school. Just about 20 minutes past three, Emily Newly entered the kitchen. It was plain to see that the young girl was very nervous. As she stood in the kitchen holding her books against her breasts, she looked steadily down at the floor. Her shoulders were shaking with the effort she was making to muffle her sobs. Mrs. Newly tried to rise from the table, go to her daughter, but Mark gently put his hand on her shoulder keeping her in her chair. Mr. Newly didn't seem angry, just resigned as he waited for his daughter to speak.

Mark said, "Emily, I think you know why we're here. Tell us about your involvement with Chief Hayward."

Emily took a seat at the table, kept her eyes downcast.

Mitz said, "Can you tell us how you met the chief?"

"He asked me if I wanted to go for a ride in the Cruiser with him. Mrs. Newly started crying softly, Mr. Newly took her hands firmly in his own as Emily's story unfolded.

Mitz asked, "How old were you when you met the chief?"

"I just turned sixteen."

"Did you—"

Emily interrupted, "Alan was nice to me. We just drove around, talked a little, then he would bring me back home. Alan would pick me up two or three times a week, just drive around, talk with me. He cared about me."

Mitz softly asked, "Did you have sexual relations with the chief?"

"Yes."

"When did the sexual relationship start?"

"Only about seven months ago. We loved, each other, Alan was going to marry me after I graduated."

"Did you see the chief on Wednesday, the day he went missing?"

"No."

"What did you do on Wednesday afternoon after school?

"My parents picked me up at school. We all went shopping at the new department store in Bethel."

Mark asked, "Did the chief tell you he was worried about anything?"

"No, we never talked about his job. He never said anything about problems."

"When was the last time you saw him?"

"Monday afternoon."

Mark told them he would need blood and hair samples from them all, he would arrange it. Mr. Newly saw them out. Mark shook his hand, told him his daughter's involvement would stay private if possible. Mr. Newly nodded his understanding.

Mitz was aggravated, told Mark she knew that bastard was a sexual sadist. Mark kept his thoughts to himself, thought that the possibility existed that the whole family might be involved in the missing chief. Mitz kept rambling on about the chief. Mark thought they were no closer to solving the case than the day they started. He felt they had definite proof that Chief Hayward was definitely a "dirty cop." He would inform headquarters as soon as he could. Every lead they turned up seemed to come to a dead-end. Not finding any hard evidence was making the case impossible to solve. He didn't think the chief's affair with Emily has anything to do with the case. Emily's parents hadn't been aware of their daughter's actions. Even if they had known, he couldn't see them for the missing chief. He radioed Trooper Wilson, told him to pick up Albert Smith, deliver him to the station.

Mark was just finishing eating when Al Smith was led into his office. He told Trooper Wilson to stand by as this interview wouldn't take long. He greeted Al with a handshake, told him, this is your last chance before he would be considered a suspect if he didn't agree to take a lie detector test. Al started to, protest, Mark cut him off. Just yes or no will do.

"Alright, I'll take the damn test."

"You'll be notified, Trooper Wilson will drive you home."

Sitting in his rented Cabin, he read a few of the affidavits that had come back. Some were easily verifiable, some were questionable, some were downright evasive. He had ordered background checks on all the respondents. He felt he was lost, powerless to take the next, positive step. He felt he had no choice but return home, awaits the far-off spring to resume the search.

ave Blake stopped his four-wheel-drive CJ-5 Jeep just before the bridge. Dave was a young-looking twenty-two-year-old. His 5'9" frame was heavily muscled. His blonde hair was shorn close to his ears, nicely framing his features. His most prominent feature was his intense gray eyes, they seemed to glow with intensity. He donned his snowshoes, shouldered his trapping basket. He hadn't trapped this section of Turner Brook because of all the Police activity. It was bitter cold, quiet, as he made his way to the running water. Slower portions of the brook were iced over, but the main channel was still ice-free. He had trapped this section of the brook for many years. He expected to catch a few mink and an occasional otter in the slower moving water just before it narrowed, turned into rapids.

He had placed drowning wires on five carefully selected sites prior to the season-opening. The use of drowning wires made for a more humane method, allowed him to use smaller traps, make more sets than he normally could working in the cold water. It was getting late in the afternoon. He was getting worn out from the long day he had spent in the Marshes setting traps for Beaver. He quickly made five sets for mink, decided to walk down to the rapids, make two sets for Otter. As he walked past the large pool full of fallen tree branches, he saw where a large beaver had emerged from the water to feed on the succulent poplar trees on the bank. The beaver was far from the nearest lodge, had the thought it was a bank beaver. He decided to continue on, make the Beaver set after he finished. Walking around a thick stand of hemlocks, he saw many weasel tracks. He noticed the weasels were feeding on a deer carcass frozen into the snow. He liked catching the white-furred ermine although they didn't earn him much money. Native people used the white pelts for trimming their dresses, he was happy to help them out. He quickly set four #1 jump traps using wax paper under and over the trap. to prevent their freezing in. He continued on to the rapids, made two sets for Otter utilizing his drowning wires.

Back at the deep pool, he had to make a set for a front foot catch as he didn't have a large enough trap with him for the preferred hindfoot catch. He cleared the exit hole from ice, placed a branch across the opening that the Beaver would hit with his chest, drop his front foot into the trap, hopefully. He had no drowning wire, so he cut a small tree down, trimmed the lower branches off, left the wide, bushy top on to stop the tree from being pulled through the hole in the ice. He finished the set by making a tent of hemlock branches over the hole to delay the set freezing over. Making this set took time. Dusk was upon him, he was very cold, especially his hands. He made his way back to his jeep, had the last cup of coffee from his thermos, relished the heat slowly warming him. It was dark when he called it a day, headed for the comfort of his cabin.

Dawn the next morning found Dave sitting in the Errol diner eating a filling breakfast of bacon and eggs, fried potatoes, home-baked bread with jam. The diner was busy, the parking lot filled with logging trucks, four-wheel-drive vehicles as another day in the north country started. While they were filling his thermos with boiling hot coffee, Dave smoked a Camel, planned his day. He decided he would check all his Beaver sets on the Marshes, re-set as necessary. He would trap these marshes for two days only. He had deliberately made sets for the larger beaver that traveled away from their lodges to feed. He did not want to catch any juveniles. Dave was a full-time trapper. He made sure not to over-trap any of his areas. Before the season opened, he had made feed beds to lure the mature beaver away from their lodges. Detailed planning was essential if he wanted to continue his life as a free trapper. He hoped he would finish in time to check his traps on Turner Brook.

Driving East back into Upton, the sun was rising in the east giving the promise of a fine day in the woods. At the first marsh, he had to chop through the ice to inspect his sets. The coni-bear traps he used were instant killers, but it was hard work pulling the sets. His pack was full of beaver which meant a long walk back to his CJ, another long walk to get the rest of his catch out.

The second marsh yielded eleven Beaver giving him a total of eighteen Beavers for the day. As the day passed, the temperature was rapidly falling. It was two thirty in the afternoon when he parked by the bridge on Turner Brook. A tired, cold, wet, Dave started down the brook. He had only his trapping basket containing a few traps as he hoped this would be quick and simple. He should have known that Murphy's law might rear its ugly head, but a tired Dave Blake trudged ahead.

Things were good so far, he pulled five minks from his sets, quickly remade them. He planned to trap only one more day in this small section to ensure he left fur for the following years. Coming to his Beaver set, he saw that his drag pole had been pulled into the hole, its bushy top frozen into the ice. He decided to leave this set for last, continued on to his Otter sets where he pulled two prime Otter from the freezing water. Following his snowshoe trail, he saw he had caught four weasels, but a wandering Fisher cat had eaten them. One hundred pounds of meat under the snow, and this Fisher eats his weasels, go figure. He made a set for the fisher using two #2 coil traps, went back to his Beaver set. He broke the ice around his drag pole, tried pulling the pole out of the water. Somewhere, the trap was caught solidly, he couldn't budge it. Discouraged, he went back to his Jeep, got his snowshoes, an ice chisel, and a length of rope. He knew he would have to venture out onto the ice on the deep pool. He would tie himself off to a sturdy tree before he would venture out onto the ice. Dave had had many experiences with the cold water and freezing temperatures. Life and death were ever-present when venturing out on running water.

He carefully edged out onto the ice. He used his chisel to test the ice as he went. He used a snowshoe to clear the snow away, chiseled a hole through the ice. Freezing water gushed through the hole he had just cut. He tried to stay dry, but his knees soon soaked through as he probed for his trap chain. No luck. He ventured out another four feet, chopped another hole that released a torrent of water against his boots. He reversed his chisel, used the hook on the end of it to finally hook his trap chain. The damn thing was still stuck. He had to kneel down in the icy water, cup his hands on either side of his face to peer into the dark water. He saw the beaver about eighteen inches under the water. He knew he could pull the Beaver out of the trap since it was a front-foot catch. He didn't want to make another trip to his Jeep to get his shoulder-length rubber gloves. He thrust his hand into the hole, grabbed the Beaver, pulled the Beaver out of the Hole. He dropped the Beaver, forced his hand inside his coat under his armpit. The cold was really getting to him, but he didn't want to leave his trap. He knelt again, peered into the water. A boot? Was his mind playing tricks on him? He peered again and thought, *'That is definitely a man's boot.'*

His knees and lower legs are starting to ache, his arm and hand are going numb. He leaves everything, painfully makes his way to his Jeep. His hand is so cold, he cannot turn the ignition on. Awkwardly, he uses his left hand to start the Jeep, turns the heater on full blast. He pours what's left of his hot coffee over his frozen hand. After half an hour later, a semblance of feeling has returned to his hand. Working around water in the north country can be a fatal attraction. He drives to the Upton Police Station to report what he has seen.

Trooper Wilson is seated in the chief's office writing in his daily log when Dave enters. Wilson can't help but notice the man is cold, wet, looks like he's in pain. When Dave relates his findings, Wilson quickly realizes the importance of it, he contacts officer Mitz, asks her to report to the station ASAP. He decides to wait until Dave's statement has been documented before notifying Mark.

Wilson verifies Dave's identity, gives him hot coffee in an attempt to make him more comfortable. A rush of freezing air precedes Mitz into the station. She writes up Dave's statement, gets a blanket to wrap around the cold trapper.

Mitz dials Mark's number and has to leave a message on his phone. She's just about to raise him on the radio when the phone rings. She relates Dave's story to Mark in a rush. Mark asks her to, slow down, repeat the message. Wilson indicates he wishes to speak with Mark. Mitz passes the phone to him, pours Dave another coffee.

Wilson tells Mark exactly where the pine grove is located, advises it was part of the original search area. Wilson ends the call by telling Mark they have to consider Dave as a suspect.

Mitz is concerned with Dave's ability to drive himself home. She tells Wilson she will drive Dave home in his jeep, can he pick her up? Wilson nods yes, turns back to his log.

Dave's cabin still has some heat in it when they entered. As Mitz adds fuel to the stove, Dave changes into warm clothing. Sitting in front of the stove, she asks Dave to recall any other details of his find. Dave replies he's told them all he knows. When she leaves, she tells Wilson she doesn't believe Dave is involved in the case prior to his findings. Wilson grunts, tells her, time will tell.

Mark is sitting on his sofa with his infant son in his arm. Carol is asleep on the couch with her feet in his lap. He rubs her lower legs as he mentally makes a list of what actions he wants to take before he notifies headquarters. Carol stirs, awakens to take the baby from his arms. Mark calls headquarters, requests a recovery team from Fish and Game, Warden Ivan Petrov be assigned to him, two Troopers to report to Upton by six the next morning. He adds that it will be a water rescue, a very difficult endeavor in below-zero weather.

Ivan has just finished eating when Mark enters, tells him he's going with him to Upton to aid him in the investigation. Marie is not thrilled to hear that Ivan is leaving, but she helps him pack a bag, does not comment on the situation.

Mark notifies Wilson he wants Mitz and Dave at the station by six in the morning. Mark turns on his blue lights, roars down the two-lane road leading to Upton. He updates Ivan on the findings, tells him he wants to find out all he can about trapper Dave Blake.

Back in her apartment, Mitz is standing under the hot water pulsing from the showerhead. As the sensuous hot water cascades down her, her mind is on trapper Dave Blake. For some reason, the man stirred her. Perhaps it was his neat cabin. Perhaps it was his quiet, soft-spoken direct manner, more likely it was his piercing gray eyes. She sighed as her body warmed under the hot water.

It was barely light the next morning when the group of officers gathered in the town hall. Mark instructed the Troopers, under Wilson to mark off the pine grove as far as the bridge with Police tape. He told Wilson he wanted both sides of the road closed off. Ivan and Mitz were seated with Dave Blake. Ivan could tell from talking to him that Dave was an experienced trapper. Ivan told him he wanted him to lead them to the pool exactly as he had gone to it the previous day. Dave nodded his understanding.

It was five below zero, and the temperature was falling with a stiff, cold wind from the north. They had no choice but to wait about two hours for the rescue team to arrive.

Mark, Ivan, Mitz, and Dave drove out to the bridge where Dave took them down his snowshoe trail to the pool. Mitz photographed the site in situ from every angle. Mark had Dave walk them to the end of Dave's trail by the Otter sets. Mitz photographed every relevant detail there was. Dave, lead them to the carcass under the snow. Mitz stepped in to take a photo, stepped on a hidden trap, which simply pushed her foot up. Mark asked Dave to undo any other traps he had placed there. Mitz photographed the carcass in situ. Mark said the forensic unit would recover the carcass for evidence. Mark was getting worried about all the people that would be walking down this trail. His hope of finding evidence in the pine grove was rapidly disappearing. They returned to the cruisers to await the recovery team.

Mark instructed Mitz to drive Dave home. Dave had been advised he was a, "material, witness," not to leave the area without notifying Trooper Wilson. When Dave asked her if Trooper Wilson thought he was involved, Mitz felt her attraction to the soft-spoken man even stronger.

"It's just procedure, Dave. Can you see why?"

Dave smiled slightly, didn't comment. Dave asked her if she had time for a coffee? She nodded yes, followed him into the small, snug cabin made of native logs. She liked, his strong hands, thought he should trim up his beard. She almost blushed as she caught herself sizing him up. Dave habits were sure and methodical, that appealed to her somehow. He didn't strike her as a man who would do anything rash. He had no criminal record, not even a speeding ticket. Mitz studied his face over the rim of her coffee cup. She knew she couldn't get involved with him until after this case was done with.

"How long have you lived alone here?"

"I started trapping full time when I was in my teens. Built this cabin six years ago."

"Where's your family from?"

"My folks are from Bangor, no brothers or sisters."

"My parents are from Montreal, moved here when I was a baby."

"Would you allow me to buy you dinner sometime?"

"Yes Dave, but only after this mess is cleared up."

Dave nodded his understanding as she left.

Driving back to Turner Brook Road, she thought, I've gone and done it now.

Ivan was talking with the lead rescue officer. He was going to lead them to the pool along the same path already in use. It took an hour for the team to bring all their equipment to the pool. Two inflatable rafts were on the ice. Two officers cut through the offending ice using chain saws while two other officers used ice chisels to free the ice from the tree branches. Mark was on the bank watching, slowly losing all feeling in his body. Ivan had taken charge of Dave's ice chisel, snowshoes, one dead, frozen solid large Beaver.

The lead officer dressed in scuba gear, slowly lowered himself into the icy water. He confirmed that there was a body attached to the boot. The body was solidly wedged under and into the tree limbs. After ten minutes in the water, he was replaced by another officer utilizing a hand saw to cut the limbs away. The men could work no more than ten minutes in the freezing water, took a half-hour to sufficiently warm them back up. Both men proclaimed it was colder out of the water than in it.

Mark could hardly feel his body when the body of Chief Alan Hayward was slid onto the bank. Mark could stand the cold no longer. He took a quick look at the body, easily saw the two bullet holes in his chest. The chief had been murdered, no doubt at all. He left for the warmth of his cruiser. After the coroner had seen the body, it was taken to an ambulance, delivered to the hospital to await the autopsy results.

Late afternoon, after a hot bath and two cups of boiling hot coffee, Mark finally warmed back up. Ivan had shown he was impervious to the bitter cold. Mark could not settle himself. His mind was awhirl with the recovery of the chief's body. While he was laying in the hot water, he thought about the probabilities of the case. The presence of the dead deer strongly indicated that a hunter—or hunters—was responsible for the shooting. He tried to formulate how the death had occurred, but without any hard evidence, he was fantasying.

The killer had fired two shots that were barely two inches apart on the chief's chest. The killer obviously was proficient in double tapping using a large caliber handgun. Not an easy thing to do. It seemed to him that the killer must have moved the chief's cruiser. How did the killer know where the cruiser was? Was Dave the killer? What an impossible find, he thought. Dave had gone to the authorities immediately after seeing the boot. That the boot was visible through the hole in the ice he had seen for himself. Ivan had told him Dave was a competent trapper, the sets he had made along the brook were well planned and in place long before the shooting. The two holes he had chopped through the ice were consistent with a trapper trying to find his prey. By the time he climbed out of the tub, he had convinced himself that Dave was not involved in the shooting. He was also convinced that the only reason to be in that pine grove, was hunting, or trapping.

Mark asked Ivan to go to Dave's house and, "feel the man out". He called Mitz, told her to make sure to give him the affidavits of interest in the morning. She advised that Al Smith had passed the lie detector test. Done for the day, he called Carol, drove to the diner for a good meal.

Ivan got directions from Trooper Wilson to Dave's cabin. He picked up two ham and cheese grinders, a six-pack, before he drove to Dave's cabin. Dave lived at the end of a dead-end logging road at least four miles in the woods. The two-track road was frozen solid, slippery going. Dave's log cabin was a small square structure with a center chimney. Gray smoke was pouring out of the chimney when he parked by Dave's Jeep.

After Ivan had gotten the grinders and beer from the trunk, Dave appeared at the front door, waved to him to come in. The cabin was toasty warm. A homemade stove that accepted a three-foot log was red from the heat it was producing. A blower on the stovepipe was blowing a steady stream of hot air.

"I hope you like ham and cheese Dave."

Seated at the table, Ivan scanned the interior of the cabin. One side held an array of pelts in varying stages of drying. The other side held a kitchen, and a single bed, neatly made. The cabin was neat and clean. Ivan asked Dave about his trap line on Turner Brook. Dave produced a notebook showing all the areas he trapped. On the page denoting Turner Brook, Ivan noted the date Dave had placed his drowning wires as well as notations Dave had made about the area. Ivan was impressed with Dave's system for trapping. Ivan thought Dave was a man who paid attention to the slightest details.

Looking at some of the pelts on plastic rings, Ivan was impressed with Dave's preparation of the pelts. He was definitely a trapper who knew his business.

Ivan spent another hour with him talking about the north woods in general. Dave had all his weapons in a rack on the wall. The only handgun he owned was a .22 Colt Woodsman with a six-inch barrel, a trapper's gun. The only ammunition he saw was .22 caliber, .30-30 factory ammunition.

Ivan tried to keep the conversation light, but he felt sure Dave knew he was under scrutiny. Dave was forthright in his conversation. Ivan thought the man was just what he appeared to be, a very competent trapper.

The next morning dawned bright, even colder. When Mark and Ivan left for the diner, the temperature was 15 below zero with a stiff north wind making it even colder. Mark was glad he had plugged in the block heater on the cruiser, it easily started.

Over breakfast, Ivan told Mark that Dave had placed sets well ahead of what happened to the chief. In his opinion, Dave was not involved in the shooting. Mark thanked him told him he was arranging to have Ivan driven back home. Told him he would contact him if he needed him.

Mitz was in the station when Mark entered. She was reading the affidavits, had put the autopsy report on Mark's desk. Mark poured them both a coffee, sat down to read the report.

The cause of death was two bullets through the chest. Either bullet would have caused death. The bullets were solid, non-expanding bullets. The entrance and exit wounds were the same size. The cold water had done a remarkable job in preserving the body. The only damage was to the soft tissue on the face that had been partially eaten away. Mark thought the lab results would confirm that the bullets were hard, solid lead, or common military .45 caliber ball ammunition. In any event, the caliber was either .44, or .45. That was the best the medical examiner could swear to.

Mark looked over the items taken from the chief's body. His hat had been found stuffed under his jacket over the bullet holes in his chest, His 9mm, was secured in its holster. An ankle revolver was secure in its holster. A spare cruiser key had been found in his wallet along with two condoms, eleven dollars. No key ring had been found. The undigested food in the chief's stomach showed he had eaten an hour or two before his death. Mitz had proven he had eaten at the local diner that day.

Forensics had reported that the chief's 9mm had been wiped clean of any prints. The Chief must have at least tried to defend himself. Mark couldn't help but wonder if the chief's actions had contributed to his own death. He sighed inwardly as he realized his only option was to interview the numerous hunters that had been in the area. One thing he knew, the chief's actions were going to come to light. Sooner or later, the press would get hold of the questionable actions of the chief.

The necropsy done on the deer carcass yielded their first solid clue. A fragmented bullet was found lodged against the buck's right shoulder. The only forensic value was the diameter, .308, with a few marks on the rear of the fragmented bullet. The report said there were not enough markings on the bullet for a positive I.D.

Mark thought it was better than nothing, but realized he had to tie the deer to the crime before it was of any value. He put the report aside, asked Mitz to pass him the affidavits of interest. They spent a long boring day going over many, many vague statements.

8

Mitz left the station, went to her apartment, changed into warm wool slacks, a white linen blouse with a high collar. She decided she would visit Dave, try to learn more about the habits of hunters in the areas surrounding the pine grove. She dabbed some perfume behind her ears, a few dabs between her breasts. She donned a wool jacket, left driving the town cruiser.

It was approaching six, pitch dark already on a moonless night as she stepped up on Dave's porch. If Dave was surprised to see her, he didn't show it. They sat at the kitchen table where Dave served coffee, cookies along with a welcoming smile that softened his features. She spent a good half hour pressing him for details on hunters in the area, in general. She couldn't understand his explanations simply because her only knowledge of the area was the tarred road leading to those areas.

Dave interrupted her. "You're missing the real importance here. The question you want answered is, 'Why did the chief go into that pine grove?' I can tell you he didn't go in because he heard a shot. Shots are fired in Maine practically year-round, no cause for alarm. He went into that pine grove because of what he saw."

Mitz simply looked at him over the rim of her coffee cup, "Go on."

"He must have seen someone cross the road and enter, then he heard the shot maybe. He probably investigated because the New

Hampshire State line is only a few hundred yards up the westerly ridge. He might have figured it was a New Hampshire hunter."

Mitz thought about his statement, leaned across the table giving him a glimpse of her ample cleavage. She had undone the top two buttons on her blouse on purpose. Dave softly placed his hand over hers. He stood up, approached her. He gently raised her from the chair, embraced her, kissed her searchingly. When Mitz felt her legs weakening, she molded herself against him, returned his kiss with passion.

It was well past dawn when Mitz awoke in Dave's bed. The cabin was warm, empty. She washed, dressed, poured herself a coffee. The note on the table said, "This was the most wonderful night of my life, Dave.

Mitz was past blushing. She had wanted this man and now she may have put her career in jeopardy. She brushed the thought from her mind as she drove to the station to update Mark.

It was a breathless Mitz that rushed into the station, hurried to Mark's office.

She started to repeat Dave's explanation when Mark said, "Whoa, slow down Mitz."

She got her breath back, told Mark Dave's theory. Mark replied, it makes perfectly good sense, but remember, it's only a theory at this point. He reminded her that another vehicle may have been involved. At this point, we just don't know.

The more Mark thought it over, the more convinced he was that Dave had the right concept of how the murder was committed. He called Ivan, asked him to get Max and trapper Alfred Holmes, if possible. Mark wanted these men to advise him when he was going to re-interview Dave.

As soon as Ivan arrived, he called Dave, asked him to come to the station with all his trapping data, and any maps he had of the area. When Dave arrived, he spread his trapping maps out on a large table. Trapper Homes said, "Forget about trapping. How do the deer move through this area, this pine grove where the body was found?

"Hunters can push the deer into this grove. I've seen it happen before. If they push the cutover area to the south, a deer could be pushed into the grove. Max asked, "This was an injured deer some hunter was pushing, why would it leave the thick cover and enter this pine grove?"

Trapper Holmes was intently looking over the maps spread out on the table. "If the wounded deer was pushed into this grove from the east, the north, or the south, your police officer wouldn't have seen them. Would he investigate a shot from the woods?"

Dave shook his head no. Ivan asked Dave to describe the westerly ridge along the New Hampshire State line.

Dave ran his finger up the map directly opposite the Pine grove. The top of this ridge is covered by a large area of beech trees. It's a magnet for both deer and bear. If you cross this small brook that leads down to the bridge, there's a logging road that leads to Route 26 just three miles from the Errol diner. There's just open hardwood from the top of the ridge to the conifers close to the road."

Max pointed out that a hunter would have to cross the brook to gain access to the beech trees. Max pointed out that the most probable place for a hunter to see a deer would have been at the top of the ridge. Holmes and Dave nodded their agreement.

Mark said, "The hunter wounded the deer in the beech grove, followed the deer down the ridge, crossed the paved road into the pine grove."

The consensus was that the chief had seen the deer and the hunter cross the road while seated in his cruiser.

Dave added that, over the years, he had seen numerous deer tracks jumping over the narrow part of the river where he had made his otter sets.

Trapper Holmes added that there should be three fired cartridges in the leaves, but would be a hard thing to find. Mitz entered the room with a bag full of sandwiches, a huge thermos of hot coffee from the diner, handed Mark the local newspaper which featured an article about the complaints that had been filed against the chief, a message from headquarters.

Mark thanked the men for their help, told Mitz to get all the statements from hunters that had been in the area.

The article alluded to the chief's involvement with a high school girl, harassment of local women. The message from headquarters told Mark not to make any statement concerning the chief's actions without clearance from Headquarters. Pandora's box had been opened.

9

Notices had been in place for two days announcing a meeting at the Upton town hall to discuss the murder of the chief. Anyone with any information was urged to come forward. Mark was surprised to see a packed house as he took his place at the lectern.

The Police are requesting any information about the murder of Chief Alan Hayward. Those of you that were requested to attend are being asked to write out a description of your activities on Wednesday, November fourth, the day the chief went missing. Anyone that has any information, no matter how trivial, please speak to me after this presentation. Hands from the reporters shot into the air. Questions about the chief's actions were being yelled out loud. Mark waved for quiet, told the packed audience that it is an ongoing investigation and he had no further comment.

Mr. Steve Larkin approached him, advised he had been hunting just a mile south of the pine grove. He stated he had heard what became a series of three rifle shots starting around one in the afternoon. A few minutes after the last rifle shot, he had heard two more quick shots. He stated he wasn't sure of the direction the shots came from. He added the chief had a very aggressive manner with out-of-state hunters. Mark thanked him, asked him to write a statement, give it to Officer Mitz. Mark noted that many of the statements coming in made mention of the chief's aggressive mannerisms. In his report to his superiors, he had stressed that the chief's mannerisms may have been a factor in his death. Public opinion of the chief was not favorable, could possibly have an effect on the outcome of a trial.

A statement from Mr. James, Obrien had stated he was hunting just north of the pine grove, about even with the log landing where the cruiser had been found. He reported hearing the shots, noted he saw another hunter just before dark. Mark immediately radioed Mitz, had her bring Mr. Obrien to see him.

Mark asked him to describe the hunter, was told the only reason he remembered the man was because he wasn't wearing any visible orange safety clothing. Could that be the killer? Mark called Mitz over, told her about Obrien, told her to thoroughly check him out.

Mitz recalled the statements from two hunters from Newport, N.H. who were hunting in Errol opposite the pine Grove. Mark now knew that area was two and a half miles from the Pine grove. Of the thirty- seven people that had submitted statements, about a quarter of them had run-ins with the law. He had requested they take lie detector tests. He would not exclude anyone from the list, but he would pay special attention to those people that had failed the test, those people that had hunted in the area. He felt that the case finally had a direction to go in. He was especially intrigued by the hunter seen in the dark woods above where the cruiser was found. He asked Mitz if she had gotten the names of all the people who had attended the meeting? She nodded she had.

Back at the station, Mitz handed Mark all the statements from the people that had failed to pass the polygraph test. Seven hunters from out of State had failed the test. He noted in particular that one of the hunters that had hunted in Errol had not passed the test. From the statements from the two hunters, he could see where they didn't seem to logically match up. The older man had admitted hunting up into the beech trees on top of the ridge above Turner Brook Road. The other hunter had claimed he had not crossed the brook, had hunted north away from the top of the ridge. Trapper Holmes had told them that it didn't make any sense for two hunters to hunt away from each other. Ivan, Max, and Dave had all agreed with Holmes's statement.

Mark felt he had to personally interview all of the hunters who had failed the test. He had decided to request that Officer Mitzven accompany him. He was impressed with her knowledge of the case, her easy way of interviewing people. He wrote out a plan of action, had Mitz send it to headquarters.

Colonel Mike Williams was seated at the big table in the conference room. He was reading the plan Sergeant Mark Schaffer had sent in. His three Captains were seated with him. The Colonel was not happy with the newspaper article in front of him. He asked Captain John Sharpe how the information had leaked to the press.

Captain Sharpe explained the many complaints that had been filed against Chief Hayward over the years, added that the chief's behavior was common knowledge throughout the area.

"What about our investigator, Schaffer? Is he up to being in charge?"

"Sergeant Schaffer is our best investigator. It's my belief he is the man to solve this case."

"Who authorized him to bring in all these people from outside the force."

"He has developed his own methods of solving cases. He relies heavily on people that have knowledge in specific areas. Over the years his methods have proven successful. He operates with my full authority."

"Very well, authorize him to follow his plan."

Sitting at his kitchen table, Ray was not overly concerned with the discovery of the Policeman's body. The most conservative newspaper in the State had written an article questioning the behavior of the slain officer. If you read between the lines, you might get the sense that the cop got what he deserved.

He had failed to pass his lie detector test, had been notified they wanted him to take another test. Boss had told him to hire a lawyer, but he didn't want to spend the money. He was confident they had no hard evidence against him. He lit up a smoke, pulled heavily on a fifth of booze. Better brush my teeth before I go take the test again.

Officer Little escorted Ray into the testing cubicle, asked him if he wanted coffee. Ray answered yes, lit up a smoke. Little watched Ray through the one-way mirror. He looked calm, with no expression on his face. He was smoking, idly turning his cigarette lighter over and over in his hand.

Ray failed the test for the second time. Officer Little watched him leave the station, drive away in his pickup truck. He thought to himself, this is a long way from being over.

10

Mark had received authorization to conduct interviews out of State. He called Mitz into the office, informed her he wanted her to accompany him, conduct some interviews. Mitz asked him, "Why?"

"Men react differently to a woman than to a man. I like the gentle manner you have when you interview people. I think you get a lot more out of people when you don't have an adversarial situation. I want you to dress in a business suit, but don't lose your femininity."

"Do you want me to look sexy, or motherly?"

"Somewhere in the middle, I guess."

Mitz gave him a smile, a soft laugh as she left to pack.

Mark had headquarters notify the relevant agencies of his planned visits.

The Hartford, Conn. Police had done a good job in interviewing the three men. Mark and Mitz read their report, told the liaison officer they wanted to conduct the interview in the subject's home. Mark felt you learned more about people when they were in their own surroundings.

They drove down Albany Avenue, turned right onto Oakland Terrace, were greeted by the sight of decaying Victorian-styled houses. Mark thought this must have been a beautiful area at one time, was shocked at how far the area had gone down. Mark was used to seeing shanties and sheds in disarray in Maine, but he had never experienced an entire area gone to decay.

The three-story house was occupied by the Patistroni family. Carl and his wife, children, lived on the first floor. Carl's son and family lived on the second floor. Carl's father lived on the third floor. As they walked up the steps, Mark told Mitz, you conduct the interview.

Their knock was answered by the oldest man in the house. He offered them coffee. The old man started to tell them about the neighborhood when he had bought the house. Back then, the neighborhood had been comprised of many different nationalities. On this one street, you had Jewish, Italian, French, Polish, and a black family all living together in peace and harmony. Over the years the neighborhood had fallen apart, was not a good place to live anymore. As the old man was sipping his wine, the whole family entered the parlor. Mitz introduced them to Carl junior who was the acting spokesman. She asked to speak to the three hunters apart from their families. Mitz stated that two of them had not passed the polygraph test, they wanted to straighten things out if possible. Mark lit up a smoke, watched intently while studying the faces of the three men.

Mitz had dressed in a blue business suit. A high-necked white blouse with its lapels on the outside of her blue jacket coupled with her dark hair falling to her shoulders, gave her a very non-threatening look.

Carl junior spoke up, saying his son and his brother had not made true statements.

Mitz instructed Carl that what he said could be used against them in a court of law. Carl junior nodded his understanding, nodded to his son. Carl's son admitted that he and his uncle had not told the truth. He explained that on that Wednesday, he and his uncle had both fired at a deer, missed it. They were afraid to put that in their statements. Mitz laid a map out on the table asked the young man to show her where they were hunting that day? The spot he pointed out, was six miles away from the pine grove. She asked the other two men to look at the map. They both confirmed the same area.

Mitz asked the young man what time they had shot at the deer. He replied, mid-morning. She asked what area they had hunted in the afternoon? He pointed out an area that was two miles away from the pine grove. She asked them if they would be willing to submit their firearms for testing? They all agreed. After all their firearms were rounded up, she confirmed all the firearms on her list were present. She asked if they owned any other firearms? They all answered she had them all.

"Did you hear any shots while you were hunting?"

"We heard shots to the north, didn't pay much attention to them, they sounded far off."

She asked them to write an amended statement, give it to the Hartford police department. They would be given another polygraph test on their new statements. Mitz glanced at Mark, who nodded to her. She thanked the men, ended the interview.

Over dinner in the hotel lounge, Mark praised her for her interview technique. He noted that she had asked the right questions, especially how she had each man identify the areas they hunted in. He pointed out that she should have asked if they had encountered any other hunters on that day. Mitz nodded, said she would add that to their statements. Mark had left instructions with the Hartford, P.D. thanked them for their co-operation.

After a good breakfast, they turned their rental towards Hookset, N.H. As they were driving north, Mitz made the comment, flatlanders, while shaking her head. Mark had a personal distaste for labels, but had to grin at her comment. After meeting with the Hookset police, arranging the meeting for the following day, Mark wanted nothing more than a hot shower and a soft bed, he was getting sick of the traveling already. Sitting on the edge of the bed, he called his wife. They talked of the baby, when he would be returning home. He fell asleep thinking about the hunter that had been seen going up the ridge opposite the log landing where the chief's cruiser had been found.

Mitz was enjoying the trip. She liked the added responsibility that Mark had given her. She studied the notes on the hunters she would be interviewing in the morning. She fell asleep with the notes on her chest.

Since both men had chosen to be represented by their lawyer, Mark had decided to hold the interview at the Hookset P.D. Both Ralph Cummings and Joe Trottier were dressed to the nines in business suits. Mitz sat opposite them while Mark sat behind her.

Mitz opened by requesting that both men turn their weapons into the P.D. for examination. Both men readily agreed. She stated that both men had failed their polygraph tests, did they want to file an amended statement? Their lawyer asked for a recess so his clients could write out an amended Statement. Mitz looked at Mark, who nodded his okay to her. They watched in an adjoining cubicle as the men wrote.

After a half hour, they re-entered the interrogation room, read copies of their new statements. Both men claimed they were in the company of two local women from Errol. They claimed they had spent the day before the shooting and two days after the shooting in their cabin with the women before leaving Errol. They gave the names of the women along with the address of the camp they had rented. Both men were married, requested their statements not be made public.

Mark sighed inwardly as he read the easily verified statements. Mitz told them they would have to take another polygraph test. Their lawyer objected, but both men readily agreed to take the test.

At dinner that night, Mark explained to Mitz that he had saved the most important interview for last. He told her the elderly man had passed the lie detector test using straightforward language, not a hint of guile or evasion. He didn't consider the man a suspect, but felt he could contribute greatly to the investigation. Mitz sipped her coffee, said, "So you are looking at Ray, the younger man as the killer."

"Everything we have uncovered leads us in that direction, but we may be off base. He may be innocent. People lie for reasons we don't know, always keep an open mind."

They were met at the Newport P.D. by Lt. Bob Harris. Lt. Harris filled them in about what he knew of the two men, told them they needed to interview Officer Little before they spoke with the two men. On the drive to Little's house, Mark told Mitz that the Lt's friendship with Don Boer had given him an idea they might later utilize. Mitz nodded, didn't press for more information. She had learned that Mark lived inside himself, was very often not very open.

Officer Little greeted them at his door with his young son peeking around his leg. Mitz rubbed the boy's head as they entered the kitchen. Larry's wife had hot, coffee, some pastries laid out on the table. She scooped up the young boy, left them. Larry spent a good half hour telling them of his suspicions about Ray. Mitz listened intently, was impressed by Larry's demeanor. She couldn't tell if Larry was afraid of Ray, or slightly in awe of the man. Larry finished by saying, "Ray is not a man that can be pushed. You push him and he will explode like an atomic bomb. Believe me, when I tell you this, I have seen it firsthand many times."

Mark asked, "What about his weapons?"

"He doesn't have a carry permit for a sidearm, but he's a hunter, has rifles, I'm sure."

Mark wanted to visit with Don unannounced. Lt. Harris told them to get to his house before dawn or they would miss him. Don hunts wild boar that, escape from Corbin Park all winter.

Mark was in the diner at four A.M. It was a cold morning and the sun had yet to make its appearance. He drove his rental to Don's house, turned the lights off on his vehicle as he entered the driveway. The front half of the house was lit up, the remaining house was dark. In the half-light of dawn, he saw Don walk to his barn, come out leading a sorrel horse to a hitching post. Twin plumes of moisture were coming out of the horse's nostrils. Don emerged carrying a saddle and a saddle blanket. Mark watched as Don ran his hand over the sorrel's back before putting the blanket on. This ritual between man and horse had always fascinated Mark since he had first seen his father handling his horses. He had thought his father a different man when he worked with the horses. His dad showed endless patience, an even temperament at all times when dealing with the horses. No stern look creased his face, no harsh words came out of his mouth. Mark snapped back to reality as he watched Don canter out into the pasture towards the distant forests. Mark's father had been disappointed that his sons had not followed in his footsteps. Mark saw his father as a manmade hard by the conditions he lived under. His dad was an independent logger. No matter the weather, he worked out on the coldest, stormiest days. Mark had great respect for his parents. Whenever possible, he had listened to his father.

When he had joined the police force, his father had said, "In this world, a man rises to the highest level of his incompetence. Be careful to stay with what brings you success. Be aware of your shortcomings, always play to your strengths." Years of experience had proved his father correct. Mark decided to go back to the motel, take Mitz out for breakfast. He thought he would spend the day riding with Officer Little, learn a little more about his suspect. He would have Mitz investigate the background on Don Boer.

itz gave her report on Don Boer to Mark. Don was a self-made man dealing mostly in speculation housing. Many of the homes he sold went through the local bank, or the Farm and Home Administration. He was a man who was considered, "narrow," in his thinking by those that knew him. He had no criminal record, possessed a carry permit for many years. He had a Federal Firearms permit, had as many as three hundred guns in his home. Mark noted he was a cautious man, had everything he owned fully insured. He was reputed to have few friends, but his friendship with Lt. Harris interested Mark.

After reading the report, he and Mitz left the diner to interview him. Mark told Mitz he would handle the interview. Their knock on the door was answered by a young girl of about ten years of age. She quickly hollered for her mother who came to the door.

Mark showed his credentials, asked to speak with Don. She sent the young girl out to the barn to get her father. Don was dressed in jeans, a white, tank top tee shirt. Mark noted he was short, darkly tanned, gave them a scowl as he entered the kitchen. His wife offered coffee which everyone accepted. She shooed the three children out of the kitchen. Don and Mark lit up smokes, studied each other across the table.

Mark pretended to read the statement Don had written out. He told Don they were investigating the shooting death of Chief

Hayward. He asked Don to tell them exactly where he was that afternoon.

Don told them the same story he had submitted in his statement. Mark asked him for his firearms records. He produced a bound notebook, passed it across the table. Mark read the entries from when the chief had gone missing, noted no sales or purchase of large caliber handguns. "Did you hunt up into the beech grove that day?"

"I barely entered it. I could see about two hundred yards ahead, saw nothing of interest, started to hunt back to my truck."

"Did you see Ray that afternoon?"

"I saw him when he returned to the pickup about twenty minutes after dusk."

"Did you see him, or any other hunter in the beech grove?"

"I never saw anyone else that day."

"Have you bought or sold any large-caliber handguns recently?"

"No."

"How did Ray act when he returned to the truck?"

"Normal."

"Was he agitated, happy, sad, smiling, frowning?"

"Why don't you ask him?"

"How long did you spend in the Beech grove?"

"Maybe five minutes."

"Did you go east down the ridge?"

"No, I told you I hunted back to the truck."

"Did you hear any shots that afternoon?"

"Yes, some shots were fired north of me. My hearing isn't too good, I really couldn't tell you where they came from.?"

Mitz could tell that Mark's questions were aggravating Don. He smoked constantly, almost had a permanent scowl on his face.

Mark asked for a refill on the coffee. Don got up, put the coffee pot on the table, told Mark to help himself. Mark poured himself another cup full, asked Don, "What was Ray's attitude when he returned to the truck?"

"I already answered that."

"You ever see Ray lose control, act with violence?"

"Look, if you want to know about Ray, ask him."

Mark stirred the sugar into his coffee, looked hard at Don, "I'm asking you."

"Do I need a lawyer here?"

"That's up to you, do you need one?"

"I already told you that Ray acted normal when he got in the truck. He told me he had not seen anything but a few tracks in the melting snow. That's all I know. I don't want to talk about Ray."

"What kind of firearm do you use as a carry gun?"

"I use many. I usually carry a three-inch Smith and Wesson Model 36."

"You ever carry a .44 or .45 caliber handgun?"

"No."

"How did you meet Ray?"

"I told you I don't want to talk about Ray."

"Were you armed with a handgun that day?"

"Yes, I had a Smith and Wesson Model 19 in a shoulder holster."

"Was Ray armed with his .44 Magnum that day?"

"Not that I noticed."

"Did he have it with him on the trip?"

"I didn't notice."

"You will appear tomorrow morning at the Newport P.D. at nine in the morning. If you don't appear, I will issue a warrant for your arrest."

Back in the vehicle, Mitz asked, "Do you think he's involved?"

"He's the key to the whole thing. Tomorrow we'll continue questioning him about Ray. I think his lawyer will advise him to co-operate with us.

"He passed the polygraph test, doesn't seem to be hiding anything."

"You're missing the point, Mitz. He's the key to getting at Ray. We want him as aggravated and upset as possible. His emotions are written all over his face. Ray knows how to read this, man, we need to use that to get to him."

Mitz didn't quite understand what Mark was getting at. *Time will tell*, she thought.

The next morning in the restaurant having breakfast with Mitz, Mark was quiet, trying to compose his thoughts for the upcoming interview with Don. Outside, the Town of Newport was living up to its slogan as the "sunshine" town. A brilliant sun was spreading across Main, street advertising the arrival of Spring. Mitz was dressed in a blue business suit, white shirt, buttoned up all the way. With her dark hair falling to her shoulders, she had attracted the eye of many diners. Mark thought, she's a beautiful woman.

Looking through the one-way glass, Mark could see Don conferring with his lawyer. Mark could tell that Don was not happy with the advice he was getting. He was agitated before they even entered the room.

Mitz turned on the recorder, identified everyone in the room. Don was dressed in jeans, a light blue shirt, and jeans jacket. His hammer holster was attached to his belt. Mark was dressed casually in light grey slacks, white shirt open at the neck.

Mark advised Don that he may be requested to take another polygraph test after the interview. Don's lawyer advised him not to agree at this time.

"How did you meet Ray?"

"He came to the job site because of an ad I ran in the papers for a carpenter's helper."

"How long have you known Ray?"

"Must be about ten years now."

"Is Ray a violent person?'

"Not to my knowledge."

"Have you ever seen Ray commit a violent act?"

"I've seen him defend himself."

"How many times have you seen him be violent."

"Two or three times, I guess."

"Which is it, two or three?"

"Three times."

"Was he the aggressor?"

"No, he was defending himself."

"Do you socialize with Ray?"

"We've become friends over the years. He comes to our home when invited. We hunt together as well."

"Does Ray own a .44 Magnum pistol?'

"Yes."

"Do you know if he has ever carried a concealed handgun?"

Don conferred with his lawyer.

"Yes, he has on a few hunting trips."

"Was he carrying a handgun on your trip to Errol?"

"I didn't notice if he brought it or not."

"You spent three nights in a small cabin. Are you sure you never saw Ray with a handgun?"

Don conferred with his Lawyer.

"I saw a handgun in his luggage, but I don't know if he was wearing it that day."

"So, he had the handgun with him?"

"Yes."

"Just to be absolutely clear, did Ray have his .44 Magnum handgun with him on that trip?"

"Yes."

"It's your testimony that you never saw Ray after you parted that morning until twenty minutes after dusk?"

"Yes."

"Why do you think Ray was late coming back to your truck."

"I don't know."

"Give me your opinion."

"He was probably watching a deer crossing is what I thought."

"How did he act when he returned to the truck?"

"Normal."

"What is your definition of normal as regards Ray?"

"Ray doesn't talk a lot, doesn't waste words. I asked him what he saw, he replied just some tracks in the melting snow."

"How about in camp that night, how did he act."

"He acted his usual self, quiet."

Mark lit up a smoke, pushed his pack across to Don. Don never made a move towards the pack.

"Do you think Ray is capable of shooting an officer of the law?"

Don conferred with his Lawyer.

"On the advice of counsel, I'm not going to answer that."

Mark grinned at Don. "Interview concluded."

Mark was sipping coffee, smoking, lost in thought. Mitz remarked that they had established that Ray had brought a .44 Magnum on the hunting trip. Mark barely nodded at her statement. He was thinking it's time to interview the man who failed two polygraph tests, admitted that he had hunted to within two and a half miles of the pine grove where the chief had been murdered. Never got back to Don's pickup until well after dusk, could be the hunter who was spotted not wearing hunter orange who was going up the ridge as dusk was falling. The pieces fit, he thought, but no solid evidence as yet.

12

Mitz argued strongly that it was time to get a search warrant on Ray's apartment and his truck. Officer Little was of the same opinion. Lt. Harris stayed neutral, glanced at Mark.

"Ray feels comfortable. He probably thinks, and rightly so, that we don't have any evidence tying him to the case. A good attorney would get him off easily. We need to get him back in here. Make him commit hard statements that he can't back away from. If we get a search warrant, there is nothing that will tie him to the case. We already know he is a hunter, a handloader, owns a big bore handgun. That in itself is not evidence. The best we can hope to achieve is to force him to make a mistake. His boss Don is our best chance to make him nervous."

Officer little offered, "Ray has a tell. Just before he erupts into violence, he turns his lighter over and over in his hand. I've witnessed him do this twice while in high school."

Mark thought a little, lit up a smoke. "We'll put a tail on him. We'll use a cruiser that he will spot, Officer Little will trail him if he leaves the area. I don't think he will run, but you never know."

Mitz said, "We should interview his wife. She may well give us some information we can use."

Mark agreed, asked Lt. Harris to set something up at her home. Little added that she was living at her parent's home since the separation.

Ray arose early, cleaned up, decided to get breakfast at the diner. He noticed the cruiser parked on the street as he drove down, South Main, street. He saw it pull a u-turn, pull in behind him, keeping pace with him. When he parked opposite the diner, the cruiser went right on by.

Ray left the diner, paused on the sidewalk to light a smoke. He noticed the cruiser parked behind him. He got in his truck, left to meet the boss. The cruiser followed him to Don's driveway, slowly drove past him.

Boss was drinking coffee on the porch, waved for Ray to join him. Boss was all wound up about the cops from Maine. They had given him a rough time, wanted to know about Ray. Ray could tell that Boss was upset. The man wore his emotions on his face. Ray had told him nothing, Boss knew nothing of the goings-on in Maine. Did the cops think Boss was involved?

"They're just fishing Boss."

"They seem to think that you're involved somehow."

Ray shrugged, poured himself a cup of coffee. Don's wife came out on the deck with her two daughters. They all said hello to Ray, piled into the wife's station wagon, drove slowly out of the yard. They got in Don's truck, left to pick up an order from the lumber yard. When they turned onto the road, the cruiser was right behind them. When they pulled out of the lumber yard, the cruiser was right behind them, followed them to the job site in North Newport. Boss never noticed it.

When they quit for the day, the cruiser followed them back to Don's house, picked up Ray, followed him back to his apartment, parked across from his apartment. Ray pulled back the curtain, saw the cruiser still parked across the street. It was still there when he went to bed.

Mark and Mitz sat across the table from Pam. She was dressed in shorts, tank top, that showed off her figure. Her blonde hair was cut short, framed her pretty face. She was reluctant to talk about Ray, kept asking why they wanted to know. Mitz talked calmly to her, told her of Ray's involvement in the investigation in Maine.

"Ray doesn't look for trouble, but if you want trouble, he'll give it to you. Everyone knows you don't push Ray unless you want to wind up in the hospital."

"Has he ever hit you, Pam?"

"He never has."

"Do you think he's violent, does he lose control easily?"

"Ray takes control only when someone pushes him. He won't be pushed around."

"What did he tell you about the hunting trip to Maine?"

"I was gone before he even came back. He's never spoken to me about any hunting trip."

"Do you think he's acted normal since he came back from Maine?"

"I haven't really talked with him since I left him."

Mark asked, "What does he normally talk about?"

"Ray doesn't normally talk. He'll answer you all night long, but he doesn't offer opinions, doesn't engage in what he calls idle talk."

Mark gave Mitz a look, who ended the interview. Mark thought it had been a total waste of time, Mitz agreed. Mark was really disappointed that the interview had not yielded more. He had hoped that Ray had said something to his wife that they could use.

Ray poured himself another cup of coffee, looked out his window at the cruiser parked across the street. He decided to drive to Claremont, see if the police followed him there. The cruiser stopped at the town line. Ray continued into Claremont, had breakfast at a fast-food joint. That they were watching him was a no-brainer. Did they have something? He still felt that they had nothing. All he had to do was stick to his original story. He decided he wouldn't need a lawyer unless they charged him. He drove the limit back to his apartment. A cruiser followed him all the way home.

Mark updated his superiors and told them he was going to wait until after the interview with Ray before he took any action. After hanging up the phone, he pulled all the information he had from all sources. Ivan and trapper Holmes had stated that the encounter probably started at the top of the beechwood ridge. Holmes had said, "It's the most logical place to see a deer."

The deer had been shot three times. Where were the empty cartridges? Could they scour the ridge and the pine grove, find those fired cartridges? It seemed like a "Hail Mary pass" to him, but what else did he have? They had enough circumstantial evidence to obtain a search warrant, seize Ray's rifles, put a real scare into him, perhaps force him to do something. He was certain forensics could match the cases to a rifle.

He called Mitz, ordered her to prepare a search warrant expressly for Ray's firearms and cartridges, told her he would have it served as soon as Ray was picked up. He called, Carol, told her it would be a few days yet before he could return home. He called Trooper Wilson, told him to check on the snow cover in the pine grove, call him back. The last four days had ushered in Spring. The snow was gone from the mountains surrounding Newport. The pine grove on Turner Brook Road can't be far behind.

Mark was awakened by the call from Trooper Wilson who reported a good eight inches of snow in the pine grove. He added the mountains to the west, were clear of snow except for scattered patches.

At the station, Mitz handed him the search warrant for his approval. He requested that Officer Little along with Mitz conduct the search. Lt. Harris nodded his agreement. Mark requested that Officer Little order Ray report to the station, follow him back to the station. They would serve the search warrant on Ray after he was in the interrogation room. Lt. Harris had two cruisers standing by in the event Ray chose to run.

Ray had just left his driveway when the blue lights flashed in his rear-view mirror. He pulled to the right, stopped. Officer Little tapped on Ray's window. Ray lowered the window, turned his head to look at the Officer.

"You need to go to the station right now, they want to talk with you." Ray nodded and said, "Can I park my truck in the police parking lot?"

"No problem, Ray, I'll follow you down."

Little breathed a sigh of relief when Ray entered the Station. He met with Mitz and two other officers, they left to conduct the search. Mark watched as Ray was led into the interrogation room, handed the search warrant. Ray showed no emotion as he read the warrant, put it down on the table, lit up a smoke, asked the officer for a cup of coffee. Looking through the one-way glass, Mark thought, come on, show me some emotion.

I'll wait, Mark thought. I'll wait until that cigarette lighter is turning over and over in his hand. The killer of Chief Hayward is sitting in that room showing no emotion whatsoever. Mark lit up a smoke, requested coffee be brought to him. Mitz reported, by phone, that they had seized a .300 win. mag rifle, ammo, empty and loaded cases, reloading dies, one .44 Mag. revolver. Mark told her, "Good job, take your time, get everything you can." Mark lit up another smoke, watched Ray sitting calmly in the room. *Cold-blooded bastard*, he thought.

Mitz entered the room, looked through the one-way glass at Ray.

"He looks very relaxed, doesn't he?"

Mark didn't respond, never letting his focus sway from Ray.

"You'll conduct the interview with me. Make sure you bring a topo map of the area and a red marker with you. Add the info on the rifle, other items you took, to the file on my desk. Send it to the D.A., tell him I need an answer ASAP.

Mitz left to get the necessary items, Ray had finished his coffee. Lit up a smoke, started turning his cigarette lighter over and over in his hand.

It took over an hour for the D.A.s office to respond. Mark read what he had expected, "A circumstantial case, not enough hard evidence for a conviction." Mitz read the report, said, "What now?"

Mark gave a little, laugh, told her it was time to chat with Ray.

Mark sat across from Ray, put a large folder in front of him, pretended to read while Mitz turned on the recorder, listed all persons present. Ray calmly smoked, kept his eye on Mitz.

"You've failed two lie detector tests. Are you aware of why you are here?"

"Not really, but I'm getting tired of all the harassment."

"Do you wish to make an amended statement at this time?"

"No."

"For the record, you stand by your previous statement as the truth?"

"Yes."

Mark pushed a topo map over to Ray, asked him to mark the route he took while hunting that day. Ray hesitated, asked, "What does this X mean?"

"That's where Don's truck was parked on the logging road."

Ray picked up the red marker, drew a red line up the road until it converged with the brook, veered northerly away from the logging road, made a circle back to the logging road just above the X. He pushed the topo map across the table to Mark, lit up another smoke.

"You're sure this is the route you took that day?"

"Yes."

"Did you hear any shots that afternoon?"

"Yeah, bunch of shots to my southeast."

"Did you fire your weapons that day?"

"You mean did I fire my rifle that day?"

"Were you carrying a handgun that day?"

"I was hunting with my rifle, never fired it."

"Where was your handgun."

"I left it in the cabin."

"For the record, you never fired a shot, you were not carrying a handgun."

"That's right."

"Did you see any other hunters that day?"

"No."

"You state that you never crossed the brook, never went to the top of the ridge?"

"I never crossed any brook."

"Do you consider yourself a violent person?"

"No."

"You don't like to be pushed around?"

"Nobody does."

"Word is when you are pushed, you push back harder."

"I don't know what you're talking about."

"What kind of Ammo do you shoot out of your handgun?"

"Any kind I can buy."

"How about hard lead non-expanding bullets?"

"Yeah, them too."

"Why do you keep failing the polygraph test?"

"Guess I'm just a nervous person."

Mark pushed a sheet of paper across the tabletop. Ray read the data, stayed non-committal.

"That's your rifle, reloading equipment, ammo?"

"You've got no right taking my gear just because I was in Errol that day."

"Do you own any other firearms, not on that list?"

"You got them all."

"Did the officer piss you off?"

"What officer?"

"The one you shot."

Ray lit up another smoke, sat back in the chair, grinned at Mitz. Mark and Mitz left the room.

Mark said, "Let him stew a bit. He's thinking back, wondering what we have, bet on it."

"He's pretty calm, not rattled at all."

"Don't kid yourself, he's burning up on the inside. We planted the seeds, now we have to let him make a move to save his ass."

"All he admitted to was having a handgun back at the camp, how does that help us?"

"It's not the handgun Mitz, it's the fired cartridges from his rifle that he claimed he never fired."

"But we don't have any."

"Ray doesn't know that."

Ray sat at the table, smoking, turning his lighter over and over in his hand. Ray thought, fucking empty cartridge case. I know I pocketed the first one I fired, but there's one halfway down that ridge, one in that pine grove. Did they find one? If they release me, they're just guessing. If they arrest me, they found a case. His insides were turning over, he wanted a good stiff drink, was getting a headache from all this shit.

It was a good hour before the pretty policewoman came in, told him he was free to go, but do not leave the area. He laughed at her asked, "How big is the area?" She turned on her heel, gave him a good view of her butt as she walked away.

Ray drove out of the parking lot, noticed Boss's truck right behind him. He drove directly to his apartment, motioned for Boss to follow him in. In his kitchen, he uncapped two beers, sat down across the table from Boss.

"What the fuck Ray, what's going on?"

"Same old shit, nothing new."

"You in trouble man, can I help you out? Are you involved with that policeman?"

"Drink your beer Boss."

13

Ray took a long pull on the whiskey bottle, left his apartment, drove to the Sportsman Club in Windsor, Vermont. There was, always a few firearms for sale, usually sold between members. Ray picked up a six-inch .357 Magnum, a box of cartridges. If he needed a handgun, he had one. He shot the shit with a few members, had a couple of beers before leaving.

Mark was explaining his plan to Lt. Harris. He wanted the Lt. to invite Don over to his house for a pool game. Officer Little was going to pretend he was drunk, blurt out that he didn't want to go to Maine on some scavenger hunt. It was imperative that Don overhear his comment. Mark felt that Don would relay the message to Ray, couldn't help himself.

Lt. Harris felt bad about using Don in this manner but quickly saw the value in it. He reluctantly agreed.

Don was working alone on the job site when Lt. Harris pulled in. He walked over to the cruiser, started to ask about Ray. Harris told him, pool game, my house tomorrow night. Got a bunch of fish think they can play nine-ball.

Don started to reply, was interrupted by the police radio squealing. Lt. Harris said, "Gotta go, see you tomorrow, seven, sharp. Don thought, can't even answer my question before he takes off.

Don picked up his cue case, checked to make sure he had his tip shaper, extra chalk. He kissed his wife goodbye, nodded when she told him not to drink too much. The driveway was packed when he arrived, parked on the lawn. Harris had a Brunswick nine-foot table with a good quality cloth. It was a relatively fast table, ideally suited Don's game. Don was engrossed in his game. He was dominating the table, beating all comers. The mood remained festive, lots of beer being consumed. Officer Little was drinking heavy, had miscued twice on easy shots. Don took a break after the game, sat down in an easy chair by the patio door. It was a warm, evening the door was open to let in some cooling air.

Lt. Harris and Officer Little were on the patio. Don couldn't help but overhear Officer Little tell Harris that he didn't want to go to Maine the following weekend on some hair-brained scheme. He told Harris he hated walking in the woods, hated search parties.

Don left the easy chair, stood by the pool table watching the play. It had been a good night for him, time to go home get some sleep.

Mark was sitting by the phone when it rang. Lt. Harris simply said, "He's got the word." Mark thanked him, hung up the phone, called his wife.

Mark had a crazy day lining up all the law enforcement agencies necessary to implement his plan. His superiors were reluctant to back him, but to a man, put the onus on Mark.

Mitz turned to Mark. "You've planned this all along. This is why you wanted Ray to commit himself." Mark nodded.

Don spotted Ray's truck parked by the diner, parked behind it. He joined Ray in a booth, ordered coffee. Ray was eating his eggs when Don told him what he had heard the night before. Ray wiped his mouth, sipped his coffee, showed no emotion whatsoever.

"I need a few days off to deal with the divorce."

"No problem, Ray, take as much time as you need. You okay for money?"

"Yeah, I'm good, Boss."

Ray wasn't thinking about money. He was thinking of the two .300 win. mag. cases laying under the snow in Maine. The finding of either fired case would put him in the gas chamber or the electric chair. There was no way to get past the fact that forensics would match the cases to his rifle. He sat, alone in the diner turning his lighter over and over in his hand.

Ray rose at three the next morning, used just the night light while he dressed, perked coffee, made a lunch. He pulled the curtains back, scanned the street. Traffic was non-existent, with no vehicles in sight. He carried a small satchel containing his lunch, a thermos of hot coffee, his shoulder holster, and his .357 Magnum. The streets were deserted when he hit the lights on south Main, turned left for Claremont and interstate 91.

Officer Little notified dispatch that Ray was on the move. Officer Little followed Ray discretely to Ascutney, where he reported Ray had turned northbound on 91.

In Upton, Mark was roused from a deep sleep by the phone call that told him Ray was on the interstate. It would take his suspect over three hours to arrive, he would have his men in place long before the suspect's arrival. Each man had been carefully briefed Mark trusted all of them to do their jobs.

Mitz dressed warmly in thermal underwear, warm wool clothing, a vest with, Police, in yellow letters on its back. She knew Mark would want to be in position early, was ready for a long wait in the cold pine grove.

The police radio was silent for over two hours before a Vermont State Trooper advised the suspect had entered New Hampshire on Route 2.

Ray turned left in Gorham, headed to the Diner on the North end of Berlin. The Sulphur smell from the mill was heavy in the moist morning air. He ate a good breakfast before heading North on Route16 along the Androscoggin River. Ray had no eye for the beauty of the North woods this day, his focus was on two cartridge cases that could seal his fate. Thank God Boss had tipped him off about the upcoming search. He would beat them to the punch, get out of Dodge, never come back again.

Mark put the phone down, advised the suspect was en route, got his men moving.

Deputy Max was dropped off at the logging road in Errol. His main weapon this day was a telephoto camera to document the happenings.

Trooper Wilson dropped Warden Ivan Petrov off before the bridge on Turner Brook Road. Ivan would work his way to the top of the beech wood-ridge where he would have a view of the brook, the ridge running down to Turner Brook Road. He also dropped Mark and Mitz off at the bridge. They would situate themselves to observe the suspect in the pine grove. Trooper Wilson would watch the road, advise when the suspect crossed it.

Ray, drove slowly through the small village of Errol. No police in sight he noticed. No police at the diner or the Motel. He turned left to go to the logging road. He slowly drove past the logging road, saw nothing but woods. He drove more than a mile north before turning around.

Max dutifully reported that the suspect had driven past the logging road, continued North.

Mark said softly to Mitz, "He's coming, he won't chicken out."

Mitz nodded, unsnapped the retainer on her holstered .38 special.

Max held his breath, tried to stay absolutely still as the suspect's truck parked at the end of the logging road. He very carefully started shooting pictures of the suspect as he exited his truck. Max documented the suspect putting on a shoulder holster, checking his pistol before putting it in the holster. After the suspect had left his vision, he keyed his sat phone, advised, he's on his way up the road, he's armed.

Ivan was carefully hidden from sight. His camera was trained on the ridge top awaiting the arrival of the suspect.

Ray stopped at the top of the ridge saw the tree he had leaned against when he had fired at the deer. Ivan started snapping photos. One of his best photos was of Ray crossing the brook. Ray walked directly to where he had last seen the deer. He looked down the ridge, recognized the boulders he had passed through before taking his second shot. Ivan got excellent photos of Ray searching the leaves, snapped a photo of Ray holding a cartridge in his hand.

Ray felt a wave of relief pass through his body as he pocketed the empty cartridge case. He had a little spring in his step as he worked his way down the ridge.

Ivan keyed his radio, softly said, "He's on his way down."

Mark turned his head, told Mitz, "Do not fire your weapon unless I do first."

Mitz solemnly nodded.

Ray carefully looked both ways down the tarred road, with no vehicles in sight. He hurriedly crossed the road, breathed a sigh of relief when he entered the pine grove.

Officer Wilson keyed his radio three times.

Mark touched Mitz's arm, drew his .357 Colt Python, braced his arms across the fallen tree. When Ray appeared between the trees, he was centered in the sights of Mark's Python.

Ray knelt, carefully searched the ground.

"Stop! Police. Put your hands on top of your head."

Ray slowly stood, turned slightly to face the voice he heard. He shook a cigarette out of his pack, lit up. He just stood there turning his lighter over and over in his hand.

"Put your hands on top of your head, do it now."

"Give it up Mitz shouted."

Ray dropped his lighter to the ground, started to pull his revolver out of its holster. He was falling into a crouch when Mark fired the first time. Ray took a step back, got the revolver out. When the muzzle of his revolver started to rise, both Mark and Mitz fired again.

Ray fell on his right side. As they approached the fallen body, Mitz could see blood coming out of Ray's mouth as he fought to breathe through his damaged lungs. In a few moments, he died before their eyes. Mark took Mitz's arm, walked her directly to the tarred road.

Half an hour later, Turner Brook Road was full of Police and Emergency vehicles. When Mrs. Al Smith was waved by, she thought, what now.

— 14 —

The forensics unit recovered an empty .300 win. mag. case close to the body of Ray Chance. He had been shot three times in the chest. Any of the shots would have caused death.

Back at the Station, Mark had turned his weapon over to the State Police investigator. He had written out his report of the incident, checked Mitz's statement before allowing her to turn it in. Mark felt no elation. He gave a brief statement to the press giving credit to many law enforcement agencies that had worked the case.

He wrote a letter of recommendation for Officer Mitz, Trooper Wilson, and Ivan. Mitz brought him a coffee, asked Mark, "Did I hit him?"

Mark looked at this beautiful young officer. "Yes."

Mark tried to relax on the drive home, keeping any thought of the case out of his mind. He concentrated on his driving, the beauty of the place he calls home.

Mark was offered the position of head of the homicide division. He remembered his father's words when he turned them down. He would keep his status as lead investigator.

Mitz was appointed full-time officer, was promised she would be chief after graduating College. She married Dave, the trapper two months after the case was over.

In the diner in Allagash, Mark told a group of officers, "It was the trapper Dave Blake that solved the case; I just followed his reasoning."

Ivan laughed and thought, "Maybe I'm finally free from Auschwitz."

END

www.ingramcontent.com/pod-product-compliance
Lightning Source LLC
Chambersburg PA
CBHW030622190726
48286CB00008B/2355